Steven Camden is one of the UK's most acclaimed spoken word artists. He writes for stage, radio and screen and teaches storytelling. His creative company Bearheart leads story-based projects across different platforms.

Steven moved to London for a girl, but Birmingham is where he's from. He also has a thing for polar bears.

Follow Steven on Twitter:
@homeofpolar

Keep up to date with all Steven's news at:
 /StevenCamdenTheAuthor

Hear from the author himself – Steven Camden's spoken word poetry can be discovered here:
bit.ly/itsaboutlove

Books by Steven Camden

TAPE

IT'S ABOUT LOVE

IT'S ABOUT LOVE

by

STEVEN CAMDEN

HarperCollins *Children's Books*

First published in Great Britain by HarperCollins Children's Books in 2015
HarperCollins Children's Books is a division of HarperCollinsPublishers Ltd,
1 London Bridge Street, London SE1 9GF

The HarperCollins website address is: www.harpercollins.co.uk

3

Copyright © Steven Camden 2015

ISBN 978-00-0-751124-2

Steven Camden asserts the moral right to be identified as the author of the work.

Printed and bound in the United States of America

For Birmingham,
my heavy armour

INT. EMERGENCY ROOM — NIGHT

Black.

Hum of a strip light and radio static as a dial
tries to find a station.

Fade up to a face. YOUNG MAN. Wheat-coloured skin.
Dark hair cropped close. Radio static settles on
'Fly Me to the Moon'.

Cut to wide shot. Emergency Room. Moulded red
plastic chairs and cream walls. YOUNG MAN stares
straight ahead, thick shoulders slumped, dark
butterfly of blood spread across the chest of his
white shirt. A POLICEWOMAN sits in the chair to
his right, her body turned towards him.

POLICEWOMAN: Do you understand me?

YOUNG MAN just stares out. Circular clock on the
wall above them says eleven thirty. Sinatra sings.

POLICEWOMAN: I need you to tell me what happened.

YOUNG MAN frowns.

Cut to black.

YOUNG MAN (VOICEOVER): Start where it matters, he said. Start in a moment where things hang in the balance. Start with a question. Then you can go back to wherever you like.

That's fine, but you show me one moment where things don't hang in the balance. Go on. Exactly.

So where to start?

PART I.
Waiting.

I.

I'm standing under the bus shelter outside the crappy little shopping arcade. I'm wearing my battered blue hand-me-down Carhartt, but I'm gonna get soaked walking up the hill.

It's Friday morning, last day of my first week.

Wait for the rain to stop and be late, or walk into the room like a drowned rat? Either way, I'm getting stared at.

It's been a week of sitting in circles wearing sticky labels with our names on. Most of them seem to already know each other from schools around here. Kids who look like money. Who speak with words my brain uses but my mouth runs a mile from. Kids not like me.

"No umbrella?"

The voice is scratchy, but well spoken. I turn.

She's wearing one of those long black North Face coats that

4

cost like a hundred and fifty quid. The top half of her face is hidden by the massive white umbrella she's holding on her shoulder, but I can see her mouth and her chin and chunky plaits of dark hair either side of her neck.

I look over my shoulder, then back at her. "You talking to me?"

She tilts her umbrella and I see her face properly. She's mixed race. Dark shining eyes. Tiny freckles dot her cheeks. And she's smiling.

No, she's staring.

"Yeah, Travis, I'm talking to you."

Rain trickles off the edges of the umbrella, her safe and dry underneath.

I feel to look away.

She frowns. "Travis Bickle? *Taxi Driver?*"

I know who she means, but I don't move.

She holds her left hand out in front of her like a gun, pointing at me. I watch the rain hit her fingers and notice a ring that looks like a mini snow-dome made of amber.

I look down. Tight black jeans and black All Stars stick out from the bottom of her coat.

"You're doing film studies, right?" she says.

I look up, turning my head slightly, trying not to seem

uncomfortable.

She's staring.

Her eyebrows are raised. "I saw you in the circle the other day," she says. My stomach and shoulders tighten.

She points at her umbrella. "You want to share?"

I look past her, but feel her eyes on me as I shake my head. "Nah, I'm good."

She stares for a second, then shrugs. "OK. See you in class, Travis."

And she walks away.

I watch her white umbrella float through the rain to the traffic lights, cross the road, then turn into the church graveyard and out of sight.

Good choice. Not here for mates, remember.

I look at my phone. 8.50 a.m., Friday 6th September. Seven sleeps left.

What's he doing right now?

An old woman walks under the shelter to my right, pumping her little purple umbrella like a Super Soaker.

"It's not dry, is it?" she says, as she opens her bag and starts looking for something. I watch the rain fall off the edge of the shelter roof.

"I said, it's not dry is it, young man?" I feel her look up.

I turn to her. Her hair is the colour of cobwebs. She stares at my face.

What you looking at?

"Strong silent type, are we?" she says, looking away.

I don't answer, as I walk out into the rain.

I chose to come here.

I chose to catch two buses to reach a college on the other side of town. Mum and Dad didn't even make me get a job. Dad said as long as I stick it out they're happy to give me a little allowance, and what I saved from working with Tommy over the summer should last me till Christmas, if I'm clever.

Never had a bus pass before. Never needed one.

They had film studies at the Community College, which I could've walked to. But Tommy had started working for his uncle properly as a builder's apprentice, and Zia had to take the supermarket job to prove to his dad he's dedicated enough to join the family business, so it's not like I would've been with them anyway. Plus the film course here looked wicked. Theory stuff, but the prospectus said there'd be lots of writing and practical bits too. Maybe I'll get to make something of all these ideas. That's why I came. New start. Blank page.

A place far enough away that nobody knows me.

And a place where nobody's heard his name.

I walk in soaked.

Everyone stares.

I try to tilt my face down without making it obvious.

Get your head up, you idiot.

The tables are arranged in a squared horseshoe facing the front. No more circles and name badges. The teacher guy's half sitting, half leaning on his desk. I look straight to the back of the room. The umbrella girl's sitting in the back left-hand corner. The chair next to her is empty.

"Is it raining?" says Teacher Guy.

A few people laugh. I feel my face getting hot as I scan the room for another empty seat. There aren't any.

"Have a seat, we're just talking favourite films." His voice is local, with a bit of somewhere else mixed in. He's younger than most teachers I've known, but what does that really mean? I avoid everyone's eyes as I walk to the back and sit down next to Umbrella Girl. My socks are soaked and my jeans are stuck to my thighs.

The ring on her finger has something inside the amber, and I think of the mosquito from *Jurassic Park*. She doesn't

8

look at me.

Don't look at her then.

Teacher Guy carries on. "So. We've had *Twilight*, *Avatar*, and, what was the last one?"

A kid with blond hair and a suntan puts his hand up. "Avengers, sir."

Teacher Guy points at him. "Right. *The Avengers*. Thank you. You can put your hand down, and less of the 'sir', OK? I'm Noah. We'll stick to first names, I think."

Great. Another 'cool' teacher who wants to be friends. Call me Noah, I'm just like you, let's be mates. Tell you what, Noah, let's not, yeah? Hows about you just teach us a bunch of stuff about film and shove the rest of it—

"Is there anyone here whose favourite film isn't a huge Hollywood blockbuster? Not that there's anything wrong with blockbusters, but something different. How about you, at the back?"

He means me. Everyone turns to look.

"Waterboy!" says the blond kid, staring back, and nearly everybody laughs. Hot needles prick my face and my hands ball into fists under the table. I spotted him first day. He looks like he should be in a toothpaste advert.

Teacher Guy's standing up now, and I can tell he takes care

of himself. His hair's the dark curly bush that mine would be if I let it grow, but he's got that stubble I'm years away from having. He's wearing dark jeans and a light blue linen shirt and his shoulders look strong. *Noah*. I dunno if I could take him, but he'd know he'd been in a fight.

His eyes are on me. Everyone's are. Umbrella Girl's turned in her seat. *Better choose something good.* I can taste rain as I look straight ahead and say, "*Leon.*"

Noah's face flickers briefly and his expression changes, like he's gone from just wanting my answers to trying to see behind my face. Other people in the room look confused as their eyes go from me, to him, then back to me again, and even though I don't want to be looked at, I feel good. I've surprised him. The blond kid's staring back at Umbrella Girl and I can feel her smiling. Noah's still looking at me, his head tilted like he's remembering something. Then he nods. "I see. Interesting choice."

Umbrella Girl sticks her hand up. "I love that film too, sir, I mean Noah."

Noah looks at her, then at me, and it's kind of like everyone else goes out of focus.

"All right then. You two can be partners."

He claps his hands and everyone's back.

"Right. Everybody turn to the person next to you. If you don't know them, introduce yourself. You've got fifteen minutes. I want discussions – best films, worst films, important films, funniest films, films that matter. Get everything down, make notes, scribbles, doesn't matter, no idea is stupid, get talking. Go!"

Shuffling and chatter. The blond kid's looking back at me again. I wipe my forehead with the back of my hand and cold water runs down to my elbow.

"It's a love story, you know. *Leon*," says Umbrella Girl. She's doodling on the cover of a new A4 lined pad.

I peel off my jacket and let it hang inside out over the chair. My black T-shirt is dry, but my arms are cold as I take my notebook out of my bag. It's a new one. Ring bound. I pull my biro out from the binding and open it up, tensing my bicep more than I need to. I don't look at her. I'm glad she's on my right. "No, it's not."

I start to write the date, like we're still in school, then scribble it out hoping she didn't notice.

"Course it is," she says. "Not a conventional one, but it's a story about love."

The fact that she's even seen it makes me like her, but it's not a love story.

"It's about revenge," I say.

My right arm is still tensed as I scribble over the date again and I can smell cucumber shampoo. Umbrella Girl stops doodling. "No, revenge is what starts it, what she thinks she wants, but it's about sacrifice. The choice to love."

I look at her. *Who speaks like that?*

Her skin's the colour of wet sand, like Dad's, and her ear has almost no lobe at the bottom, like an elf's.

"I guess we saw it differently," I say.

"Which is why it's so good! Tragic love story. Amazing soundtrack, too. I'm Leia."

I blink longer than I should do. *You're kidding me.*

She drops her pen and holds out her hand.

Leia? I look around the class. Everyone's deep in discussion and right now, in the moment, I feel older. Like school was a long time ago.

I shake her hand. It's smooth and cool and only half the width of mine.

"I'm Luke."

And she smiles, our hands still together.

2.

Whenever I go to a new place I always imagine it as a movie set. I think about how every brick and wall and door and corner and roof had to be chosen and built by somebody. How the people who move through and around the spaces are characters playing their roles and, most of all, I'm aware at all times, somebody could be watching me.

I'm walking past the refectory to the college car park. It's not raining any more, but the sky is still dishwater grey and my socks are still soggy. Sitting through two hours of comms & culture and then an hour of English was hard and I'm wishing I could just do film studies without the other two, but I'll need them for the points if I'm even gonna consider getting to uni. *Uni? One week at college and now you're Stephen Hawking?*

"Later, Waterboy!" The blond kid shouts. He's standing with a chunky rugby type and a skater-looking ginger boy outside the double doors. He raises his thumb sarcastically, flashing his grin. *Prick*. I stare at him as I walk, holding his eyes, face up, until the wall of the reception block cuts the shot.

"Prick."

"Talking to yourself?"

And she's right next to me on my right, out of nowhere, her steps matching mine. Her umbrella's rolled up and she's holding it like a cane. Her eyes are level with my mouth. She is so fit.

"Didn't mean to scare you," she smiles.

"You didn't scare me." I stare ahead. The footpath's made from the same red bricks as the buildings.

"You forgot my name, didn't you?" Her eyebrows are raised. I glance at her, then look away.

"How could I forget your name? You're the princess."

And as we walk towards the car park, I'm imagining the camera moving out and up, circling round us.

"Where did you go to school?" she says, and the camera hits the floor like a bowling ball. My stomach knots. Tommy's picking me up. "Not round here," I say, as I scan the car park for a blue Peugeot 306, praying he's not already here. Then Leia's phone rings and saves me. We stop walking. She looks at the screen, then pushes decline.

"Not important?" I say.

She's still looking at her phone. "Brothers," she sighs, and slips it back into her pocket. "What other subjects are you doing?"

She's got a brother. I'm looking over her shoulder for Tommy. "Communications & Culture and English."

"Me too, English, I mean. We must be in different classes."

"I guess so." Why is she still talking to me? *What does she want?*

"Why were you at the bus stop if you drive?" she says. "Are you seventeen?"

Jesus, she asks more questions than Lois Lane.

A small gang of girls who look like a pop group walk past us and start down the hill. I shake my head. "Not until next month. My friend's picking me up."

Leia nods. "He's pretty cool, right? Noah, I mean?"

I nod back. She says, "The thing he said about keeping a notebook is so true, I've kept one for years."

I think of the notebook in my bag right now and picture all the ones under my bed, filled with ideas; random lines, things people said, thoughts, dreams, memories, snippets of scenes, things I couldn't say to anyone but that felt like they had to come out. I say nothing and just stare at her. There's something about her eyes.

"It's lazy." She points at her right eye. "Not loads. I used to have a patch when I was a kid."

I look away and pretend I'm checking the road. Leia hits my elbow. "Don't worry, I'm not offended. Aaaaaaarrrggggghhhhh."

I turn back to her and rub my elbow even though it doesn't hurt.

She shrugs. "Like a pirate? Eye patch?"

"Good one."

That sounded sarcastic. "I mean, not good that you've got an eye patch…"

"I don't have an eye patch. I used to have one."

"Yeah, that's what I meant. I've gotta go."

"I thought your friend was picking you up?"

"Yeah, I need to ring him. I'll see you later."

I start to walk back the way we came and take out my phone, hearing her voice. "Yeah. Later, Skywalker."

I can feel her watching me, but I don't turn back. I'm not here for friends. Even pretty ones who know about films.

I hear the horn before I see the car. Our navy blue carriage to freedom. Passed down through three older O'Hara brothers and now it's Tommy's. He pulls up outside reception and the passenger door swings open.

"Yes, Shitface! How's big school?"

Tommy's my oldest friend. We've been mates since we were three. He's the youngest of four brothers, all of them one year apart, all of them carbon copies of their Dad, Micky; Irish catholic, black hair, sharp chin, long limbs and blue-grey eyes. Dad and Micky have known each other since school.

Tommy was the best footballer in our year by far. I'm all right, but he was something else. He played for the Aston Villa youth team until they kicked him out for trouble. Tommy's skinny, but he can fight. Even though I'm bigger than him, when we mess around, he's always a handful.

One time he bit a dog. We were nine and being chased by Mr Malcolm's Doberman, Dusty, after we'd been stealing apples from his garden. As we were running down the alley behind the supermarket, Tommy just stopped and turned round, gave this weird howl like a werewolf, and when Dusty went for him, Tommy wrestled Dusty to the floor and bit him on the neck. Dusty yelped and ran off and Tommy just sat there looking up at me, grinning. He still brings that up proudly whenever he gets the chance.

He insisted on picking me up today. The car's seen better

days, but it's real and it moves.

"So how was it then?" he says, leaning forward to check out the campus buildings through the windscreen. Something about him being here feels weird. Like I don't want to be seen.

He's wearing dirty grey overalls and a black T-shirt and his hands and cheeks are speckled with white paint. His voice is deep and his top lip's got the shadow of a potential moustache.

An older girl wearing expensive headphones and a denim jacket walks past the car. I feel my stomach drop as Tommy beeps the horn. I look down as the girl turns round.

"Yes, princess! Need a lift?" He's leaning out of his window.

I pretend to tie my shoelace, waiting for it to be over.

"Whatever then, your loss!" He slaps my shoulder. "You know her? She was banging. What you doing?"

I sit up and shake my head. "Can we just go?"

As we drive down the hill, we pass Leia, umbrella under her arm as she talks on her phone. I turn away from the window.

"So come on then?" Tommy lights a cigarette as we pull up at the island behind a black BMW.

"It's fine," I say.

"Fine? It better be more than just fine, Luke. It took me nearly half an hour, man. What bus you get?"

I crack open my window. "The 87 and the 50."

"Two buses? Shit, they better be teaching you some important stuff." Tommy whacks my thigh. "Girls though, yeah?"

And I picture Leia, her fingers pointing at me like a gun. "Dunno. Not really noticed."

"Yeah, right, dark horse Luke Henry? Them posh girls love a bit of rough, eh? Just don't forget to sort me out once you're plugged in, yeah?" He raises his finger like a politician. "Share and share alike, Lukey."

"You look like your old man, Thomas."

"Like you don't?" He takes a long drag and looks down at himself. "Some of us have to work in the real world, mate. We can't all be nerds."

3.

```
INT. CAR — DAY
Close-up of TOMMY's mouth as he pulls on a
cigarette. YOUNG MAN next to him and scenery
outside blurry in the background.
```

Tommy turns the engine off and the pair of us sit, staring up at the back of the supermarket. Next to the fire door, a row of industrial-sized bins are lined up and there's a greyness in the air that I don't want to say is just this side of town. *You just said it.* Whatever it is, it feels familiar and I can feel my body starting to relax.

"What did Zia say?" I ask.

Tommy flicks his cigarette out the window. "To wait out back and he'd dip out. What time is it?"

I look at my phone. "Half four. You should get one of them air fresheners, man, them little trees."

"What you saying? You saying my car stinks?"

"Like an ashtray."

"You wanna walk?"

My phone beeps. It's a text from Dad.

How wis fist wk big man? Dodx

I picture him lying on his back under some battered old car, taking ten minutes to type the message, his thick thumb hitting four buttons at once.

Good thanks. See you tomorrow

Tommy tuts. "Where is he, man?"

I look up at the concrete building. "He's probably being watched. What did he say the manager guy's name was again?"

"Dunno. I'm starving though."

Then the fire door pops open and Zia pokes his head out, like a meerkat sentry. He looks both ways, then nods at us. He's shaved his beard back to rough stubble and he's wearing a hair net. Tommy laughs. "He looks like my mum after a shower."

"Yeah, 'cept your mum's beard's thicker."

He tries to dig my thigh, but I grab his fist and squeeze.

21

"All right, all right, get off, Luke!"

I hold him a second longer, then let him go and open my door.

"Yes, boys!" whispers Zia. The whites of his eyes sparkle next to his skin. Fists bump, then he says, "Wait here," and he's gone. The fire door clicks closed and me and Tommy are standing with our backs against the wall.

Tommy points up at the security camera facing the car park. I nod. The door opens again and Zia hands me a small, torn cardboard box. I can see Babybels, a ripped pack of Jammy Dodgers and a can of Relentless. I look at Zia.

"What's this?"

Zia frowns. "Dinner."

Tommy looks into the box. "Dinner for who? A crack head?"

"If you don't want it, don't eat it, man. I have to be careful what I take, don't I? We have to put the damaged stock out the back and if I tear expensive stuff, Pete the Prick flips out."

Tommy takes out a Babybel. "Couldn't you just get some crisps or something?"

Zia pulls the box back out of my hands. "Look, if you wanna give orders, go Chicken Cottage, yeah? I'm not a waiter. You want this or not?"

I put my hands on the box. "Course we do. Thanks, man.

What time you finish?"

Zia lets go of the box and sighs. "Ten. We gotta stack up the shelves for the staff working tomorrow." He scratches his velcro stubble. Tommy pulls open a Babybel and the three of us just stand there. One supermarket employee, one builder's apprentice and me. A year ago we'd all be in school uniform.

Zia clicks his fingers. "Yo, check this out. I thought up a new bit. Upgrades, yeah? Like with phones, but for your friends and family."

Tommy looks at me and rolls his eyes. Zia carries on. "So I'd be like, OK, I've got the standard Tommy friend, yeah? But I wanna upgrade, cos the new one has got better features and that, like he never asks to borrow money, and he doesn't say dumb stuff and get us into trouble."

Tommy pushes Zia. "Shut up, man. Why am I the one who gets upgraded? You say dumb stuff all the time."

I smile. "That's not bad, man. You think that up today?"

Zia nods. "Nothing else to do while I'm stacking sugar."

"Yeah, well I've heard it somewhere before," says Tommy.

Zia frowns. "Shut up, that's mine. It needs work, but it could be good."

Tommy smiles through a mouthful of cheese. "So you gonna sort out an actual gig then?"

Zia stares at him. "Maybe I will." Something clatters from inside. Zia looks back over his shoulder. "I gotta go. Come get me later, yeah?"

We nod. Fists bump.

Me and Tommy start towards the car, but stop when Zia calls out, "Lukey!" We turn back. "One more week, eh?"

Tommy looks down. I give an awkward shrug. Zia does his good Samaritan smile. "Ring me if you wanna talk, yeah?"

Then he slides inside and the door shuts, leaving me and Tommy standing there, silent. I stare at the ground.

"You all right, Lukey?"

"I'm fine." I start walking.

As we get to the car, Tommy points at the box. "Yo, the Relentless is mine."

I look at him as I open my door. "Course it is."

He opens his. "What you saying then? FIFA at mine?"

I nod. He smiles. "Friend upgrades, that is pretty funny."

I stare up at the supermarket building, at the security camera, and picture a dark room with a wall of black-and-white screens. I zoom in on one and see me, standing next to the car, staring up into the lens.

One more week. Is he thinking about me?

4.

Mum said: Life's a record on loop; we just have to learn to love the song.

It's after midnight when Tommy drops me off.

Mum works nights at the weekend and she turns the heating off when she leaves, so the house feels like an empty cave. I kick off my shoes and climb the stairs.

The landing light has no shade so the bulb shines a circle across the ceiling and walls. Standing outside my room the landing stretches away to my left, towards his door. I feel it pulling me. Like I always do. Like part of him is always here. So I walk towards it.

The gloss painted wood, something pulsing behind. The cheap silver handle. The dark jagged letters carved into the white:

MARC'S ROOM

I remember sitting in my pyjamas on the landing right here, my hair still damp from the bath, listening to him play the first Eminem album. Knowing the words were bad, but not really understanding and feeling like I wanted in on the secret.

I picture inside now. The perfectly made bed with his barbell underneath. The football posters. The black veneered shelves full of trophies, nearly two years untouched. Two years of waiting, weighing everything down, pressing things into their place. My hand moves up to my face. *Not long now.*

I push my bedroom door closed behind me, take *Leon* from my DVD shelves. I switch off my light, open my laptop on my bedside table to face my pillow, slide in the disc and lie down on top of my covers. The Columbia Pictures logo comes up, the lady holding the torch as the trumpets play, and I feel the tingle in my blood. My heads sinks into my pillow as the camera flies over the water, then trees, and the strings start to play and the names of actors appear and everything's all right. I get to go somewhere else.

Morning sunlight splits my ceiling in half. I stare at the crack in the ceiling plaster that cuts from the corner in towards the lampshade like a thin black root and I feel my face.

I reach down into my bag, pull out my notepad, grab a pen from my bedside table and…

A waterfall of rain.

Leia's staring from behind it. Her hair's out in a big afro like from some old 1970s cop show. She's wearing the big black coat, but the front is undone and there's a clear V of naked skin. It's like inside a tent or a cloud or something, everything washed in white. Leia licks her lips and raises her hand to point straight at me with two fingers. The water hits her hand and her face goes out of focus. Then there's fire, behind her and on both sides, tall flames that don't touch her but feel like they're all around. Her face becomes clear again and she's wearing an eye patch and the water is gone. Her head tilts. She smiles, then her mouth mimes a gun shot and she's stepping forward, fingers still pointing, as she moves closer and her coat is falling open. Flames dancing. Closer, and her skin, and closer, and the fire behind her, and more skin, and closer and closer and

I lower my pen and stare at the ceiling. What the hell's all that about? *You think she dreamt about you?*

My laptop's still open from last night. I close it, then slide off my bed down into press-up position on the floor. Back level, I feel the warmth spread across my shoulders and I smile. Thirty reps, then fifty crunches and repeat. Every morning for two years. At least my body will be ready.

I can hear the TV as I come downstairs.

Mum's lying under her duvet on the sofa, half watching a chunky man cooking something with fish. The curtains are open. Dad's old varnished wooden clock, shaped like Jamaica, ticks like a mantelpiece metronome in between Marc's trophy for under-sixteens' 800m champion and a glass-framed photograph of a younger me and him on a climbing frame, me watching as he swings from the bars.

"Make us a coffee, Luke." Her heavy eyes don't leave the screen.

```
INT. — DAY
   Close-up: Bubbles and steam cloud clear plastic.
```

I stare out of the window over the sink, holding the milk, as the kettle starts to boil. Our small square of back garden is overgrown and next to the fence I see the old deflated leather football nestled into the grass like a white rock.

I spoon coffee into the big mug with the black cat on it and keep stirring as I pour the hot water three quarters to the top. I shake the plastic milk carton like I'm making a cocktail, bang it on the sideboard to bubble it up like Marc showed me, then stir slowly as I add a little to the coffee, making a whirlpool of froth to the top edge of the mug.

Some people have machines that do it for you; in our house you do it yourself.

Mum's eyes are closed and she's mouth breathing. I kneel down next to the sofa, resting the mug on the floor and see she's still wearing her nurse's clothes under the duvet. Her skin's pale and, with her mousey hair in a ponytail, she looks young for a mum. I hold my hand up next to her face. My skin's darker than hers, but lighter than Dad's, and I think about genes and twisted strings of code. Then I notice the photograph of Marc in his Aston Villa youth kit tucked between the cushion under her head and the arm of the sofa.

"Mum. Mum, why don't you get into bed?" I put my hand on her shoulder.

She jerks awake and sits straight up, kicking the coffee all over my lap. I shout out and fall back as the hot coffee burns my thighs through my jogging bottoms. Mum looks terrified.

"Luke!" She falls forward off the sofa half on top of me, grabbing my shoulders. "Are you OK?"

The photo of Marc drops on to the floor. I can feel the heat branding my skin. "I'm OK, Mum. It's all right."

She sees the photograph and lets go of me to pick it up. Then she pulls the duvet away and looks down at the dark brown patch on the cream carpet. "Oh, look what you did! You need to be careful, Luke."

"Me?"

"This is gonna need shampooing. Get a cloth, hurry up!"

So I go to the kitchen, my thighs pulsing from the heat, to get a tea towel to clean up the mess I didn't make.

Walls work both ways. What keeps you safe, keeps you separate.

5.

"Of course there's a difference! These ones are *Honey Nut*, Dad. They've got honey and nuts in…"

"But I don't want honey and nuts."

I laugh. Zia's putting on a voice for his dad, playing both parts in this little comedy routine, hunching over and everything, pretending to adjust his glasses. Me and Tommy are his audience, sitting on the lime-green leather sofa. I can see our dark reflection in the black screen of the massive TV behind him.

"Are you kidding, Dad? Let's treat ourselves, yeah?"

"I don't want a treat, I want breakfast."

"But Dad, you're the West Midlands Carpet King, you can afford to splash out on a better cereal. Look, these ones are called clusters, they look good."

"Cornflakes."

"How about Cocopops?"

"*Cornflakes.*"

"Fine, but let's at least get the Crunchy Nut, yeah?"

"*You think I became successful by eating crunchy nuts? What's wrong with you? You used to love cornflakes, you too good for cornflakes now?*"

I laugh and Zia stops his routine.

I nod at him. "This is good stuff, man."

Zia bows. "My life is my scrapbook."

He's got no idea how cool that sounded, and I make a mental note to write it down later.

"Has your dad seen you do it yet?" says Tommy.

"Are you mad? In fact, we should go. He'll be back soon."

Me and Tommy stand up.

"You should show him, man. You're getting good," I say.

"Oh yeah. 'Hey, Dad, Tommy and Luke reckon I should jack in the supermarket job you're making me do and sack off your plans for me and the family business. Yeah yeah, they think I should try and become a stand-up comedian. They think I've got potential.'"

His face is pure sarcasm. Zia's dad doesn't even like us in the house, let alone giving his only son career advice. Tommy looks round the room. "Yo. Your sister about?"

Zia digs his arm. "Shut up, yeah? It's not funny."

"What? I'm just saying."

"What are you just saying, Tom?"

Tommy blinks slowly. "I'm just saying, that I think Famida is a rare beauty and I'd like to make her my wife."

I laugh. Zia stares at Tommy. Tommy carries on. "My older, foxy wife." He closes his eyes and smiles like he's just tasted the best ice cream in the world. Zia goes for him and they're in a two-man rugby scrum. I watch their reflection in the TV.

Zia joined our school in Year Five, but he really came into his own when we moved up to secondary. He was the kid who always said the cool thing at just the right time. Some of the one-liners he rocked to teachers were incredible. Like the time when Mr Chopping was laying into us in chemistry and shouted, "Do you think I enjoy spending my time with immature young boys?" and without even blinking, Zia was like, "I don't know sir, I'd have to browse your internet history." Brilliant.

I punch them both and they stop wrestling. Tommy cracks his neck and takes out a cigarette. Zia cuts him a look. "Don't even joke you idiot, come on, let's go."

"Where we going, anyway?" I say.

Tommy puts his cigarette back and shrugs. Zia puts his hands on our shoulders. "Doesn't matter. We got wheels!"

INT. CAR — DAY
Close-up: A pine tree air-freshener swings from the rear-view mirror to the sounds of boys laughing.

We don't have anywhere to go and Tommy's happy just driving around, so that's what we do. I get shotgun and Zia's in the back behind me. There's no stereo in the car, but it doesn't matter cos just driving with no sound feels good. Like a music video on mute.

Then I have an idea.

We drive round to old Mr Malcom's house and nick apples from the tree in his front garden, then park outside our old school. It's only been a summer since we left, but it feels like forever. The black metal front gates are locked and it looks kinda small.

"Shithole," says Tommy.

Zia nods. "Load up."

Standing in a line in front of the gates, we cock our arms back and try to hit the technology block windows.

I'm the only one to reach, my apple exploding on the thick

double-glazed glass. "Eat that, Mr Nelson."

We stop by West Smethwick park and watch the second half of an under-twelves game. It's Yellows vs Reds. Within minutes, Tommy's shouting instructions to the Yellows' defence.

Some of the parents stare.

The Yellows win 5:1.

At about four we stop at Neelam's on the high road and get masala fish and ginger beers, then park up near the bus stop and eat in the car. Heat from our food steams up the windows.

"We could go anywhere," says Zia through a mouthful of naan just as I was thinking the exact same thing; how we could just choose a direction and drive. All we'd need is petrol money. Tommy nods and I wonder what places they're both imagining. London. Manchester. Paris.

"Wolverhampton," says Tommy.

"What?"

He looks at me. "We could drive to Wolverhampton."

I stare at him. "Wolverhampton? That's where you wanna go?"

"Yeah, what's wrong with that?" He takes a big bite of his naan. "Jamie says wolves girls are well up for it."

Zia leans forward in between our seats. "I never went

to Blackpool."

Tommy scoffs. "What the hell's in Blackpool?"

"What the hell's in Wolverhampton?" says Zia. "At least Blackpool's got a rollercoaster."

Tommy thinks about it. "Oh yeah, the Pepsi Max one, eh?"

Zia's nodding. "Exactly. The Big One."

Tommy nods back. "Yeah, sick. I'd go Blackpool. We should go to Blackpool. What you saying, Lukey? Blackpool road trip soon?"

The two of them look at me, chewing in sync, and it feels like they're on one side and I'm on the other.

I shrug. "Yeah, Blackpool. Wicked."

6.

Zia said: My life is my scrapbook.

```
INT. PUB — NIGHT
The cackle of old man laughter.
```

I step out of the toilet into the noise of The Goose. It's already pretty full and I can't see across the room, but I can hear Dad's deep laugh from the corner. I weave between bodies, tensing my shoulders the whole time in case I'm bumped.

Most people in here know each other, or at least they know of each other. I'm Little Lukey, Big Joe Henry's kid, to the older ones, and to everyone else, Marc Henry's little brother. I've been getting served at the bar since I was fifteen.

As I pass the bar, Donna smiles at me. My brain sends mixed messages to my face and I half smile, half grimace. *What the hell was that, you idiot?*

The flatscreen TV up on the wall shows *Sky Sports News* and it looks out of place, like a rectangular piece of future pasted into an old photograph. *Don't start with that stuff. Not here.*

Dad's sitting in the corner on the leather bench with two workmates from the garage on either side of him, all five of them still in their dark blue overalls, like some old boy band with Dad as the lead singer. The wall behind them's deep burgundy and holds cheaply framed pictures of the local area from like a hundred years ago.

Whenever I see Dad with other men, even now, his size still hits me. He's another half bigger in every direction than the closest guy to him. I think of kids looking up at him when we're in town, their eyes wide, like they've discovered Big Foot.

"You OK, son?" He's looking at me as I sit down on my stool across the circular table.

"I'm fine, Dad. Just déjà vu."

Dad's mate Lenny sticks out his bottom lip as he looks at me. "Catching your old man up, aren't you, college boy?" He bends his arms like he's a posing body builder and I turn in my seat.

"He'll be bigger than me," says Dad, smiling proud and

nodding at me. I sit up straight and look at him. His square face is tired and scuffed with oil, but his eyes sparkle. I think of him driving me to pick up my GCSE results and the pair of us sitting in silence in the car after I opened them and got what I needed.

Lenny points at me. "Just don't forget us when you're rich and famous, eh?"

He nudges Dad. Dad does his polite laugh and I watch the little fans of wrinkles spread from the outside corners of his eyes.

"What's on your mind, Lukey?" His voice is like thick gravy and everything about him has that calm that comes from knowing that nobody can really mess with him. It makes you feel safe. Mum used to call him her 'handsome Shrek'. He knows what I'm thinking about. Him asking me what's on my mind is his way of letting me know that he knows, and that now isn't the time or the place to talk about Marc coming home.

It's never the time or the place.

I shrug and shake my head and he carries on his conversation about fan belts. I sip from my half of Guinness, letting the metal taste swim around my teeth, and watch him, turning the volume down in my head so the scene goes silent. I try to picture him my age, nearly seventeen and unsure of himself, or scared, or confused or even slightly nervous, but I can't. Dad's emotions only seem to do the primary colours; happy, sad or angry. I know that can't be true, all the other shades must live underneath his skin.

I look round the room of mostly men. A collage of weathered faces from different generations and I think about how each face has a life attached to it. A string of details that stretches out of the door, along local roads to where they sleep. A wife, a kid, an old sofa, an empty fridge. The spaces they own, somewhere else. How they choose to come here, and how people like to keep the different parts of their lives separate.

"Stop thinking will you, Lukey?" Dad's frowning. I stare back at him, trying to let him know how stupid his statement is, but I know what he means, and sometimes I wish I could.

Dad finishes his pint and sighs. "You know where too much thinking gets you."

By the time Tommy shows up with Micky, Dad and his mates are telling the same story for the seventh time, with slurred edges. Micky rubs his knuckles over my head. "And how's Mr College?" I look at Tommy as Micky grabs my shoulders. "Shame some of your brains couldn't rub off on this one." He points at Tommy with his thumb, then sits down and gets immediately absorbed into the group of grown-ups.

Tommy doesn't say anything. Dad sends me to the bar and Tommy takes my seat to go through the same customary greeting and piss-taking from each tipsy mechanic in turn that I got an hour and a half ago.

Donna's changing a vodka bottle from the spirit rack. She smiles as I place my empty glass on the rubber beer mat.

"Same again, Lukey?" Her voice is a beam of light cutting through the coarse bush of testosterone. *What the hell are you talking about?*

I look down.

"Two pints and two halves please. Micky and Tommy are here."

Donna puts the vodka bottle down and starts to pour the drinks. I'm watching her as she moves, like she's operating a machine she's known forever and, like I do most times I speak to her, I get a flash of lying on my side on our living room floor under my duvet. I'm ten years old and pretending to be asleep while her and Marc fool around on the sofa behind me. Getting a sneaky glimpse of her black bra.

"So how's college?" She places two halves on the bar and starts on the pints.

"All right, yeah," I say, and even as the words are coming

out of my mouth, I know they're too quiet.

"What? I can't hear you, babe, speak up." *She just called you babe*.

I punch out my words to cut through the pub noise, just as things fall quiet. "It's all right. Just started this week."

My stomach drops as people turn to look at me. My head goes down as I wait for them to stop staring. Donna puts a full pint next to the two halves and they look like a single parent Guinness family. I stop myself saying it out loud. She's laughing.

"That's good. Knew you were the one with the brains."

Her eyes lift my head up and I'm looking at her. Her black hair cut short like only some girls can do, her chocolatey eyes, the warmth in her smooth face. Her mum's Italian and you can tell. I crack a smile and feel the skin of my cheek, and I want to say sorry. Sorry for what happened.

"Be uni next, eh?" she says.

I hold out the tenner Dad gave me. "Dunno about that."

Donna holds my hand as she takes the money. Her thin fingers are strong.

"You get out of here first chance you get." And she's smiling, but there's something else in her face, and she knows I see it. I look down again and she lets go.

"You do what you want, handsome. Ignore us bitter

old ones."

I take my change and feel Marc's name crawling up my throat. I know she's been counting days too, walking around under the same cloud of my big brother. *Handsome?*

I swallow, then look back at Donna. "You're not old."

Donna leans forward on the bar, her thin arms pushing her boobs forward. I try not to stare.

"Just the bitter I need to work on then."

And then she's gone, down the bar to serve an old man.

She called you handsome.

And I know it doesn't mean anything, but I feel warm, and I'm wondering if this is how Marc felt every time he was with her.

Some old timer leans over the bar and stares at Donna's body. I feel my muscles tensing as I look at his cracked blotchy face. Then he's looking back at me, staring with cloudy eyes and he nods the nod, the one that lets me know that just like everyone else in here, he respects what Marc did.

Assault Occasioning Actual Bodily Harm.

It sounded like something from an ITV courtroom drama.

ABH, with greater harm and higher culpability.

One year and six months.

I remember I had to look at Dad to see whether that was better or worse than they'd expected. Dad's face didn't move. Mum was already crying. I was wearing my funeral suit, my eyes trying to find somewhere to settle that didn't feel wrong.

The room was four different shades of beige and the wooden gate that separated Marc from everyone else was so low it didn't make any sense. The magistrate gave a little speech about Marc's disregard for another human life. How Craig Miller could've died and how, by driving round looking for Craig, unashamedly asking people where he was, Marc had demonstrated a premeditated intent to cause harm. Nothing about Craig's history of terrorising people since I could remember.

The charge, combined with Marc's record of minor charges for affray and violent conduct, led the magistrate to extend the sentence to twenty months.

Mum wailed, like twenty months was so much worse than eighteen. Dad's face still didn't move. I stared at Marc, standing firm in his white T-shirt, his chin up, like he was posing for a photograph, and I wanted to shout at the judge. To explain. Make it better.

But I didn't. I just stood there, next to Dad, watching my

older brother as the magistrate spoke.

The hammer banged. Dad held Mum as she cried and reached out towards the stand. Marc sighed and shook his head. "It's OK, Mum. I'll be all right."

Then he looked at me, as the two officers led him away, and he smiled.

Marc Henry. The convicted hero. Wrong to the law, but right to anyone from round our way who knew Craig Miller, the nastiest piece of work around. Marc Henry. Local superstar. Guardian angel. Completely oblivious to the dead space he was about to leave behind.

7.

"She is so fit!"

Tommy's voice is almost angry as he speaks, the smoke flowing out of his mouth like exhaust fumes. We're standing outside the pub. He shakes his head. "I swear down, your brother, man. Lucky bastard."

I cut him a look.

"What? I'm just saying, prison or no prison, Donna's amazing. I'd… man, I don't even know what I'd do."

"Shut up, Tom."

He's right though. Donna would look sexy dressed as a chicken, and Marc was lucky to be with her. I rub my arms and feel my biceps tighten. Tommy takes another drag of his cigarette and the pair of us watch a wide smoke ring float up in front of us.

"Will you have a party? I mean, when he comes out?" he says, and I see a shot of me, wearing a shiny party hat, limp party blower hanging from my mouth, staring out.

"He'll probably be even more hench, eh?" says Tommy, holding his thin arms in front of himself like a gorilla. I shrug. "No idea."

"Course he will." Tommy grabs my shoulders. "He'll get a shock when he sees you though, eh? People's champion." He shakes me back and forth, like I just won a title fight. I shrug him off and then a car moves past and I recognise the driver.

"Noah?"

I watch the car drive past the chippy and turn up Barns Road.

"Who's Noah?" Tommy's squinting at me, and I'm not sure if it really was him, or if I just thought it was.

"Who's Noah, Luke?"

"In the car. I thought I saw someone, from college."

"Round here?"

"I dunno, probably wasn't him. He's a teacher." I feel myself shiver from the cold as I try to picture Noah standing at the front of the class, but all I see is Leia, pointing her gun fingers.

Tommy snorts and spits a greeny. "No teachers round here, Lukey."

I stare along the empty road and try to imagine where Leia is right now, what she's doing.

"What's your favourite film, Tom?" I turn to him. His

47

shoulders are up by his ears, trying to hide from the cold.

"Dunno," he says. "Don't really have a favourite."

"I know it depends on the mood and that, but if you had to say one, like now, what would you pick?"

And I watch him think, picturing shelves of DVDs stretching out either side of him, like Neo choosing weapons in *The Matrix*.

"*Die Hard II*."

"What?"

"*Die Hard II*. Die Harder." He's smiling proudly.

I frown. "*Die Hard II*? That's your favourite film?"

Tommy nods. "Right now, yeah."

"What about the first one?"

Tommy lifts his hand like he was expecting me to ask.

"Number two is the same but with aeroplanes, so it's better. The bit when he lights up the runway with the petrol from the plane and it blows up… that is so sick!"

I picture the scene, Bruce Willis lying bloodied on the snowy runway, throwing his lighter and watching the trail of flames jump up into the air, making the plane full of bad guys explode.

So many of our favourite things are passed down. It's the younger brother template. The first *Die Hard* films were made years before we were even born, but through older brothers and our dads, we've taken them on as our own. We have that in common.

Tommy mimes flicking a cigarette – "Yippee Kayaaaay!" – then pulls open the door. Noise from inside spills out over us and, just for a second, I get the feeling we're being watched.

Dad was actually on TV.

He never went to drama school or anything. He was in town with Uncle Chris and some agent spotted him. He was training to be a mechanic.

I know the story well.

Straight away, the agent got him a walk-on part in a science fiction series called *Babylon 5*. He told Dad it would be his big break. They flew him to California to film it and everything.

'Big Alien Pilot' was his character. His scene happened in the space station bar. He starts a fight with one of the main characters and gets beaten up, even though he's twice the size of the other guy. We used to sit around as a family and watch it on video, Dad doing live commentary from the sofa. I reckon I've seen it a hundred times.

When you're seven and you watch your dad on TV in blue skin make-up, a pair of prosthetic horns and a leather waistcoat, looking bigger than everyone else, it's pretty cool. *That's my dad!* type thing.

Then, as you get older and you start paying more attention to the 'what if' expression on your dad's face as he watches, and you can feel your big brother and your mum doing the same, the magic kind of wears off.

Dad said they wanted him to come back as a different alien and get beaten up again and it turned out that would be all he'd ever get to do. The agent told him he could make a good living playing 'the heavy', but that nobody wrote decent parts for big men. Dad said he didn't want to spend his life pretending to be monsters and bodyguards, so he came back, and finished training as a mechanic.

A year later, a nineteen-year-old student nurse having trouble with her first car came into the garage where Dad worked. Dad started checking it over and noticed that the girl wouldn't stop staring at him. He tried to ignore it and went under the car. As he lay on his back, he realised that the girl was lying down on the floor next to the back wheel, just so she could see him.

Turned out she was a huge *Babylon 5* fan and knew every scene from every episode. She also had a thing for big men.

Less than a year later, a giant and a pregnant nurse were married, and a month after that, Marc was born.

By the time I arrived Marc was nearly four. Four years of being the only child and then a baby shows up, crying and needing help with everything.

Mum always used to tell people that Marc's first word was 'ball' and that mine was 'Dad'. Kinda messed up that there are moments that end up defining your character before you even have a choice.

Marc's face.

Blank expression, but he's blinking. His hair's shaved. Mouth closed. Thick neck. Strong jaw. His Adam's apple moves as he swallows. Skin is perfectly smooth.

Then there's something on his left cheek, a dot underneath his left eye. It's red. And it's turning into a line.

~~Like someone is drawing it.~~ Like he's being cut with an invisible scalpel.

The cut grows, curving up towards his eye, splitting skin. But there's no blood. Just a clean red line. His expression shows no sign of pain.

His left eye closes as the cut crosses over it on to his forehead. It reaches half way up and then stops.

His fingertips dig under the skin at the bottom of the line and he pulls.

The skin comes away from his face, like wrapping paper, but there's no blood, just more skin underneath that's a shade lighter and it's someone else's eyes. It's a younger face. Skin perfectly smooth.

It's my face.

It's me.

8.

I'm walking through the graveyard before the hill up to college, reading the epitaphs of strangers on the mossy gravestones.

Most of them seem to be for kids and there's something really creepy about seeing a name carved into stone above two dates only three or four years apart.

Noah asked us to watch a film we like and choose a scene to use in the lesson and I realise that I'm excited.

As I step out of the graveyard on to the pavement, I see Leia across the road, starting up the hill. I think about calling out to her, but it doesn't feel right, then the blond kid from film studies comes up from the underpass steps behind her.

I hang back, pretending to check my phone, and watch him catch Leia up. I stay on this side of the road and keep a good distance as they walk together, and I want to know what they're saying. The blond kid is talking and gesturing, using his hands like he's pitching an idea. He's probably chatting her up. I hate him.

Everyone sits in the same seats.

I'm staring at the blond kid as Noah starts saying how he believes the best way to learn is to actually do stuff instead of just talking about it, and how, by Christmas, he wants us all to have our own draft scripts. A sheet of A4 paper goes round the class for us to all write our personal email addresses on. He wants them so he can send us links to check out. A couple of people look at each other wondering whether that's even allowed. They gave us individual college emails in the first week, but everyone still writes their real one down for him.

Leia's wearing a big grey sports sweater. The kind that looks like a hand-me-down, and that you can only wear if you have that 'I don't care what anyone thinks' air. The sides of it are hugging her chest and I'm absolutely not stealing looks whenever I get chance.

We're supposed to write a description of the scene we chose from our film and hand it in at the end of the lesson. Noah says it's a good way for him to get to know us – that he wants to get to know us through our choices. I look at him and try to figure out if it was him I saw in the car on Saturday night.

It could've been.

The room is bubbling.

It's not like at school, where the teacher would be telling people to shut up every two minutes. People are chatting and moving around and nobody else seems to be surprised by it, so I try not to be. The blond kid keeps looking over at Leia and I can feel myself staring at him like a guard dog or something, and I know I'm being stupid, but I can't help it. I want him to see my face.

I'm writing about the scene in *Reservoir Dogs* where Tim Roth is practising his monologue so he's got an anecdote about something criminal and nobody else in the crew will suspect that he's an undercover cop.

I'm writing how I like that we see him practise. How I like it when we get to see the little things that happen before or after the action.

How I think most people don't really consider what happens before they show up at a party, or what someone who isn't the 'hero' is thinking in the moment, and even though I don't like a lot of Tarantino movies, *Reservoir Dogs* would probably be in my top ten films ever. I'm writing all this stuff and it feels brilliant.

"Not saying much today are you, Mr Jedi?" Leia doesn't

look up from her page as she speaks.

I can't see what she's writing about and I want to ask, but the blond kid watching us is making me angry.

"Let me guess," she says. "Another love story?"

"No." And the word comes out of my mouth much colder than I meant it to.

"All right, easy Skywalker." She's looking at me now and I read the word RUSHMORE at the top of her page.

"My name's Luke," I snap, and I look at her without blinking. Leia looks a bit surprised and she's about to say something back when the blond kid is standing in front of our desk.

"How's it going?" He's looking at just her. His voice sounds like he's completely relaxed, like the lesson is happening in his house and we're just guests.

Leia says, "Fine. Simeon, have you met Luke?"

Simeon?

Simeon looks at me, then back at Leia.

"You always find the interesting looking ones, don't you?"

What did he say? I feel my face turning away from them and I go over the last word I wrote with my pen. He already knows her. Leia puts her pen down. "He's the strong silent type." And the fact that they clearly know each other and are talking about me is making my skin crawl.

Simeon holds out his hand.

"Good to meet you, Luke. I'm the platonic ex." *What?*

"What?"

I look up at Simeon. His skin is perfect. *Platonic ex?*

"Yeah, me and Leia go way back." He smiles his Marks & Spencer smile.

I feel completely awkward, like I'm the new cast member on some teen sitcom that's been running for years and my eyes are darting round the room, checking if people are watching. Nobody is. Leia turns in her seat. "Ignore him, Skywalker. He likes to cause trouble."

Take his hand. Let him know.

I shake Simeon's hand, trying not to squeeze too tight and be that pathetic guy who has to demonstrate his masculinity, but firm enough to let him know I'm choosing not to.

Our hands part and Simeon leans forward, trying to read my writing. My arm instinctively curls round my paper, covering it up. Simeon smirks. "All right Scorsese, I wasn't trying to steal your ideas." Him and Leia are smiling and I know it's uncalled for, but I just want to punch him in the face. He wouldn't be able to stop me and it would pop the awkward bubble he's got me in. One punch and he'd be out.

"Anyway, we still up for the Electric later?"

Leia says, "Yeah," then looks at me. "You up for it? They're showing *Ghostbusters* One and Two. Classics."

And it's horrible. All of it, the staring, the nickname, his face, the fact that they're cinema buddies, her smiling.

"No," I say. "I'm busy."

Leia's face straightens, but she doesn't seem that bothered.

Then people start packing up for the end of the lesson and I'm so glad I get to leave, I think I actually smile.

I buy a jacket potato from the refectory and take it all the way down the hill to the graveyard to get away. I sit on a bench dedicated to a man called Harold who used to clean the graves. A couple of crows are fighting over what looks like a chicken bone in front of a dirty white marble stone slumped at an angle.

I'm telling myself I have no real reason to be angry, that I knew a lot of people would already know each other and be all confident and that. But him? Her ex? Mr Squeaky Clean 'I'm a young Brad Pitt' Simeon?

Forget her. Keep to yourself. You're not like this lot.

I dig a crater into the tuna with my white plastic fork. She said he likes to cause trouble. Maybe he was just saying it to wind her up, test me out.

She didn't deny it though, did she?

She didn't. How long did they go out for? Why are they still friends? Is that the kind of boy she likes?

I'm digging into yellow potato now. If he's her type, then...

Digging with my fork.

They're just a bunch of rich kids, they're not like you, forget them.

But she seemed cool. Still digging.

Did she stare?

The fork hits the bottom of the box.

Did she stare?

I'm still pressing.

The fork snaps.

Yes. She stared.

9.

I get off my second bus early and walk round to Dad's place.

I use the key he cut for me and, as I climb the dark stairs, I remember the afternoon I helped him move in. A year and a half ago. I remember watching his big body almost get wedged between the walls as he climbed up to the small attic studio flat. It'd been coming for a while; Marc getting sent down was just the rock that tipped the scales.

I come here sometimes when Dad's at work. Mostly I just watch a film and then leave. The whole place is the size of our living room.

The only window is the skylight and in the afternoon it shines a rectangular spotlight on to the floor where the white lino of the kitchen corner meets the mud-brown carpet. It's like a rubbish fairytale:

The Giant Who Lived in the Box Attic.

The sofa bed's still folded out and the sheets are strewn. There's an extra-large pizza box on the floor by the TV and empty lager cans on the draining board. I open the skylight to try and let out the man smell and start to tidy up. I stuff all the rubbish into a bin bag. I scrub the two plates and mug that have clearly been there for a few days. I fold the thin mattress of the bed back into a sofa and I use the dustpan and brush to sweep the carpet underneath. It feels like setting up a board game.

When I'm done, I sit on the sofa and look round the room. I always imagine this place is mine. My own flat, away from everyone. Just a toilet, sink, fridge, sofa, TV and enough DVDs to get lost in.

Simeon. The platonic ex. *Forget them.*

On the tiny chest of drawers in the corner to my left there's a photograph of all four of us at Frankie & Benny's. Dad got the waiter to take it. Him and Mum are in the middle, with Marc and me on the outsides. I take it from the drawers and hold it in my lap.

It's Marc's fifteenth birthday, so I'm eleven, fresh-faced, smooth skin, my hair longer and parted at the side. I remember Mum burning her mouth on her calzone and sucking an ice cube, Dad doing the ice-cream sundae challenge and winning a T-shirt.

I touch my face in the picture, feeling the smooth hard

glass. Then it catches the light and I see my reflection. My face now, superimposed over our family. Breathe.

The afternoon quiet of the room. Just me on a fold-up sofa, in a shady attic, holding the past in my lap. Somewhere now, in a house probably twenty times bigger than this place, Leia is getting ready to go to the cinema with her platonic ex and his perfect skin.

I leave the photo on the sofa and lower down into press-up position, but on my clenched fists, like Marc used to do them. My weight presses down through my knuckles into the floor as I start and the pain is good. *One, two.* I turn my head to the side and my eyes run along the spines of the DVDs against the skirting board. *Three.*

Guilt is the worst. *Four.* Burn me with angry, choke me with sad, anything but guilt. *Five, six.* Guilt lives in your skin, like lead. *Seven.* Sitting there, heavy. *Eight.* And poisonous. *Nine.* Telling you not to forget. *Ten. Eleven. Twelve.*

I see *Ghostbusters*, the white letters against black, and I stop. I can feel the muscles across my back pulled taut as I stay there, suspended, my knuckles raw from the friction and the pressure, and I see Leia, giggling as she hands the usher her ticket, Simeon smiling next to her as he wraps his tanned arm round her shoulders. I stare at the DVD.

"Come on, sleepy." Dad's voice wakes me up. I feel the pain in my neck as I sit up from resting on the sharp arm of the sofa bed. The light is on and through the skylight I can see a rectangle of black sky.

"Your mum was worried. Since when do you come on a Monday?"

I shrug. Dad nods. "I'll drop you back." His hands are smeared with oil as he ejects the *Ghostbusters* DVD and files it back into the row on the carpet.

I look at my phone and see four missed calls from Mum. It's half ten. She'll already be at the hospital. Dad hands me a twenty pound note. "Here, for cleaning up the place."

He smiles. I take the money. "Thanks, Dad."

"Come on, I wanna get to the chippy before it shuts." He rubs his barrel stomach as I pull on my trainers and follow him out the door.

```
EXT. — NIGHT
An old black Vauxhall Astra drives along the
night-time road, reflected streetlights rolling
over its bonnet.
```

*

63

"So it's going all right, then?"

He's watching the road as he drives and I'm thinking, every conversation feels easier in the car. Staring forward and talking should be standard procedure.

"Yeah," I say, "It's fine."

"Not too much homework?"

"We've only just started really. It'll be fine, Dad."

We're behind the same bus that I catch home from town.

Dad glances my way. "And what about girls?"

I think about Leia and Simeon and my legs tighten. "No."

Dad shrugs his boulder shoulders and I notice he's not wearing his seatbelt again. "What? I'm just asking. New pond, new fish, strapping young shark like yourself. You'll make a killing."

I shake my head. "What the hell does that even mean? Sharks? In a pond?"

And he's laughing. "I dunno. It's an analogy."

Now I'm laughing. "Oh, it's an analogy, is it, Joseph? And since when do you make analogies?"

"Well, when your boy goes off to college and starts mingling with college types, you need to step your game up, don't ya?"

He grips the steering wheel dramatically, pretending like he's trying to control a spiralling jet fighter, and waits for my reply. I just look at him, then blow a raspberry with my tongue. "There's your analogy, old man."

And we laugh together as we turn on to the high road.

Our laughter fades out as we drive down ours and he pulls up outside the house. You can see the hall light is on through the glass top of the front door, but we both know the house is empty.

"You wanna cup of tea or something?" I say. Dad looks at the house.

"Better not, wouldn't want to get too comfy, eh?"

I unbuckle my seatbelt. "OK. Enjoy your chips then."

"Luke," he says and I sense something coming. He turns to me, his chunky hands in his lap. "We can talk. I mean, if you want to."

It's not what I was expecting. I know how hard it is for him to bring it up. I've thought about it lots of times. All his size and strength didn't count for anything when they sent his son down, and I know he would've done the same thing as Marc if he'd found out first. I know he doesn't speak about it to anyone. I know not speaking about it drove the nails into the coffin of him and Mum.

"He couldn't handle you seeing him, you know?"

And, just like that, there's a tiny crack in the wall of him.

I can't help staring. "What?"

Dad won't look me in the eye, but he carries on. "He made me promise not to bring you, for visits. Your mum too. He didn't want either of you seeing him in there. Me either. That's why I stopped going."

It's the most he's said about Marc since he's been away and I don't know where to look. Our road is dark and quiet.

"I told him. I told him, Luke. One's enough. One good punch and walk away. One…" He breathes through his nose like an animal. "Him who can't hear, must feel. Eh son?"

I say nothing. Just sit next to my old man, feeling more like a grown-up than I ever have.

Dad shifts in his seat. "Anyway, that chippy'll be shutting. I'll see you, Lukey." And the moment's over and I'm about to get out, when he grabs my head with his big hand and pulls it towards him, kisses me on the crown, then pushes me off. "Go on, get home."

I watch the car drive away, the red brake lights as it reaches the corner, then it's gone. One small scene. The least amount of words, but it feels like somebody just lifted up the heavy rock of my dad and showed me something growing underneath.

10.

I'm walking up the hill to college. It's Tuesday.

I've convinced myself that 'brooding loner' is my persona of choice. I'll find a different seat in film, and if there isn't one, I'll just style it out and keep quiet till Leia gets the picture.

As I get to the campus, my phone beeps. It's a message from Tommy:

Yo, hurry up and hook me up with one of them posh girls, Lukey, don't be tight. T

I picture him sitting on a stack of paving slabs, smoking a cigarette in between middle-aged builders with thick necks and rubbish tattoos as I type a reply:

Sorry mate, they're all only interested in me. Animals they are. I'm knackered to be honest. See you tomoz

I read the words and stare past my phone at the floor as I click send.

Groups of people are walking towards different lessons in different buildings and even though he'd probably do or say something to properly embarrass me, I'm wishing Tommy was here right now.

Leia isn't there when I walk into class, but there aren't any other spare seats besides the one next to hers so I just sit where I did before, and prepare myself to play it cool. A pale girl with the sides of her head shaved and a ponytail is playing music through her phone to the blonde girl next to her. They both stare at me as I sit down and I make myself not look away. *Get a good look if you want.*

Noah's sitting at the front, just watching people as they talk, then Leia walks in with Simeon and I pretend not to notice.

"Hey," she says, as she sits down next to me. She's wearing a black Stussy hoodie and it's probably a birthday present he got her when they were going out or something. *Definitely*. I nod without speaking and stare forward like I'm ready for the lesson to start. I watch Simeon slap palms with the chunky rugby boy as he sits down and I try and give him a nosebleed with my mind.

Just forget them.

Noah slams his hands down on his desk and everyone jumps.

He stands up slowly and turns to the whiteboard. He's acting differently, like he's waiting for something, and pretty much everyone's eyes are trained on his back as he pulls out a marker and starts to write.

He does a big letter S, then a capital H. A couple of people look at each other, then back at him. As he starts the straight line of an I people are starting to chatter. Noah steps back from the board without turning around and holds his arms out like a conductor.

What's this guy doing?

And it shouldn't be a big deal really, a teacher about to write the word SHIT on a board, but it feels like we're all breaking the rules together. Then Noah steps forward and curves the I round and up into a U and writes SHUT UP. And everything's quiet. He turns round and he's smiling and I'm thinking, right now, that must feel amazing.

"You hear that?" he says. People are looking round, out of the window and shaking their heads. My eyes don't leave him.

"Somebody just fell in the shower." He tilts his head slightly as though he's listening for it himself. "You hear it?" He raises his index finger.

People don't know where to look, but I've played this game. I still play this game all the time on my own and I like him. *I like you, Noah.*

"No one?"

He's starting to look a bit let down. Nobody else even seems like they might be getting ready to speak. Then my hand goes up. *What are you doing?*

"I heard it."

Get your hand down now.

But I just keep it there, as everyone's eyes turn to me. Noah cracks a smile. "Thank you…" He's leaning forward, waiting for me to say my name.

I lower my hand. "Luke. My name's Luke."

I can feel Leia looking at me on my right, but I stay with Noah. He nods. "Good. Now the real question is, Luke, are they dead?"

And it's like the scene is ours. Me and him with an audience either side of us. Simeon's staring back, but I don't care. This is why I'm here. *What?* This is why I'm here.

"No. He's not," I say, and my blood is electric.

"Ah," says Noah, "so he's a he?"

And the room is gripped and I can feel ideas flicking

through my head like holiday photos in fast forward.

"Yeah, he's a man. A young man, and he's not dead, he's just lying down."

As the words come out of my mouth I picture Marc, curled up on his side in a white shower cubicle, like Michael Biehn at the start of *Terminator*, steam rising as water falls on him.

The girl with the shaved head frowns. "That's stupid."

People look at her. I stay on Noah, as he says, "Is it?"

"Yeah," says the girl. "Why would somebody just lie down in the shower?"

Noah looks at her. "And that's why it's brilliant." He points at her with one hand and at me with the other. "Because you want to know."

My throat's dry as I swallow, but I feel great. He said my idea was brilliant.

Then Leia speaks. "It's what he does." All eyes move to her.

I turn in my seat. She's leaning forward, like she's getting ready for a race. I stare at her mouth as she says, "He waits until his family have gone to work and then he runs a shower and he lies underneath it in the bath. It reminds him of the rain."

Then she's looking at me with those dark shining eyes and I'm looking back at her and it's so clear. *There's something there.* There's definitely something there.

"Amazing!" Noah's clearly excited. "You two have to work together."

No wait… Brooding loner, remember?

But then Noah claps his hands and says, "OK, everyone! Pair-up and wait for your sound. Find your character. Start where it matters. In a moment where things hang in the balance. Show us that moment, offer us a question that we need to know the answer to. I'll come round and hear ideas. Ready? OK. Go."

II.

For nearly an hour we talk ideas.

I suggest something, Leia listens, then she gives an idea and I respond, and back and forth again and again as we build up our character and his backstory together. Her ideas are brilliant, and the whole time we're talking it's like I forget everything else as I just watch this story we're creating grow out of nothing on the table in front of us.

By the time Noah works his way round to us we've got a sketched-out scene and both of us are charged.

"Come on then," he says, squatting down in front of our desk. His eyes are excited.

I look at Leia, she looks at me. "You wanna start?"

"No, you can."

And her face lights up. "OK, so it's morning, right, Luke?"

I nod. Noah watches her.

"So it's morning, late morning, like half eleven or something,

73

and he's lying down in the shower. It's a bath actually, one of those cool free standing ones with the feet and there's steam as the shower's raining down on him. He's nineteen."

"What's his name?" Noah asks and we realise at the same time that we didn't give him one.

I hear Marc's name in my head. Then Leia says, "Toby. His name's Toby."

Noah nods. Leia carries on. "OK. The house is empty. His dad's at work and his younger sister's at college. She's nearly seventeen."

She uses her hands as she talks, like Mum does, and it hits me that maybe Toby is her brother's name in real life and if she's using real details then he's the same age as Marc.

"So he's a scientist. Physics, actually, and he's working on a really complicated theory. The shower helps him think." My stomach's dancing as she speaks and my pen rings a circle round her email address that she scribbled on my pad.

Noah frowns, but in a curious way rather than unhappy. "Where's Mum?" he asks.

Leia taps her pad with her pen. "She left, but when Toby was little, she used to have baths with him. They used to sit in the bath together and put the shower on and pretend it was raining. It's a good memory, like his happy place, and now it's his best place to think."

Did her mum leave?

Noah's eyes are narrow, like he's following her train of thought. "I see. So it's like his connection to Mum, even though she's gone?"

Leia nods. "Yeah. Exactly. It gives him clarity."

"I like it," says Noah, then he looks at me. "And what's this theory then?"

I glance at Leia and clear my throat. "Time travel."

Noah's eyes widen and I feel my face smiling. "Time travel?"

"Kind of. Not backwards in time, that's not possible, but he thinks he might have figured out a way to see into the future. Maybe."

Leia cuts in. "We're not sure yet. He's like this super brain, but kind of a recluse. He finished his first degree when he was fourteen."

"And he has these dreams," I add.

I made the dreams bit up on the spot and look at Leia nervously, but she nods with wide eyes to let me know she's cool with it and for some reason I feel the urge to hold her hand. I don't, obviously. Then it's the end of the lesson.

Noah stands up and scratches his chin like he's thinking

and I don't want this to be over. Leia looks up at him. "What do you think?"

The pair of us watch him. He slides his hands into his pockets and I can see the muscles in his upper arms through his thin cream shirt.

"I think it's brilliant."

And I laugh, out of nowhere, like a fat HA!

What was that? I feel myself shrug, but it's all right because Leia's beaming. Then Noah says, "I think you've got something here. Something to run with. Well done. Keep working on it together, yeah? You're obviously a great team." And I feel myself straightening up in my chair.

"We will," says Leia.

I start to pack my bag and I'm glowing, like I just won a race.

Then Simeon is standing in front of our desk. "How lame was that?" he says, and my glow flicks off, like the bulb just popped.

Simeon's rolling his eyes and pointing with his head towards Noah at the front of the class.

"What's this guy's thing for picturing people in the shower? What a perv." He forces a laugh and I feel my shield coming up.

"Lame?" says Leia. "That was amazing! Wasn't it, Luke?"

And even though it was, even though it was easily the best

lesson I've ever had in my life, and even though she's looking at me knowing that we just shared something that felt sort of magic, I just shrug.

"Dunno." And I get up and leave.

Good lad. *Keep it cold.*

Sometimes I feel like I could turn myself inside out. Concentrate my mind, tense every muscle, and burst my skeleton out of my skin. One total action and then done. Let everything out and explode. Sometimes I feel like I could do that. Push the detonator and make a massive mess for other people to clean up.

But whenever I think it, the voice in my head tells me I'm all talk.

"What the hell was that?"

Leia's walking after me as I head down the hill. I don't turn around.

"Oi, wait up a second!" She moves round in front, facing me. I carry on. She walks backwards and it's almost like we're dancing.

"You're in my way."

She doesn't move. "What's wrong with you?"

And I think about the scene in *Goodfellas*, when Karen comes looking for Henry after he stands her up and she's angry and shouting at him and his voiceover is describing the spark in her eyes.

Leia stops walking and I have to stop so I don't walk into her. I look straight at her. "What do you want?"

"What do *I* want? We're supposed to be working together!" I see three boys walking up the hill on the other side of the road. They're looking at us.

"Stop shouting, man."

And she instantly gets more angry. I can see her jaw tensing and her right eye is kind of twitching. "I don't know what your problem is, but we've got work to do."

"Why don't you just work with Simeon?" And as I say it, I realise how pathetic I sound.

"What?"

"Forget it." And I step around her and carry on to the underpass.

Leia skips after me. "What's Simeon got to do with anything?"

And it's like we're in *Hollyoaks* or something, and I just want to press rewind and not open my mouth. Things go darker as we walk into the underpass and the strip lights make it feel even more like a staged scene.

"Luke. What's the matter? What's your problem with Simeon?" Her voice is soft and confused and I wanna hit myself. I want to bury my fist into my own face.

I shake my head. "I don't give a shit about Simeon. I don't even know Simeon. I don't even know you."

She's looking right at me now, trying to work me out.

What's she staring at?

"Forget it," I say. I start walking away faster and feel the disappointment as Leia doesn't try to keep up.

"So you don't want to work together?" she calls after me. I turn back and she's just standing there, wide shot, framed by the underpass entrance, looking at me and I hate the fact that she can't just read inside my head. *I'm an idiot. I know I am, but there's something here. Between you and me. I've felt it. Just gimme a chance.*

Why can't she do that? Why can't I say that? I want to. But instead I say:

"I'm gonna do my own idea. By myself."

Then I turn and walk away.

12.

I used to watch the girl next door wash her BMX.

From Mum and Dad's bedroom window she couldn't see me.

Every Sunday morning, she'd wheel it out on to the dirty slabs by their back door, flip it over and clean it with a toothbrush.

Her name was Becky.

Something about the way she moved, the care she took, mesmerised me.

I wanted to tell her, let her know I thought she was amazing.

So I wrote her a note, on Dad's yellow pad, and posted it the day we left to go up and see Uncle Chris in Yorkshire.

The two weeks we were away I thought about her every day. Yorkshire was so boring. Dad and Uncle Chris fixing old bikes. Marc cooking with Mum. There was nothing to do but walk in the wet fields and think about Becky. Her face as she opened the letter. Her writing one back. Me running alongside her as she rode her BMX to the park.

The drive home was all butterflies.

Then we pulled into our road and I saw the SOLD sign straight away. I didn't even know her house was for sale. Through the front window I could see empty walls and stripped floorboards.

On our door mat, among the post, was a sky-blue envelope with my name on it. I ran upstairs, shut my bedroom door and sat on my bed to read it. All it said was:

I always liked you watching me, Luke.
You should've said sooner.
Bye
Becky x

I'm on my bed, staring across at my bookcase of DVDs.

My bedside lamp's pointed up at them like the Twentieth Century Fox spotlight. Mum's at work at the hospital. It's just after midnight.

Forget her.

I stare at the DVD spines and picture Leia standing in the underpass, staring confused as I walk away.

Forget her. She's no different.

But she feels different.

She stared just the same, didn't she?

My hand comes up to my face. *Didn't she?*

My fingertip traces my scar. The curved sickle of torn skin that swoops from above the middle of my left eyebrow, down over my eyelid, across my cheek towards my ear. The glossy smoothness of it. Branding me.

I think about how there's a version of me, somewhere else, in another universe, without a scar. A sixteen-year-old Luke Henry with a face that isn't torn, who doesn't live his life through the stares of strangers. I think about cells. How they die and regenerate and replace themselves and why can't the cells of a scar be like all the others?

Nan said every scar is the memory of a mistake. A reminder to learn from. I get that. I understand. But do I have to see that memory every day for the rest of my life?

Look at you.

I picture Simeon, head cocked back in laughter, his perfect skin. It's all so cliché. It can't be that simple. Surely she can see past it.

What does she see when she looks at me?

Trouble. That's what she sees. *Just like everybody else.*

I open my notebook in my lap and stare at the page. Zia's words from the other day are written at the top: My life is my scrapbook.

My eyes close and my head goes back until it touches the wall behind me.

I use my neck muscles and push back, feeling the pressure in my crown.

"My life is my scrapbook." Deep breath. "My life is my scrapbook."

I stare across and read the spines on my top shelf, a jumble-sale mix of films I stole from Dad and Marc and other ones I don't think either of them have seen; *The Conformist*, *A Room For Romeo Brass*, *Somebody Up There Likes Me*, *Buffalo 66*.

And then I have an idea.

I'm on my knees pulling out my notebooks. All of them. I spread them out on the floor around me. They're all A4. Some have scribbled words on the front. Some have doodles and rubbish sketches. One of them has a crude picture of a hand gun in black biro against the brown of its cover. I open it up and flick through, looking for something, then I find it.

We sit opposite each other across the plastic table.

The room has small square windows pushed up near the ceiling and through them it's afternoon. Spaced out pairs of people all sitting across identical tables from each other. The walls are off-white. A thick-set prison guard stands next to the door. I look across the table at Marc. Nervous. He just stares and says, "You shouldn't have come." I want to tell him I wanted to. I had to. He's my brother. I can help him get through this. But I don't. I just sit.

Then his skin is changing. Becoming dotted. Grainy. His facial expression doesn't change, but his skin is becoming sandpaper. Rough and speckled.

"Marc. What's happening? Marc?"

He doesn't respond, his skin getting darker and rougher. And then his chin breaks off, the bottom of his jaw crumbling into sand, spilling down his chest. "Marc?" Then his shoulder, like old stone, disintegrates. Then his chest, caving into itself. "Marc!" Then all of him. His neck gives way, then his face, his expression never changing as all of him crumbles away.

I lay the notebook on the floor, open at the page. I can see it. I can see him. And I can use it.

I pick up my new one and I write: Marc

What you doing?

I write Nineteen

What are you doing?

I cross out Nineteen and write Marc. 20 yrs old.

You shouldn't be writing this.

But I don't listen. I just carry on.

Marc showers. He dries himself and walks back to his cell. He gets dressed. We can hear shouts and the occasional clank of metal on metal. He folds his towel up and lays it over the back of the chair, watching himself in the small shaving mirror stuck on to the wall above the sink. His dark hair is cut close, light stubble on his top lip and chin, cheeks smooth and fresh. Chiselled.

He stares at his reflection, lowering his chin until it's almost touching the grey of his sweater, his shoulders rise and fall as he breathes.

Then he speaks. "I'm coming home."

13.

I'm staring out of the window in comms.

From where we are on the second floor I can just make out the dimpled curve of the Bullring. The teacher lady's leading a class discussion on immigration and it feels like I'm sitting in the audience on *Question Time*. An annoying girl with an anime face, dressed fully in American Apparel, has been talking about how disgusting nationalism is and how tabloid newspapers are to blame for most of the lesson. She's really enjoying having centre stage and I've been trying to picture her and Tommy on a date. Him looking confused by the menu as they sit in some posh restaurant, her regurgitating snippets of popular opinion that she's stolen from blogs.

The girl scans the classroom checking everyone's paying attention to her and I remember Dad saying that people with the freedom to talk mostly do only that.

"It's all just fear mongering," she says, and I imagine Tommy in blue overalls in front of an open furnace, hammering a piece of metal that's shaped into the word FEAR.

"They use our insecurities about money to whip up hatred," she goes on.

I look down into my open bag at my notepad and think about how it's film after lunch.

"What about you, Luke?"

The teacher's talking to me. Louise. She looks like she might've been the lead singer in a band a long time ago. Her hair sprouting out of her head, like blonde fire with dark roots.

"Where do you stand on this?" And a room full of eyes are burning me. My feet are digging into the carpet as I try to look like I have an opinion.

"Where are you from?"

What the hell's that supposed to mean?

"Birmingham," I say, and a few people laugh. I can feel the cords in my neck.

Louise smiles and says, "No, I mean your family, originally?"

I look round the room. There's a handful of other kids who aren't white, so she's not singling me out, but my back is still up.

Why is she asking me? What do I say?

Dad's mum came from Jamaica and married an Irish man she met five minutes from where we live now, and Mum's dad was French and married an English woman he met when she put a plaster cast on his broken arm. Where do I stand on this? To be honest it's not something I ever really think about. We don't talk about it at home. I know that I've never felt English, but I've never really felt Jamaican or French or Irish either. We're from Birmingham. The one time we went abroad as a family, to Corfu, a girl from Belgium asked Marc where he was from and that's what he said. The girl asked what country and Marc just smiled and said Birmingham was enough.

Louise changes her approach. "Question is," she says, "should there be one rule for people born in a country and one for those who've come from somewhere else?" and the eyes on me are getting hotter.

What the hell is her problem?

I don't know, Miss. Probably not. I don't care. Ask someone else. *Everybody's shit stinks.* I try not to hear it. Say it. My teeth grind together.

Louise shrugs. "Well?"

I shake my head. *Say it, you chicken.*

"No." I cough out the word.

She stares. "And why not?"

Say it.

"Everybody's shit stinks." And Louise's face drops as the

whole class breathes in, and the words are just there, on the table in front of me like a puddle of invisible puke.

I wipe my mouth. My legs are twitching. Louise nods. "OK, thank you, Luke. Interesting angle, if perhaps a little coarse."

And I can feel people fighting the urge to whisper and giggle, but it's different somehow. It's all right. The bell goes and as I stand up, I catch the eyes of the ginger skater kid, who was with Simeon, across the room. He's wearing a grey Supreme hoodie. He nods at me, his bottom lip sticking out, like he's agreeing.

I am the brooding loner. I nod back. And walk off, buzzing inside.

You're welcome.

In the refectory I sit on my own near the wall at the end of a long fold-out table, eating a tuna-melt baguette.

I can see the ginger kid from comms a couple of tables down sitting with a gang of friends. I script their conversation in my head. He's telling them about what I said in class and how I don't give a shit. A couple of them sneak glances and I hold my head up proudly like, yeah, I'm *that* guy.

I take out my phone, then Leia walks in. I drink all of her in from bottom to top without blinking. Skinny jeans, oversized black woollen jumper with flecks of white in it hanging past her bum and a bright neon pink scarf. Her hair's up in a high bun and there's a pencil speared through it. She looks like an artist. I swallow my mouthful and try not to look up from my phone. *Time to go.*

But I don't move. I think about the idea in my notebook, Marc getting ready to leave prison. How I want to show her. How I think she'll like it. But I was such a melodramatic knob yesterday. She's not gonna want to speak to me, and I don't know what I'd say if she does. I take a massive bite, pushing the rest of my baguette into my mouth, trying to be done, and a flap of hot melted cheese drops on to my chin. I go to wipe it, conscious of Leia, still holding my phone. Then my phone beeps and I drop it. It bounces off the table and smacks on to the floor. *Smooth.*

As I pick it up, I glance over at Leia in the queue. She's not looking. The boys at the other table are though, staring right at me. Mouthful of baguette, cheese goatee. I play it cool and open the message, nonchalantly pushing the cheese into my mouth like an afterthought. There's a fresh crack that curves from the top middle of the phone screen to the right edge, like a personalised scar in the glass.

It's Tommy.

Yo. Footy at six. I got us a game with my cousin. Zia's in. I'll still get you at three yeah?

I tap: **Cool.**

And carry on chewing.

"Are you on contract?"

I almost choke as Leia sits down opposite me. I don't get it. She points at my phone. "They're real idiots about replacements. I dropped mine down the toilet and it took a month to get a new one."

She opens the packet of her sandwich. I read the label. Rocket and crayfish. *Crayfish?* Maybe yesterday didn't really happen. *Yes it did.* I look at my phone and don't tell her that Tommy's brother Jamie got us all the same knocked off Samsung Galaxy from a guy he knows who works at Argos.

"It's just a crack." I stare over her shoulder at the ginger kid and his friends, then say, "Listen, I—"

"I dreamt about you last night," she says, putting her untouched sandwich down.

"I just… what did you say?"

"I said I dreamt about you, Skywalker. Well, you and me." *She what?*

"We were working on the script, in this big loft apartment

in New York or something. It had these wooden floors. Have you seen *Big* with Tom Hanks?"

I'm still thrown. "Course."

She points at me. "That apartment. That's where we were."

And I picture the apartment from *Big*, with the bunk beds and all the cool toys and I try to put Leia and me there in my head.

She dreamt about you?

And I don't know where from, but words come tumbling out of my mouth in a rush. "I've got a lot on at the minute. Home stuff." I look down as I say home, then look up when she doesn't say anything. "That's why I was a bit funny, I mean, in class and that."

Leia shrugs. "Whatever. You know the only vegetables they do here is cauliflower cheese. Does that even count?"

"Leia, I'm trying to tell you, to say—"

"It's fine." And her eyes are telling me to shut up, but not in a 'you should know your place' kind of way. More like she gets it. Like she can read between my lines.

She picks up her sandwich and looks straight at me. "I dreamt about us working together. That means something. Doesn't it?"

And suddenly I'm a car crash of confusion and excitement.

She dreams stuff too.

I reach down into my bag, take out my notebook and drop it on to the table in between us. Leia looks at it, smiling, and lays down her sandwich again.

"You like dropping things, don't you?"

And our conversation feels like a script. I rack my brains, trying to come up with a better response than *yeah*.

"Yeah."

"So?" She unscrews her bottle of water and swigs.

I suddenly feel like there might still be cheese on my chin and wipe my mouth with the tiny serviette. "So, I had an idea." I open the notebook to the page I started last night and twist it round so it's facing the right way for her to read. She presses the pages open with her fingers and I stare at her amber ring as she reads.

"This is good." Her eyebrows are raised as she nods.

I feel my chest rising. "Yeah?"

"Yeah. Really good, and it's giving me another idea." She leans forward. "Do you want to go somewhere with me, Luke?" The way she says my name is like she owns it.

"What d'you mean?" And I find myself leaning in too.

Leia's biting her bottom lip, and I'm trying not to stare.

"There's a place I like to go to, when I'm working on ideas.

It's in town."

"Town? But we've got film in quarter of an hour." I look at her lips again, full and biteable.

She sits up straight and rolls her eyes. "What? You never skipped lessons?"

"Course," I say, though apart from a couple of sickies over the years, we never fully bunked off. Not because we were scared, it just always felt like sneaking around was more trouble than it was worth.

"Let's go then." She's already standing up. "One thing though, Skywalker," she says.

"What?"

"No more of the moody boy crap, yeah? I get enough of that at home," she says, walking off.

Who is this girl?

I follow her out of the refectory, staring at the red and black pencil in her hair and neon pink against the skin of her neck and I know it sounds dumb, but as I walk, it's almost like I can feel myself growing.

14.

```
INT. BUS — DAY
GIRL sits staring out of afternoon bus window.
YOUNG MAN sits next to her. Both silent. He
watches her faint reflection as the bus heads
to town.
```

We get tea in little silver pots on brown trays like school dinners. The guy who serves us has the face of someone who just accidentally dropped a winning scratch card down the drain. He stares at my scar as we pay.

The seating area is flooded with light from the far glass wall. We're on the sixth floor and I can see the tops of city buildings and déjà vu creeps over me. Nan used to bring me here when I came into town with her as a kid. She'd get a tea and I was allowed a coke in a glass bottle that made me feel American.

"I haven't been here in years," I say. "Mad."

A few old people are scattered around in couples, or on their own. None of them are speaking, they just stare, like somebody pressed pause. We sit at a table near a tiny fenced-off children's area. The whole place smells like coffee and cats.

What the hell are you doing here?

Leia pours her tea. "Perfect right?" She smacks a sachet of sugar against the table. "My dad used to bring us here when we were little. We used to sit, watching people, giving them names and making up stories about them. It's still the same. It's like a time warp or something." She scans the scene. "Imagine that? If this little cafe was the only place in the world stuck forever in the same year? I come here on my own. A lot." Her smile is tinged with embarrassment. I look down and notice that the carpet looks like a massive furry chocolate chip cookie, doughy beige dotted with dark triangles.

Then I remember Tommy.

"Shit."

"What's wrong?"

"Nothing."

Leia stands up. "Good. So I'm going to the loo, then we talk ideas. Yeah?"

I nod and watch her as she walks away.

In the corner an old man and woman are sitting silently at a small table next to the floor-to-ceiling window. The woman is mixed race. She's taking tiny sips from her white tea cup, staring out at the city rooftops. The man's skin is lighter, but not pale. He's arranging small packets of sugar into a grid on the table. They look like they've been there a while, but they both still have their coats on and in my head they're two retired spies who spend their days daydreaming about old missions.

Maybe they're us. Me and Leia from the future. Maybe this place really is a time warp. *Don't start.*

I text Tommy:

Yo. Don't need lift after all. Got a college thing

I feel myself shrugging as I push send. I haven't even taken a sip before my phone beeps with a reply:

What about football? We need players yo!!!

Yeah Luke, what about football?

An old man wearing a grey flat cap shuffles past our table holding a tray and I think of Alfred, Bruce Wayne's butler.

Soz man. Can't do it. Speak tomoz

I imagine Tommy's face, screwing up in anger as he reads it. Then I picture the two empty seats at the back of film studies, Simeon staring back at them with the same screwed up face, and I smile.

My phone rings. It's Tommy. Leia's walking back towards me.

Stare at phone. Look at Leia. Stare at phone. Think of Tommy. Look at Leia.

Tap deny and put my phone on silent.

"Not important?" she asks as she sits back down.

"Nah. It's nothing," I say, sliding my flashing phone into my bag.

We talk for nearly three hours, referencing films we've seen and loved and ones we thought were complete crap, as we flesh out the characters for our potential script.

She loves Wes Anderson, especially *The Royal Tenenbaums* and *Rushmore*. She thinks Judd Apatow films are ugly. Natalie Portman is her favourite actor and we both agree that the original Japanese *Ring* is the scariest horror movie we've ever seen.

As we speak, our eyes meet, and look away again, doing the dance of two people both trying not to admit we've noticed something.

Leia's idea is that our character, Toby, and the one I started writing last night, Marc, are twin brothers. We scrap the time travel thing. Their parents split when they were young and Toby lived with Dad while Marc lived with Mum. Now they're thrown back together to live with their… "Mum," says Leia. "I just think it makes more sense."

I shake my head. "I reckon Dad. Two boys can be hard work."

"Why not both?" she says, and it strikes us at the same time that we never thought of their parents being together as a possibility. Leia says, "OK, cool. Mum and Dad are making another go of it. But it's tense."

"Course it is."

She goes to get more tea after an hour or so, and when I check my phone I see fourteen missed calls from Tommy. I know I'm letting him down, but this feels important.

We split a flapjack and it's like we're partners working on some investigation. An investigation into characters we've made up.

I feel a slice of guilt knowing that I'm writing Marc, but

talking about him, even indirectly, feels like taking off a chainmail coat.

I exaggerate details and I'm pretty sure she's doing the same, with Toby, making him this child genius, but it's fine. It's like we both know we're talking about our own families, without ever admitting that we are, and the whole time we talk, I'm aware that the distance between us is less than an arm's length. That I could reach out and touch her at any point. That I'm dying to.

By the time we finish our fourth cup of tea, the light's fading through the glass and shadows cut across the building tops. The pair of us nod, as we look at our pages of notes and if we really were detectives, this is where we'd high-five. But I want to do more than high-five. She feels it. I mean, I feel like she does, and we're looking at each other like something should happen to celebrate the moment.

Then her phone rings, and the moment's broken. I look around the room as she answers and notice that all of the old people have cleared out. Like they all disappeared at the same time.

"You're joking!" Leia's annoyed.

I start to tidy up the cups even though there's no need.

"And he's locked the door?" she says, and I'm drawing

arrows between sentences in my notebook to seem busy.

"Because I *am* pissed off, Dad. I'm kinda busy…"

I think of Dad kissing my head in the car the other night and wonder if it's her dad who's black or her mum.

Leia mimes an apology, then stands up and walks away as she speaks.

I think about how long it takes to feel like you know someone.

How it can happen after one chat. Like when you go on holiday, and you make a friend on the first day who feels like your best mate ever for the whole week you're there and when it's time to leave you're both crying and promising to write to each other and visit, but after you're home you can't even remember his name.

"I've got to go," says Leia, peeling her coat off the chair. "Sorry." And for the first time all afternoon, I notice frayed edges on her confidence. Her voice pretending to be upbeat.

"It's OK, we've made a start," I say, "and it's really good. Everything all right?"

"Yeah," she says. "It's just my brother. He's hard work. Long story." There's a pause and I'm not sure whether I'm supposed to ask to hear it. Then Leia says, "We should swap numbers, right? So we can talk ideas, I mean?"

I look to the window.

"Bad idea?" Leia says. I shake my head.

"No. Great idea. For ideas, I mean."

"Exactly. That's it."

And I'm Captain Awkward. I want to say something cool. Some little throwaway gem that will swim round her head and make her think of me later on. But nothing comes.

She types my number into her phone and I try to disguise the beam on my face with a yawn as I lean down to get my bag.

When I straighten up again, she's looking at me.

"How many stitches?" says Leia, and my bag hits the floor.

My stomach muscles pull tight as I bend down to pick it up again and when I stand up, I turn my body slightly away from her.

What's her problem?

But, as I look at her, it really doesn't seem like she has one. She's staring at me, but smiling, and I want to trust her. *You don't even know her*. And I don't, but man, I want to.

I turn to face her straight on.

"Twenty-eight."

Her mouth twitches slightly, just the hint of a wince, but her eyes aren't pitiful, just curious, I think. So I let her look, feeling her move along the soldered tear in my face.

Then she smiles. "Cool."

And I don't want to move. I want to stay right here. I want her to stay with me and I just want to curl up next to her and go to sleep.

I5.

Tommy said: *If you've never even had the thought, like, just the idea, for a second, of having somebody's name tattooed on to your body, you don't really love them.*

It's nearly six when I head to the bus stop and I'm caught in the stream of after-work businessmen and women packing the pavements. Tommy's probably slagging me off right now to Zia as they warm-up ready for kick-off. But I'm still buzzing from the afternoon with Leia. *She took my number.*

I tell myself I'll ring Tommy later, then I see Noah and it stops me in my tracks.

He's standing outside the museum with a woman who looks a bit like Donna, but with longer hair, and older. She's wearing one of those rain coats that could be a man's or a woman's, with a posh-looking handbag over her shoulder and she's pointing right in Noah's face, like she's telling him off.

He's just standing there, like he's not allowed to speak and finding it hard to look her in the eye. Then she's walking away. Noah grabs her arm and tries to stop her, but she shrugs and storms off. She looks so much like Donna it's kinda freaky. Mediterranean and proper pretty and she's got that look on her face of angry satisfaction that people have when they get to be the one who storms off and steals the scene.

I watch Noah watch her leave. He runs his palm down over his face and I see him think about going after her, his eyes following her trail. Then he gives up and looks down, probably replaying what just happened or chipping loose an old memory.

Usually when you see a teacher out in the real world it's weird. Like, if you see them outside of school – coming out of the cinema or something – it's just creepy, like you're reading their diary. But seeing Noah's different, somehow. It's almost like he belongs in the real world and college is the weird part.

I watch him walk along the side of the museum and turn round the corner and, for a second, I go to follow him, then I remember that I skipped his class this afternoon. Besides, my head is full of Leia and ideas and how, even though I can't really talk about Marc to anyone in real life, I now get to pour him into a story. One that I can control.

I decide to walk, rather than poaching on a packed bus that'll just sit in traffic for half an hour. My whole body's still buzzing with ideas and I always think better when I'm moving. Noah thought our idea was brilliant – wait until he hears how we've built on it. He asked for backstory, he's gonna get it, and I'm trying to think of a single teacher at school who I wanted to impress as much as I want to impress him. I'm trying to think of a teacher whose opinion I even cared about. Is it just cos he knows film stuff? But my gut's telling me there's something more about him.

I check the time as I pass the hospital and think of Mum inside hanging her jacket up and tying her hair back, ready for her shift. How much blood and bone will she see between now and morning? How many stitches and x-rays and cardboard bowls full of concussed puke will she have to deal with, and I remember her saying, "Not everyone can be a nurse, Lukey. Not everyone has it in them."

I see her face when she came into the treatment room that afternoon. The emergency room nurse recognised my surname and called Mum from whatever ward she was working on. The white of her eyes as she stared, her face frozen as she took me in. She made them let her do it. She wanted to make sure it was perfect. To fix me. *Imagine.* Having to stitch up your own son's face.

I turn off down the high road, towards ours, and take out my phone to call Tommy, preparing myself for the riot act. I picture Leia, biting the end of her pencil and smiling across the table as I shared an idea, backlit by the window, the blurred figures of old people out of focus behind her. Worth a bit of grief off Tommy any day.

I'm about to push call, then I hear an engine. The kind of engine that's obviously been beefed up so it's too big for the car.

The kind that growls.

I turn back and the road is quiet. No headlights or movement, so it must've come from the high road. But the feeling that I'm being watched crawls over my shoulder around my chest and my skin goes cold. I scan both ways and the road is empty.

Everything's still. Lifeless. But I put my phone away and sprint the last fifty metres to our front door.

I'm shopping with Nan. She's letting me push the trolley around and getting to steer is a big deal.

We go up and down the aisles, her placing things gently into the metal cage, me wishing she'd go a bit quicker, trying to perfect my corner manoeuvres. By the time we reach the tins, I'm itching to put my foot down and see what the trolley can do. Nan keeps reminding me to stay in control, but I have to know what it feels like. So I take off, imagining I'm pushing a toboggan as I speed past cans of Heinz soups, Nan calling out from behind me.

I don't crash.

I push my soles into the floor as I reach the end of the aisle and lean right, skidding in a smooth arc and coming to a stop next to the jars of honey.

A man in supermarket uniform stares at me and, back up the aisle, I can make out Nan scowling in my direction, but I don't care. I'm buzzing. Then as I straighten up the trolley to push it back up to her, I nick the shelf to my right. The jars wobble and one from the top falls.

I feel my stomach drop as I watch it dive towards the floor, waiting for the crash, but when it hits, the only sound is a kind of muffled crack. A sticky thud. I stare down as the amber ooze of honey starts to spread out like lava, shards of glass trapped in it.

Then Nan's next to me, scowling as I just stand there covered in trouble.

"Him who can't hear, must feel, Luke." I say nothing, the

sound of the impact replaying in my head.

Years later, I hear it again. I'm in Year Seven and watching a fourteen-year-old Marc square up to a bigger kid from Year Eleven. The bigger kid swings, Marc bobs, and as he comes back up he throws an uppercut that connects square on the kid's chin. The kid buckles like his body is a tower block and someone just pushed the demolition plunger, but it's the sound that hits me. That same muffled crack, only this time, instead of glass and honey, it's flesh and bone.

16.

I'm in the middle of my bedroom floor on a small island of carpet surrounded by a sea of open notebooks. A sea of ideas.

My life is my scrapbook.

I'm building backstory for the Marc in our film, using memories, made-up stuff, bits of me, things people have said, mining treasure from six years of noted-down dreams and ideas, and I'm writing it all into my new notebook, ready to show Leia. I could use my laptop, but typing isn't the same. I like feeling the pressure of my pen marking the page.

Across town, maybe on her bedroom floor, Leia's doing the same. We've been texting each other since I got home. It's nearly half one in the morning now and if this is what it feels like to make a film then I don't want to do anything else.

Marc used to be captain of the football team

Definitely. Toby used to collect worms and give them names

Ha ha! Marc got caught with a teaching assistant in the gym cupboard

Course he did! Toby likes girls, but only at a distance. Why Marc with a C? x

Some of her texts have 'x's and some of them don't. It doesn't mean anything, but the ones with an 'x' make me smile slightly wider. She doesn't do a stupid winking face once. My wrist is aching from scribbling things down in between texting, but I don't care.

Their mum is half French? Marc used to get Toby to punch him in the face to show how hard he was

Really? Like the French thing. Layers

Yeah. But if anybody messed with Toby in school, Marc would sort them out

OK, but it's not just Marc muscle, Toby brains, that too easy. What Marc into? Maybe not everyone knows about?

Food

???

He wants to be a chef

Brilliant. And Toby has a temper. Not that strong, but he can lose it sometimes.

Agreed. Toby taught Marc to tell the time, even though they're the same age. And spell. And he did his science coursework for him. Are there photos of them together? Round the house?

No. Neither of them like photographs. It's a thing they both have. Although Toby did make a pinhole

camera in year 5!

Love it x

I risk an 'x'. There's no reply. Bollocks. Then:

What the hell happened to you shithead?

My stomach drops, before I realise it's Tommy. He's probably up playing FIFA. My eyes are starting to sting and the phone screen is blurry as I start to reply, then a new message lands from Leia.

Thanks. I'm very talented xx

Two 'x's? Wicked. I reply back to Tommy:

Sorry man, college thing. You win? x

And the second I click send I see the 'x'. Cack.

What the hell you kissing me for bumboy?

113

Play it cool.

Cos I love you, gorgeous. What? You don't want a kiss?

Piss off Luke. And I scored twelve. You better be at The Goose tomorrow night.

Course. My hero. Night Tom xxxxxxxxxxxx ;)

No reply. I win.

Eyes burning. Must. Sleep. Good working with you Skywalker. Nite x

And I'm picturing her lying on top of her duvet, covered in note paper, her soft hair spread out against her pillow like a thought bubble, and another idea starts to grow.

I'm sitting on a stool. Marc is sitting on my lap, but it's not him. It's a life size ventriloquist's doll version of him. My hand is up the back of his grey T-shirt and I'm controlling his mouth. Leia is sitting next to me with a life-size doll version of Toby on her lap. He has black glasses with thick frames. His face and body are lean, but not skinny. He's wearing a flannel shirt and Leia has her hand up it, controlling his mouth. We're on a stage. We're smiling at each other as we direct their conversation, her doing Toby's voice, me doing Marc's.

Marc - You're such a nerd

Toby - You're such a thug

Marc - Baby

Toby - Caveman

Marc - I love you

Toby - I love you too

Me and Leia are laughing and cameras are flashing, because there's an audience. It's a press conference for our film. We are the writers and directors. Like the Cohen Brothers. There's a banner behind us that reads THE BROTHERS DIFFERENT. That's the name of our film. Our first film.

THE BROTHERS DIFFERENT. THE BROTHERS DIFFERENT.

I text Leia.

We should call it THE BROTHERS DIFFERENT

Then I crawl on to my bed and fall asleep.

17.

I wake up in my clothes.

Straight away I can tell it's too early. I should be knackered, but I'm still buzzing. I check my phone. No new messages.

It's ten to seven. Mum's not due back until half past. I could make her breakfast. If I go to the shop now I could get stuff for a fry-up and be back and cooking for her when she walks in. I could do that.

I skip over the notebooks on my floor, grab my jacket from the landing banister and leave.

It's one of those crisp mornings that look nice but feel freezing. I keep my hands in my jacket pockets as I walk. I cut through the back of the new houses that look like they're made of cardboard and across the little playground in front of the flats to Sandhu's shop. Everything's early-morning quiet.

Sandhu's is shut.

Doesn't open until half seven. I contemplate just going home, but decide to see my gesture through. It'll surprise Mum and be a good start to the weekend, so I walk back to the playground and sit on the only swing that hasn't been tied into a knot.

I stare up at the flats. The dark windows look like buttons on a giant grey remote control and I try to figure out which one is Tommy's. His place is on the ninth floor and from his living room window you can see pretty much across town.

The playground's only a few years old but it's already battered. The chipped paint makes the metal spring-mounted animals look demonic.

My phone beeps.

I love it! Perfect title. This is going to be ace Skywalker. Happy Saturday! x

And I'm smiling. All's good as I watch a brand-new white Mini with black trim pull up across the road.

A curvy blonde girl gets out dressed like she's been clubbing. Her black skin-tight dress looks like it's shrinking as she shuffles in her high heels towards the lobby doors of the flats. Tommy's second oldest brother Jamie gets out of the driver side and shuts the door. He's dressed in black too, jeans and designer T-shirt. Him and Marc were tight in school, but I don't see him much these days. He works in some office in town selling things on the phone.

The headlights flash as he sets the car alarm and then he's looking at me. He raises a hand with his thumb up and nods my way. I do the same. He watches the blonde girl disappear inside and turns to follow her, then changes his mind and starts walking towards me. I put my phone away and then he's standing there.

He's not as big as I had him in my head and his hair looks like he got it done in one of those posh places, all slick and side parted.

"Yes, Lukey, what you saying?"

I shrug. "Not much, Jay, you good?"

"You know, can't complain." He glances back at the flats.

"Good night?"

"Yeah, fine, mostly just watching her dance. Funky House, not really my thing, eh?"

I smile a sheepish, little-brother smile. Jamie rubs his hands together. "How's your mum?"

I look past him up at the flats. "Fine."

"Good. You waiting for Tommy?"

I look down. "Nah, just waiting for the shop to open."

Slightly awkward silence.

"Tommy says you're getting a house," I say.

He slides his hands in his pockets and hunches his shoulders from the cold. "Yeah, we've been on the council waiting list for a couple years now. Think they've found us a place."

"Whereabouts?"

"Other side of town pretty much, near the cricket ground."

"Cool."

Tell him he looks like a pretty boy. Why's he trying so hard? I look at my feet and try not to listen.

Jamie says, "Tom said you're going college, that right?"

"Yeah."

Oi, pretty boy! Who cut your hair? Who you trying to impress?

Jamie's nodding. "Good lad. Always knew you had the brains, Lukey."

I keep my eyes down. I know what's coming.

"It's tomorrow, right?"

I nod, still looking at the ground. "Yep."

"Messed up, man."

I look up at him. His face is wrestling two different expressions.

"He did what had to be done, Luke. Everybody's glad he did it."

I'm biting my teeth together as I nod. He turns to walk away, but then turns back. "It's shitty how things work out, Lukey, you know? I think that sometimes." He's looking at me but seeing something else. "Got balls, your brother. Just went too far."

I want this to be over. He can feel it and walks away.

I rock back and forth on the swing until he's inside, then I kick off and start to fully swing, pushing my legs forward on the up and bending them back on the down. I keep swinging until my back is going horizontal each time. I'm gripping the cold chain with my hands and tilting my head back and with every swing, the world turns upside down.

18.

Nan said: Him who can't hear, must feel.

I step through the front door and smell bacon. The house is weirdly warm and I can hear *Buffalo Soldier* and the crackle of the frying pan from the kitchen. I look down at the feeble bag of breakfast ingredients I waited half an hour to buy and can't help but smile. Why's she cooking? I walk to the kitchen. Who's she cooking for, me? Why's she playing Bob Marley after a twelve-hour shift?

"Hello, son." He's sitting at the little kitchen table holding Mum's mug and straight away it feels false. Mum turns from the cooker and smiles with closed lips.

I look back at him. "What are you doing here?"

"Oh yeah, I'm good thanks, good to see you too."

"Sorry, Dad."

Mum puts a plate full of bacon and beans and egg and fried

dumpling in front of him.

"Thanks, Ange, this looks amazing." He breaks open a dumpling and I watch the steam. Mum nods without looking at him and goes back to the cooker.

"Sit down, Lukey."

I sit down. Mum puts my plate in front of me, then sits in the chair in between us, holding one of the cups we never use in both hands.

"You not eating, Mum?"

Mum shakes her head. "Your dad came over."

Classic 'state the obvious cos something bad is coming' line.

Hi, son, it's really sunny outside today, isn't it? By the way, the dog died.

Dad finishes chewing. "We need to talk."

I spear a crispy rasher of bacon and watch it crack in half.

"It's tomorrow, son."

He's looking at me. Mum's eyes are flicking between me and her mug. My hands are getting hot.

"We thought it was a good idea to talk about things," he says, then looks at Mum. "The three of us."

My fingers are strangling my fork. I'm supposed to say something, but my legs are twitching and it's them two versus me and I have to concentrate on breathing.

Then Mum speaks. "He's coming home, Luke. Marc's coming home."

And my stomach's churning.

Dad adds, "We need to prepare, big man. All of us."

Every single part of this is pissing me off. How long have they been planning it? Why are they acting like they can stand to be in the same room together? I know they can feel me squirming. Dad's chewing, Mum's sipping, both of them hiding behind the music and the breakfast.

Dad carries on. "He'll come back here, to start with."

"To start with? What does that mean?" I stare straight at him as I speak. Dad swallows.

"Things have changed, Luke. We've changed, all of us. Marc's nearly twenty-one. You'll be seventeen next month."

"What's that got to do with anything?" My eyes move between the pair of them. Mum puts down her mug. "Luke." Her voice has the same 'calm down' tone it used to have when I'd get excited in the car.

"Why now?" I blurt out.

Mum fakes confusion. "What do you mean, love?"

"I mean, why wait until the day before he comes out to 'talk about it'?"

Dad leans forward. "Easy, Luke. We've thought about this."

"Easy? What the hell part of this is easy, Dad?"

"Steady on, big man, don't forget yourself."

But I've started. My engine's running. I look at Mum. "Now we need to talk about it? Not then, not once since, but now?"

She can't look me in the eye.

I'm on the attack. "So what, then? What are the points of discussion? Do we lay out some five-step plan to deal with the return of the family convict?"

"Luke…" The mug's shaking in her hands. "We just want to do what's best, for everyone."

Dad's hands are balling into fists. "Stop it, son."

But I can't stop, and he knows I can't, and this all feels like some shitty scene from *EastEnders* and I'm the emotional teenager who's just gonna storm out cos he can't handle it and leave them looking at each other, shaking their heads as the front door slams.

"This is bollocks," I say, and I'm standing up and looking at them and I know they're trying – however rubbish they are at talking, this is them trying – but all my brain's doing is searching for something to say that will cut them, something sharp that will stick in their skin before I leave, but all I can seem to think is, can I take the food with me? *What's wrong with you?*

"I don't know!"

And they're both looking up at me with big eyes, like I'm some stray dog they've just found and I want to hit them. I want to punch them both in the face.

"Sit down, son." Dad holds up one big hand like a traffic warden. I don't move.

"Sit down, Luke, please," Mum pleads.

But all of me is hot and I'm looking at my plate of food and it's just dead meat and burnt eggs and I want to smash it and smash the table and tear the walls off this stupid little kitchen and bury them in rubble.

"You're so full of it!"

I used to find him at lunchtime. I'd just started the infants' and we had a separate smaller playground to the juniors, but if you went round the side of the building you could get to theirs. Some days knowing he was in the same school was enough. Other days I needed to see him in the flesh. I'd make Tommy come with me and we'd snake through the crowds of big kids playing *Gladiators*, to where Marc and Jamie would be playing football, and we'd just watch. The way he moved and how people reacted to him felt like watching a film star to me and, standing next to the fence, I'd feel safe. I'd feel cool. *That's my brother.*

Sometimes a Year Four or Year Five kid would come up to me and try and have a go, then another one would be like, "Yo, that's Marc's little brother," and that would be the end of it. Squashed. A free pass from fear, but one that came with a contract to live in his shadow.

"Go in, son."

Dad's standing at the top of the stairs. His body almost completely blocks out the landing window behind him.

I look at Marc's door, then back at Dad, and with a sigh, anger melts into resignation. "Mum doesn't like it."

"I'm not Mum." He walks towards me and it hits me that one day I really might be that big. Fill-a-doorway big. What will that feel like?

Dad pushes open Marc's door and the pair of us stare in.

"Jesus. It's like a museum." He lays a hand on my shoulder.

I stare at Marc's perfectly made bed. "It *is* a museum," I say.

Dad's hand is squeezing my shoulder and it feels like we're breathing at the same time. Then he's pushing me from behind, not rough, but firmly, into the room.

We sit on the bed, the space in between us too small for

Marc to fit in. I look at the black bookcase of films. Dad shakes his head. "You're not kids any more."

I'm reading film titles from left to right. *Predator. Raw Deal. Commando.*

Dad's looking at me. "You know?"

Last Action Hero. Eraser.

"We haven't been kids for a while, Dad."

Nowhere to Run. Timecop.

"Yeah, I guess not."

Bloodsport. Kickboxer.

"Two birthday cards, Dad. That's all I've got."

Crouching Tiger, Hidden Dragon. Romeo Must Die.

Dad sighs. "He didn't forget us, Luke."

"Happy Birthday, Lukey," I say. "Stay strong, Marc. Same message. Two years. Twelve words, Dad." The DVDs go out of focus as my eyes start to well-up. "Twelve words."

"It's how he chose to deal with it, son."

"Why?"

Another sigh. "I guess because it made sense to him that way."

My cheeks are wet. "What will you say to him?"

Dad's shaking his head. "I honestly don't know, mate." Then his arm is round me, and it feels as heavy as when that guy from the zoo came into school in Year Six with the boa constrictor and me and Tommy had it across our shoulders.

"We live our choices, Luke. Sometimes it gets messy." And I'm not sure whether he's talking about Marc or himself, but sitting here next to him, my eyes full of tears, the two of them don't feel so different. *We live our choices*.

"Hold on." Dad sits upright and his heavy arm slips down my back. I follow his confused eyes to the shelf.

"*Universal Soldier III?*" He's pointing at the DVDs, but looking at me.

I sniff and smile. "And Van Damme's not even in it."

Dad's confusion goes up a notch. "I don't understand. Why would he buy that?" Then a smile creeps up and he gently digs my thigh. I close my eyes and breathe out, as the camera slowly fades to black.

INT. OPERATING ROOM — NIGHT

The washed-out halo of a circular light.
The beep of a heart monitor.
Muffled voices.

DOCTOR I: We're going to need more blood.

The clink of surgical tools.

DOCTOR 2: Do we have a name yet?

DOCTOR I: More gauze please. No idea. It's not looking good.

The tearing of plastic and paper.

DOCTOR I: The bone's completely shattered.

Swing door. Brief hallway noise.

NURSE: We've got a name. Henry. Marc Henry.

PART 2.
Facing.

I.

"You ready?"

I'm staring at the gravestones, sitting on the bench.

I try to guess how Leia's got her hair before I turn to look at her. *Bunches?*

It's the thick plaits. She's standing a metre away. She's got her big coat on. It's Friday the thirteenth. You couldn't make it up.

"Well?" she says, and I notice A4 paper rolled up in her hand. "Big day, Skywalker." She's clearly excited. We're supposed to share the character dialogue we've prepared in front of the class. Marc and Toby's first conversation after Marc gets home. I'm supposed to be Marc, she's being Toby. We've practised on the phone.

"There's no better description of your character than the words you let him speak." She's quoting Noah; he said that on Tuesday.

My stomach's empty. I didn't eat breakfast. Mum was up and scrubbing the bath before I even got out of bed. I look at Leia. "The hero returns."

She smiles. "You up to it?" She's talking about class, I'm thinking about home. I picture Dad driving, right now. Marc sitting in the passenger seat that's been mine for two years, driving through Cape Hill back to the house.

"Luke." Leia kicks my foot lightly. "Come on."

"I can't do it. I'm not coming to class today." I make my eyes stay on her, waiting for her to get angry. We've been working hard and the dialogue scene is good. We've really got something.

Leia frowns, then nods and says, "I know."

"What?"

"I know, Luke. It's all right. I know about Marc."

And she's smiling and nodding and it feels like a weight is lifting from around my neck. She knows. I didn't have to say anything; she knew and everything is all right.

Then her face is fading. Her face is getting fainter, the gravestones behind her coming into focus, as her body dissolves into the air.

A pigeon flies through her, landing on the ground, and she's gone.

The real Leia will be walking into class now, at the top of the hill, ready for the lesson. Ready to share our idea. And I won't be there.

I stare at the old gravestones ringed with moss and I remember the last time I saw him. Chin up, smiling as they led him out.

Come on, big man. It's time.

"I know. I'm coming, Marc."

People say 'It doesn't make sense' a lot.

When bad stuff happens and there's a space to fill, an awkward silence, that's what they say. Like if we don't understand what's happened maybe we don't have to feel so bad.

But he was such a good boy. It doesn't make sense.

He was on his way to great things. It doesn't make any sense.

That's not the young man I knew. It really doesn't make any sense.

Maybe sometimes they're genuinely confused.

Maybe sometimes it does honestly feel like the jigsaw pieces of what's happened don't fit together to make a picture of something they can recognise. Maybe sometimes it's true.

Mostly though, I think it's something they say to cover up the fact that even though what has happened is so bad, so horrible and shameful and cold, deep down, they know it makes complete sense.

Underneath all the talking and confused faces and shaking heads and cups of tea is the knowledge that, in their gut, everybody knew it was coming.

2.

I feel him straight away.

The house is different. Like the air's charged.

I can hear Mum in the kitchen. Dad's car wasn't outside and I'm wondering how long he stuck around before he left. Before he felt like he had to.

I pass the living room. Just the dead TV screen and the same empty chairs. I breathe in and walk to the kitchen.

"Luke!" And Mum's hugging me like I just came home from the war or something, pinning my arms to my sides. My bag drops on to the floor. He must be upstairs. "He's home, Lukey. Marc's home!"

She's wearing perfume. *Why the hell is she wearing perfume?*

"OK, Mum. You can let go."

She steps back but holds my shoulders in both hands and stares at me. Her hair is up and she's got that eyeliner stuff under her eyes.

"He's upstairs. Go say hello to him."

Then she's back at the side chopping whatever she was chopping before I came in. My throat's itching. It's time. Mum calls after me, "Lukey, tell him dinner'll be ready at six."

I climb the stairs.

I see light from both our rooms cutting on to the landing carpet. The bathroom door is ajar and steam's coming from inside, like someone's had a hot bath. This is it.

He'll talk. He always did the talking. I'll just have to nod and stand there. I can't swallow. My feet are planted, my toes trying to burrow themselves into the floorboards. Two years. What do you say? What will he look like? What do I look like? What if he feels like a stranger? *Stop being such a baby, just walk.*

And I'm walking, expecting to hear something, expecting to hear him, but as I get closer to his door I hear nothing. I picture a shot of me standing there in his doorway, a comic speech bubble next to my head. *Hi, Marc! It's me, Luke, remember?*

He's asleep.

He's lying on top of his duvet on his side in just a towel, the same old maroon towel I used this morning, and he's asleep.

I don't know what to do. I'm supposed to do something, I

have a line, but I've lost my script. Part of me's actually glad I don't have to speak, but the rest of me feels weird about having to wait. I've been waiting long enough. My head's torn as I stand there, taking it all in. The room seems like it's smiling, happy that its missing piece just got slotted back into place. His arms are folded and the one I can see is thick and powerful. His bed against the wall isn't touched by the sunlight and from here his skin is the colour of parcel paper. His stomach's lean and toned and there's a thin line of dark hair from his belly button running down behind the towel. I can only see part of his face, but his hair is definitely shaved close. I try to picture him in the same position, lying down in the bath, shower water falling on him as he sleeps.

He looks like a man. I mean, obviously he is a man, he's nearly twenty-one, but he looks like an actual man. And I'm just watching him, a sleeping lion, through the glass at the zoo.

He's here.

He's really here.

Then a memory.

I'm standing in front of him with my fists up. He's sitting on the bed holding up his palms ready.

He's telling me to aim past his hands, to not just hit them, to

138

punch through them.

My stomach is dancing. I think I'm eight. His duvet cover is red with thin white diagonal stripes.

He's wearing a black vest and his muscles are like grown-up muscles. I can hear music from downstairs and Dad trying to sing along. It's that 'More Than Words' song.

He's nodding at me. I throw a punch and feel my knuckles tap his palm. He's smiling.

Telling me we've got plenty of time.

"Luke?"

His voice is sleepy, but the same as I remember, the tone thick and sure. How long have I been standing here?

"Lukey?"

I feel young. I'm a little brother again.

He slides his feet off the bed and sits up, his palms pressing down on the mattress either side of his hips, and he's big. Broader than I remember. I try not to stare.

"Yeah. It's me," I say.

He looks like a boxer. I feel my shoulders rising as he rubs his eyes.

"Holy shit. Look at you."

And our eyes meet. I watch him take me in and I know I've

grown, I'm stronger, I've made sure I am, and watching him see it feels good.

He nods a smile. "You look like Dad."

He's really here, speaking to me.

"Come in, man." He beckons with his hand. "Can I get a hug?"

And I'm stepping into his room, small steps, and the air is warmer from the sunlight through the window and I'm going to hug my brother.

"Come here, big man," he says, and he starts to stand up and I'm almost at his bed and his arms are reaching out towards me and we're the same height. I'm as tall as Marc. I feel my arms coming up too, ready to hug him and then his towel falls from his waist. My brother is standing there with his arms out, completely naked, and I freeze.

"Shit! Sorry, Luke, stupid, let me get…" and he's scrambling for the towel and looking around for clothes and there aren't any and I'm trying to not look but it's impossible, the black patch of hair, the darker skin of his… and my feet are backing out of the room. He grips the towel next to his hip with one hand and reaches out with the other.

"No, hold on, mate. Gimme a sec."

"I'll let you get dressed." I start to leave. "Mum says

dinner's at six."

"Yeah, OK. Thanks."

And I'm walking out, pulling his door closed behind me, hearing him curse himself under his breath as he fights to get his bearings.

3.

The three of us sit at the kitchen table eating Mum's lasagne.

Marc opposite me, Mum in between us on my left, the empty space where Dad should be on my right.

Forks clink against plates. Every now and then Mum clears her throat like she's going to say something, but doesn't. Her eyes keep going back to Marc.

"This is lovely, Mum," he says, and holds up a forkful of lasagne, like it's evidence, before putting it in his mouth.

"Thanks, love. I remembered you liked it." She smiles proudly.

I'm digging at my food, not eating it. I stare at the layers of meat and pasta and think about the diagram of the Earth in cross-section from the wall in science back at school. The layers of mantle and rock and crust and how the plates underneath shift and make earthquakes.

"So. College?" says Marc, and both of them are looking at me.

I shrug. "Yeah."

He looks like one of the cast of *The Fast and the Furious*. The rough but handsome one, who doesn't get many lines, but has one decent fight scene. I get another flash of him curled up in the bath under the shower and then I think of Leia, sitting in class earlier this afternoon, face fuming as Noah asks her where I am.

"That's good," Marc says and it's like we have absolutely nothing to say to each other. How can we have nothing to say?

Then Mum slaps the table and both of us jump.

"I forgot! I got you something." She's up and leaving the kitchen. We hear her climb the stairs.

Marc lets out a sigh. "Man. This is kinda full on, eh?"

I nod. What things has he done inside? What things has he had to do?

He takes a sip of his tea. "She'll calm down soon enough, mate. You know what she's like." And him saying it is annoying. Like he somehow thinks things haven't changed in two years. Like we're just the same as before. I stare across at him. He's looking at my scar and I don't want him to say anything about it. Please don't say anything about it.

"It's healed good."

I resist the urge to cover my face with my hand. He points

with his fork. "Actually looks pretty cool." His face betrays the fact that he knows how lame that was to say. I tell myself this is how it'll be for a while, and that it's OK. Then he says, "So you got a girlfriend then?" And it's like he's laughing at me. Like he doesn't think I could have one. Maybe he doesn't mean it like that, but it's annoying. He's annoying.

I squeeze my fork and stare at his hands as I answer; his knuckles are scratched and scarred.

"Nothing serious," I say, and it sounds like the dumbest reply ever. Marc laughs and my back teeth are grinding.

"I see," he says. "Playing the field are ya?" And I don't want him to know me. I don't want him to know anything about what I'm doing. I don't want him to take it over and undermine it. You don't know anything about me, Marc.

Mum walks back in and places a small white box on the table next to Marc's plate and sits down again.

"What's this?" He picks it up. I recognise the Apple logo.

Mum looks at him excitedly. "You'll need one. It's a good one."

She's bought him an iPhone. She's gone and spent like three hundred quid on a brand-new iPhone for him.

"You bought him an iPhone?" I say and I know I sound like a little kid, but I can't help it.

Mum looks at me briefly and frowns. "He's gonna need a phone, Luke. It's important."

Marc puts the box down. "It's great, Mum, thanks."

"An iPhone?" I say again. I'm trying to remember the last time she bought me anything. My laptop cost me a birthday and a Christmas and that was Dad's idea.

Marc can see I'm pissed off.

"Maybe you could show me how to use it, mate?"

And it's too much. This is like some twisted two-person reunion scene with me as the third wheel. Help him use it? Like he's some caveman who's just been dug out of ice after ten thousand years, or something?

"Forget this." I'm standing up.

He's looking up at me. "What you doing, Lukey?"

"I'm getting out of here, that's what I'm doing."

"Don't be daft, sit down, man."

He points at my chair, like he's some mafia boss who doesn't need to raise his voice. Mum won't look at me.

"I just got home, Luke. Sit down and let's finish our meal." His eyes harden slightly, letting me know not to mess this up, but I don't care. What's he gonna do?

"She'll show you how to work it," I nod towards Mum, my stomach twisting. Marc seems surprised and it feels stupid, but it feels good. I'm stealing this scene.

"Welcome back," I say, in my most sarcastic tone and they're both looking at me and I should just leave it there, but out of nowhere I look right at him and say, "your highness." And I leave.

4.

I just walk.

I'm so stupid.

I was so concentrated on storming out that I forgot my jacket and my phone. The second the front door shut behind me I realised, but what could I do?

I walk round to the playground and keep going past the flats. I think about buzzing for Tommy, but I don't want to have to answer a bunch of questions about Marc so I carry on to the high road.

It's not even seven yet but it's nearly dark and there's already gangs of people starting on their nights out. I pass a group of three girls at the cash point that I recognise from a couple of years above us at school. They're all dressed up for town in outfits that scream 'try hard'. The kind of clothes Leia would never have to wear. *What? You think she's better than us?* That's not what I said. *Yeah it was.* So what? It's true.

I get a waft of sickly sweet perfume as I pass them and as I walk away, I swear I hear them whispering.

I can see a line of men heading my way further up, so I cut down Poplar Road, by the petrol station, and walk past the big houses. I think about going all the way to the reservoir, walking through the trees, finding a bench and sitting by the water, but I'm already cold and at this time on a Friday night it'll just be creepy guys walking their old dogs. So I carry on down City Road, walking faster than normal to try and keep warm.

By the time I reach the bottom my arms are freezing. I've gotta go home soon. Stupid. Then I hear the growl.

I'm standing on the corner and look down both streets, but I can't make out where it came from. That same engine.

Both sides of the road are lined with parked cars and I can't see any headlights, but it definitely sounded close. Someone is watching me. I can feel it. My gut is telling me to move.

```
INT. SUPERMARKET — NIGHT
Furry bristles where sliding glass doors come
together. Cases of Carling on special offer.
Supermarket sounds.
```

"What the hell you doing here?" Zia's on his knees, stacking tinned tomatoes on to the bottom shelf.

"What do you mean?"

He points at me with a jar in his hand. "I mean, you can't just show up, Luke. You need to warn me, yeah?"

"Why?"

"I dunno, it's just weird, innit?" He carries on stacking.

"How's it going?"

"You kidding? I'm on my knees stacking tomatoes." Zia shakes his head. "You seen Tommy?"

"Not since Saturday," I say.

"He's pissed off with you." Zia neatens the front tins. "We needed you the other night, man."

I look away. "Yeah. Sorry, man, something came up at college."

Zia stands up holding the empty cardboard box. "So who is she?"

"What you talking about?"

Zia shakes his head. "Come on, Lukey, who you talking to? The only reason you're letting us down is for a girl." He expertly flattens the box against his chest. "So?"

"Shut up, man."

"Fine." He starts walking away down the aisle. I step after him.

"OK, OK. It's someone at college, all right? It's nothing

serious. Happy?"

Zia stops walking and smiles. "What's her name?"

Then a man with greasy blond side-parted hair is standing in front of us. He's wearing a dark blue fleece with the supermarket logo sewn into it. I reckon he's late twenties, or older. He's my height, but he looks weak.

"No time for chat, Zia," he says. The tone in his voice is one of a teacher who's not sure you're gonna listen to him. Zia looks at me like dogs look at you, trapped inside parked cars on summer days.

"So you think long-grain rice would be best, then?" I say.

Zia understands straight away. "Yeah, I'd say so. We've got a couple of different brands, all at the top end of aisle three." He points.

The fleece guy's eyes narrow. "Is he helping you, sir?"

I nod like I'm grateful. "He really is. I'm trying to get things together for an important meal and he's been a big help."

That was too much. The man looks at Zia. Zia forces a smile and turns to me. "Is there anything else I can help you with?"

I shake my head. "I don't think so. I'll get the rice and if I'm stuck I'll come and find you, if that's OK?"

"That's fine, sir, I'm here to help."

The fleece guy knows he's got nothing and walks away,

frowning.

I slap Zia's shoulder. "You're welcome."

Zia's shaking his head. "You think he's not gonna remember that later and make me clean the toilets?"

"You're just doing your job."

"You don't understand, Luke, you haven't got a boss."

And for the first time, I can feel resentment in him.

Zia punches my arm lightly. "I'm sorry, man. Ignore me, just been a shit day. Shit week."

I want to say something to make him feel better, something to make things less crap.

"Marc's home."

Zia's face drops. "Course he is! Sorry, man, I completely forgot. You OK?"

I shrug. "I'm fine. Pretty weird, but what you gonna do?"

Zia's face is sheepish. "Dunno, look, I'm done at ten, you wanna come to mine, I mean, if you wanna get out of the way and that? We could watch something, you could stop over?"

But I'm only half listening, because Noah just walked past us along the end of the aisles and turned down the next one.

"Luke?" Zia's staring at me. "You wanna?"

"Nah, I'm good, man. Thanks, though. I better go."

And I walk after Noah, feeling Zia watching me.

5.

Noah's choosing cereal and I think about Zia's shopping with his dad routine.

I'm walking straight towards him. *What are you doing?*

"All right?" I say, immediately lost for words.

"Luke," he says, looking a bit confused but not weirded out.

"You don't like my Friday lesson much, do you?"

I look down, embarrassed, and stare at his shoes; they're a grey pair of those dusty suede desert boots.

"Yeah, sorry about that. Family stuff."

Noah nods. "Can't hide from blood, can you? What brings you over this side of town, anyway?"

"I live here."

Now he looks confused. I point in the direction of home. "I live in Bearwood."

And he's laughing. My body's tensing up on the defensive

and all kinds of comeback lines are starting to brew on my tongue.

"Why's that funny?"

Noah sees my face and stops laughing. "Oh, no, no, I'm not laughing at you, Luke. It's just funny that we're both from Bearwood."

And he's holding out his hand for me to shake it and that's what I do. I shake his hand and his grip is just firm enough and he's smiling and I'm smiling too. It's weird. I never would have said he was from round here.

"Well bloody hell," he says and lets my hand go. "A boy from Bearwood who's into film. What are the chances of that?"

I just shrug, unsure what to say, but a connection's been made. He's from where I'm from.

"Noah? Noah Clarke?"

Zia's boss with the greasy hair and the fleece is walking towards us. Noah's face freezes and I can see his body tightening.

"It is you! Bloody hell!"

And fleece guy is standing next to us, his hands on his hips, shaking his head.

Noah's smile is painful. "Hello, Pete."

"What the hell you doing here, Noah?"

Pete moves on the spot like his knees and elbows don't bend, like he's an excited robot who just won a game show. "I'm shopping," Noah says, deadpan.

Pete snorts a laugh that's either fake or really unlucky. "Classic Clarkey! Smart arse."

Noah looks at me and he knows he doesn't have to explain. "Is this your little brother? I've heard about you, trouble."

Pete's looking at me now. I don't move. He's got a little brother? Trouble? Noah nips it in the bud.

"No. This is a friend from work. Luke, this is Pete, Pete, this is Luke."

Pete sticks his hand out. I take it. It's like shaking a fish. His eyes stay on Noah. "Noah Clarke. I thought you were off living the big life in London."

Noah shrugs. Pete's waiting for more. So am I. Big life?

"You were in a film, weren't ya?" he waits, like a dog, for Noah to throw him a bone. In a film?

Noah shakes his head. "No."

"Yeah you were, I heard all about it off Tuffy. It was a couple of years back."

Noah's face stays straight. "Think you heard wrong, Pete. I'm not an actor."

Pete looks at me and rolls his eyes. "He's playing it cool,

eh?" Then he slaps Noah's arm. "Back in the hood, Noah, we should go out."

Noah doesn't respond.

"I'm manager now." Pete pats the company logo on his fleece. "Give it two or three years and I'll be going for regional."

He's nodding proudly. Noah nods back. "That's great, Pete. Listen, we need to go. I need to drop Luke home. We'll see you later, Pete. Good to see you."

And he starts walking down the aisle towards the tills. I follow.

Pete calls after us. "All right, Noah, good seeing you! I'll make some calls, sort a night out, eh? Like old times! Shiland boys on the town!"


```
INT. SUPERMARKET — NIGHT
Close-up: Girl's hand moves over scanner. Baby
blue nail varnish.
Too many rings. Barcode beeping.
```

Noah loads the stuff from his basket on to the conveyor belt in silence. I stand next to him like his sidekick.

The girl on the till is not much older than me but she looks hard, her hair pulled back, eyebrows forced up. Her name badge says Kylie. She cuts Noah a look like she knows him, but he's not paying attention to her as he packs his bag and puts his card in the machine.

"I'm on Park Road, bottom end. You near there?" he asks.

I nod. "Linden Road. You sure it's all right?"

"Course it is," he says.

Then Kylie points at me. "Aren't you Marc Henry's little brother?" And every muscle goes tight.

She's looking right at me and I want to say no, but something won't let me.

So I nod, and I can feel Noah's eyes on me too, and I slide my hands into my pockets to stop them shaking.

"I thought so," Kylie says. "Liam, right?"

"Luke."

"That's it! Little Lukey. With the scar. You're bigger than I remember. You look a bit like him, you know."

I'm just nodding nervously like one of those little plastic dogs in the back of cars. Please let this be over. Please let this be over.

"We proper fancied Marc at school you know. All of us."

I watch Kylie drift off into a memory. Noah can see me squirming and says, "We should go, come on, Luke."

Kylie looks at Noah like she couldn't care less, then turns

back to me.

"He's coming out soon, right?"

And I want to disappear. Not in front of Noah, please.

"Everybody was proper glad when he got Craig."

I can feel the heat in my face. She's staring right at me. "He got what he deserved, eh?" And I swear she's literally about to point to my scar, then Noah walks away.

I stand there, caught in her tractor-beam stare, then I follow him, walking sideways, split between where I'm going and where I've been.

"See you later, Lukey," she says. "Say hi to Marc for me, yeah? Kylie Burdle! I was in the year below him!"

I walk out the exit into the cold air. The side of my face on fire.

6.

It's a Fiat Punto.

My legs are squashed against the glove compartment, but I don't say anything as Noah pulls out of the supermarket on to the main road. The air inside the car is thick with what just happened. *Please don't ask about Marc. Please just leave it.*

He's got one of those little traffic light air fresheners hanging from his rear-view mirror and his stereo is far too good for the car. I feel proper awkward. I should've walked.

We pull up to lights and we're just sitting there, looking forward. I shouldn't be here. I should get out the car.

I think about Dad and how he's probably in The Goose, talking to his work mates about everything except Marc, and it suddenly makes the most sense. What good will talking do?

"You said Linden Road, right?" Noah looks at me. I nod. The lights change and we pull off.

We're driving along streets I've always known but in this

different car, with this new person, who says he's from here too, but who I don't really know. I pull my shopping bag closer into my lap, gripping the handle.

"A bag full of the past, eh?" says Noah.

And it sounds like a fortune cookie or something, but it makes perfect sense. A bag full of the past, that you have to carry around, weighing you down.

"Yeah."

I put my left elbow on the inside of the door and rest my face in my hand, staring out. I think of Leia. I wonder how pissed off she was. If she spoke our dialogue on her own, or if someone else helped. Simeon probably came to the rescue. I should've gone to the lesson. Should I ask Noah what happened? I should call her. Say sorry.

We're waiting behind a number eleven bus and he must know as well as I do that it's the bus that goes to the prison. Is he gonna say something?

Noah bangs both his fists on the steering wheel and I jump, nearly hitting my head on the inside of the roof.

"OK. Let's do it," he says. "One each."

"What do you mean?"

"One question each. You get one, then I get one, deal?"

We're both staring at the back of the bus, the amber

indicator flickering.

"OK."

"Cool. You first."

"What did he mean, you were in a film?" I say.

Noah nods as he weighs up his answer, then shakes his head. "I wasn't in a film. I wrote one."

"You wrote a film?"

"Yeah. It was a while ago."

The bus pulls away and we follow.

"What was it called?"

"Hold on, that's your one question. My turn."

He glances at me. I look out of the window.

"So Marc Henry's your brother?"

Bam.

He knows Marc. Or he knows of Marc. Maybe he's heard what happened. He's from Bearwood, course he has. Maybe he already knew who I was. My throat's itching again.

This is too much. It feels like somebody just pulled my towel away. I press my face against my hand, feeling the heat pass from scar to palm as Noah waits for me to say something. Silence.

We pull up to the lights at the top of City Road.

My mind's racing. I can see Mum and Dad smiling at me

from the kitchen table, and I can see Leia standing in the underpass and then Marc's there too, standing next to her.

"Luke, are you all right?"

But I'm already clicking my seatbelt and opening the door and my heart is going and I'm out of the car. *What the hell?*

The cold air is on me and I'm in the road. I don't know what I'm doing and the cars behind are honking their horns and I'm slamming the door shut, and walking off.

What's wrong with you?

I reach the pavement and see a black metal lamppost. I kick it full on and pain shoots through my toes into my right foot and up my calf. I'm so stupid, but I keep going, limping now.

"Luke!" Noah's calling through his open window, and the cars behind are honking more and I'm just hobbling, the cold biting at my neck and arms as I reach the alleyway between the flats. My heart is punching the inside of my chest, my foot's throbbing, and my face is on fire, but I'm not looking back. I don't look back once.

7.

Fortune cookies are only good if they make sense. Otherwise it's just a greasy piece of paper inside a shit biscuit.

The warmth of the hall is amazing. I don't know how long I sat in the dark playground, but I'm cold, my foot still hurts and I still feel like an idiot as I watch Marc walk back into the living room. What must Noah think?

I ease the front door closed, letting the latch catch in slow motion. The living room's dark and I can smell Mum's lasagne as I stand in the doorway and squeeze my trainers off. Why's he sitting in the dark?

"You all right?" he says, in that patronising big brother way. I can't be bothered right now. I should text Leia. I need to watch a film.

He's sitting in the corner chair, his legs crossed in front of him, like he's meditating or something. I can see the white iPhone box in his lap.

"It's late, Lukey."

And it feels like one of those spy films when they have the mysterious meeting in the car park in the middle of the night and the informant speaks from the shadows. I can't make out his eyes, but he's wearing a dark vest and jogging bottoms, are they mine?

He clicks the lamp on and just sits there, staring at me. His strong cheekbones and full lips, his thick smooth shoulders on display. "I was worried, mate," he says, and I tell myself that this is what he's done for the last two years. Somehow, every night, he's escaped from his cell, made it here, quietly broken into the house and just sat in the corner chair, in the dark, all night, like some silent guard dog, leaving before we wake up, making it back to prison just before sunrise.

"You OK?" he says, and I can't deal with him. He was *worried*? I turn to leave the room. "Don't go, Luke." And something in his voice throws me off completely.

"I'll leave you to it." My voice stumbles over the words and I force a kind of smile as I step towards the door.

"Please, Luke?" And it's like the living-room carpet moves. A tiny tremor underneath my feet. *Please*? I cant remember him using that word to me, ever.

I sit down on the two-seater next to his chair, leaving a space between us and we're both just staring forward at our faint reflection in the TV and I feel the fingertips of déjà vu tapping lightly on the back of my brain. Like we've been here, me and him. Or maybe I've dreamt it.

"There's stuff to be said, mate. Things we need to talk about. I know that." His words sound prepared. Like he's been rehearsing this. I don't say anything.

"It's OK," he says. "It'll take time."

And my mind is a montage of moments. Shots from the past playing silently on the inside of my skull. The pair of us in the car on the way back from the cinema, Dad driving, Marc in the front, me asking question after question from the back seat. Me and Marc vs Mum and Dad in a living room pillow fight, me switching sides and Marc almost crying with laughter as Dad holds him down and me and Mum pummel him with the throw cushions. Marc and Donna laughing in our kitchen, flour everywhere, their white hand prints all over each other as they try and make pancakes.

"I don't know what's gonna happen, Luke."

He's looking at me now, waiting for me to look at him. So I do.

"I honestly don't."

His face is telling me he wants me to say something that'll help, that I've got the power to do that. And I want to, but I can't.

I stand up.

"Luke." He's looking up at me. I'm looking down at him and it's weird and good and too much and I'm tired.

"I'm gonna go bed."

Marc nods, defeated. "Course. Night, big man."

He holds the iPhone box in his lap. I point to it. "You figure it out then?"

He looks down and shakes his head. "Not even opened it, to be honest. Who'm I phoning?"

And he's less man and more boy.

A boy who doesn't know what's gonna happen.

"What about Donna?" I say, and picture her behind the bar, pulling a pint.

Marc doesn't look up. "Yeah."

And I watch him picture her too, in a memory of his own.

"All right then." I'm walking out of the room.

"Lukey?"

I stop at the door again. "Yeah?"

"I was wondering, I kinda need to get some stuff, clothes and that, and thought you'd maybe come with me, tomorrow, like?"

"What, shopping?"

He shrugs and shakes his head. "Yeah, forget it, stupid, don't worry, it's cool—"

"I'll come."

"Yeah?" And it's genuine happiness on his face. I nod and walk out, my eyes starting to sting, my foot still aching, but my chest full.

What the hell? I had to do the dialogue myself. L

Yo. You cool? Lemme know if u need to get out house. T

You couldn't even send a message? L

Evrythinh ok? Ring me if nd too. Dod x

Cld cum pick u up tomoz? Jamie said tell Marc ring him. T

Sorry man. Should've remembered. Bell me if you need to talk. Z

You ok? Ring me? Lx

I read them all, then I read them again. I leave the others and click reply to Leia. I didn't mean to let her down. The empty square and blinking cursor. The crack in the screen. What do I say? I don't want pity, I just... I'm an idiot. Click phone off, leave it on the floor. I'm tired. I'll text her tomorrow. I picture my two best friends and Leia sitting behind a desk like a panel in front of me. I put Dad on the end next to Tommy and Noah on the other end, next to Leia. All five of their faces staring out, expecting, waiting for me to do something.

Marc's still downstairs, sitting on his own in the corner. Tomorrow we go shopping. I almost laugh at how normal that sounds as I strip down to my boxers and start to do my press-ups, my fingertips in the carpet like a cat clawing fur, the heat in my arms, pain in my foot, breathing through my teeth. *Five. Ten. Fifteen. Twenty.*

My notebooks are loosely stacked on the carpet. Arms extended. Elbows locked, I hold my body off the floor and it feels good. This I can control. Pushing up and down, I read the names scribbled across the papers, Marc, Leia, Toby, Zia, Tommy. Breathe in. *My life is my scrapbook*. Breathe out. Done.

I stand up and rub my eyes, feeling my knuckles fill the sockets.

Then I slide under my duvet and sink into sleep.

8.

The cold air scratching my exposed cheekbone.

The flap of skin hanging on by a thread.

The sting as I touch the open wound. I look down at my hands and there's blood. It's all over me.

My chest and stomach and legs. Splashed down my arms and it's in my eyes when I blink and he's just staring at me. Arm's length away. Eyes wide. Like he can't believe what he's done. There's blood on him too. My blood. I look down. The broken pieces of the green bottle and a puddle of beer soaking into the cracked concrete. It doesn't hurt. It's just cold. I can feel the air on my eyeball and I want to touch it. I want to feel what he's seeing. My legs start to go and I look up again and he's smiling. A crooked smug smile and I'm dizzy. I'm falling forward. Things go blurry and, just before I black out, I see Craig Miller running away…

"Lukey."

"Leave him alone man, he's sleeping."

"He just said something, though. We can't just sit here while he sleep-talks. What if he says something dodgy?"

"Like what?"

"I dunno! Something. It's just creepy. Luke, wake up, man."

The blurred outline of Tommy at eye level. My eyes start to focus. He's sitting on the floor next to my bed, a dark grey hoodie pulled up on to his head. He smiles.

"What you doing here?" I say, immediately tasting my own mouth, and pulling my duvet up in front of me.

"He's watching you sleep." Zia's smiling from the windowsill, leaning on it like a guitar stool. "He was trying to hear your dreams."

"Shut up, Zia! I said it was creepy."

Tommy shuffles back to the wall and sits next to my film shelves. "We came over."

And all three of us laugh at how stupid his statement is.

"Was it a nightmare?"

My hand comes up and rubs my face. "Same as always."

Zia stands up. "Come on. It's Saturday. Time to do nothing." He rubs his hands like he's about to do a magic trick.

"So check this out, yeah…"

"No, Zia. No more, man." Tommy's rolling his eyes. "Yo, if I have to hear one more joke about old ladies trying to choose shampoo, tell him, Luke."

I sit up and lean against the wall, the cold wallpaper on my naked back. My foot feels better, but there's still a dull ache.

"Shit, Luke!" Zia's staring.

Tommy nods at me. "Told ya, he's massive, eh?"

I feel to pull the duvet up over my chest, but don't want them to see me do it. "Shut up, man."

Tommy points. "You look like a James Bond baddie." He's sticking his tongue out. "With them muscles and the scar and that. You just need, like, a nickname or something."

"Stop staring, will ya?" I roll down my bed and reach for my black T-shirt from yesterday.

"Igor," shouts Zia, like he's calling a full house in Bingo.

"Igor?" I pull my T-shirt on.

"Nah," says Tommy. "That's crap. You want something powerful, like The Hammer, or The Hound." And we're all laughing again.

"We saw Marc," Tommy says, and the laughing stops.

Zia looks out of my window. "He let us in. He's making breakfast with your mum. You OK?"

I look at them both and realise it's been ages since all three of us have been in my room. Our house hasn't been much of a meeting place for a while.

"I'm fine."

Tommy stands up. "He looks hardcore man, proper UFC."

I picture Marc, flipping bacon at the stove in his black vest and my jogging bottoms, Mum buzzing around him.

Zia throws my jeans at me. "Get dressed, man, let's go nowhere."

"I can't."

"What d'you mean?"

"I said I'd go with Marc into town. He needs to get stuff, clothes and that." I pull my duvet off and my jeans on. "We can link later on?"

Zia nods. "Yeah. Course. Come on, Tom."

"Who's Leeya?" Tommy's bending down and picking up my newest notebook.

I jump forward and snatch it out of his hands, quickly scoop up the others and push them under my duvet. "No one."

"Is that her name?" says Zia.

Tommy's frowning. "Whose name? Who's Leeya, Luke?"

The blood's rushing to my face. Both of them are staring at me.

Tommy nods. "Leeya." He says the word like he's trying to remember someone. "She Chinese?"

"What?" I'm telling myself I've got nothing to be embarrassed about, and that I still haven't texted her to say sorry. Tommy stares into space. "Leeya. Feel like I know that name. She Swedish? I love Swedish girls. And Chinese girls."

"What the hell, Tom?" I say. "Since when do you know anybody from China or Sweden? What are you even talking about?"

"It does sound Chinese, to be fair," says Zia. "Leeya."

"Stop saying Leeya! Her name's Leia, all right? Leia." And hearing her name coming out of my mouth feels funny, like the word's in a different language or something. Tommy and Zia look at each other then back at me.

Tommy says, "Leia? Like the *Star Wars* princess?"

I nod.

Zia's beaming. "Luke and Leia. Man. Who's writing this story?"

9.

EXT. STREET — DAY

Over-shoulder shot of walking through town. Busy
with shoppers. Looking up at buildings. Taking in
how tall the city actually is.

"Happy?"

Marc's leaning forward holding his menu like a hymn book.

"Yeah. You didn't have to though." The right shoe of my brand-new Air Jordan IV's is balanced on my fingertips. New-trainer smell and perfectly clean. "Thank you."

"Forget about it. I still want to go look at some kitchen stuff, yeah? Mum's pans are ancient."

"Cool."

Marc nods and scans his menu. I put the shoe back into the box and slide it into the bag between my legs.

It's nearly one o'clock and we've been in town since ten looking for clothes for Marc. We have multiple shopping bags. Mum's rung every hour to check in with us. Marc made me choose some trainers, saying mine were too battered. I didn't ask where the money came from.

I watch him read, and I wonder whether this feels normal for him. Sitting in a crowded restaurant choosing food. Whether prison feels like a dream he just woke up from that's already starting to fade. I'm guessing it's not that straightforward.

We're sitting next to the window and through the shaded glass I can see the old church, nestled among the modern walkways and purple grey bricks of the Bullring. Not everything changes.

"Marc Henry!"

The waitress is next to our table holding two Cokes. Marc looks up. The girl's mouth is wide open. Mine's closed, and I can feel déjà vu. Supermarket check out girl, take two.

"It's you, isn't it?"

And I can't tell whether her voice is cracking from excitement or just crazily high.

Marc looks at me like he's about to apologise, but I save him the trouble and get up.

"Where you going?" he asks.

"Toilet." And I leave him there, the waitress staring at him like he just came back from the moon.

INT. RESTAURANT BATHROOM — DAY

I splash cold water on my face and stare into the mirror. The floor and the walls are the same beige tiles and it smells like a swimming pool. I'm trying to leave it long enough so whatever conversation Marc and the waitress are having can be long over before I go back out there. I should text Leia, or ring her, to say sorry about yesterday, maybe even explain about Marc. *What's she doing right now?*

"I'll text."

I watch my mouth move in the mirror.

"I will!"

Marc's on my phone, probably giving Mum the latest update.

There's two full glasses of Coke on the table. I can't see the waitress anywhere.

"Of course I will. No problem. I'll drop him off myself."

Myself? Who's he talking to?

"Seven o'clock. He'll be there. You too, Leia. Bye, bye."

I nearly fall off my chair.

175

Marc's smiling. "She sounds lovely, mate. Good work."

"What the hell, Marc?"

He holds my phone out. "Not a problem, big man. She's expecting you at seven."

My left eye's twitching. "Seven? What are you talking about? What did you say to her? Did you tell her? How did…? *What the hell?*"

"Easy tiger. Your phone rang and I thought it was Mum again, so I picked it up before I looked at the screen and then it was Leia. We had a little chat. You shouldn't have stood her up yesterday, mate. It was out of order. I said you could watch a film at hers, for research. I told her you do that a lot." He's smiling like we're sharing an in-joke, and I'm crumbling. The thought of him talking to Leia is breaking me into pieces.

"You can wear your Jordans." He smiles like he's just offered me my dream job. *What did he say to her? Expecting me at seven?*

"I don't know where she lives."

"It's over by Cannon Hill. Man, me and Jamie went to some bangin' parties over that way back in the day. Few scuffles with posh boys. Them college girls. Man. Anyways, she said to ask you to bring snacks."

Then the waitress brings over two half chickens and more

sides than two people need. She smiles as she taps the table and walks away, grinning over her shoulder at Marc. He waves a chip at her and smiles back and it's all that simple. I'm eating lunch with the King.

I've done stuff. With girls, I mean. Not everything, but stuff.

Leanne Bullock taught me how to kiss in the food tech store cupboard in Year Ten. She pretty much walked me through it, like furniture instructions, putting my hands where she wanted them, her tongue leading mine in a mouth dance. She thought my scar was cool. It was only a few months old at that point and she said it made me look older, which seemed to be the most important thing to her and all the other girls in our year. I knew she fancied Marc. In between kissing she'd just ask questions about him. Stuff he was into. If he had a type. She got bored of me by Christmas, but by then I felt like I knew the basics.

Alison Pike. Naomi Langford. Denise Phillips. All older than me, all in charge of the situation, and all full of questions about the superstar who shared my surname.

Tommy and Zia started calling me a dark horse and it was stupid, but I felt cool. Even though I knew every one of them was picturing my brother while we swapped spit.

At Tommy's sixteenth, Maria Brandon from Marc's year put her hand down my pants behind the social club. She made me hold her Malibu and Coke and I thought she was gonna fix her tights or something. Next thing I knew, her cold fingers were on my warm skin, grabbing and rubbing me. I remember the concentration on her face, like she was working out an equation in her head and for some reason all I could think of was when we made our own pizza dough in Year Nine.

Then Tommy ran round the corner and threw up next to the bins. Maria stopped, downed her drink and went back inside, leaving me holding her empty glass, watching my oldest friend paint the tarmac with puke.

10.

EXT. — EARLY EVENING

Bay windows and primary-coloured front doors,
like one of them little kids' shows.

Nobody seems to close their curtains, even though it's getting dark. I see widescreen TVs, huge fireplaces and expensive sofas in rooms that stretch back to French doors and gardens.

Number twelve.

Number fourteen.

Sixteen has a huge painting above the mantelpiece of a face made out of multicoloured shapes and there's an old man sitting in an antique-looking armchair reading a book, and my stomach is twisting into a fist.

I look down at my blue corner-shop carrier bag. Pringles and chocolate cornflake cakes. Idiot. I should've gone Sainsbury's and got some of them posh biscuits with bits of real ginger in or something. *Shut up. It's not an audition.* I picture Marc driving back across town, beaming to himself about playing matchmaker. He wanted to drop me right at the door so he could get a look at Leia. No chance.

I text Zia to let him know I'm not around tonight after all and notice how new my Jordans look. Too new. Like I bought them especially. I step to the tree next to the curb and scuff them in the dirt and now I can smell the aftershave. There was an old bottle of Dad's Davidoff in the bathroom cabinet and Marc made me put some on. Why did I wear aftershave? I don't even properly shave.

Number twenty has squares of that frosting stuff on the glass so you can't see inside but there's the outline of people and a massive paper lampshade hanging from the ceiling.

Twenty-two.

Twenty-four.

The door is red with stained-glass panels. The curtains are open but the front room is dark and lifeless. I pull a big leaf off the bush and rub it on my neck to try and absorb some of the Davidoff. *Just relax.*

And right now, my finger poised over the doorbell, it's so obvious that I really like this girl.

*

Dad said: The best ducks can swim in any pond.

The back room's like a grotto. Lit by a real open fire and a standing lamp behind the TV in the far right corner. The high wall behind them is completely filled with DVDs and books. The TV isn't actually any bigger than ours, but everything else is and through the glass of the patio doors the dark garden looks massive. My toes wriggle into the deep carpet and I'm glad I got to take off my shiny Jordans. Leia's been gone a while. How long does a tea take?

What do her parents do?

I shrug and scan the room. There's a glass-framed full-size *Empire Strikes Back* poster above the fire. It's got a couple of scribbled signatures in the bottom right-hand corner in black ink. Underneath it, on the mantelpiece, a photograph sits in pride of place. It's a black-and-white picture of a boy, about nine, with a younger girl on his lap. He's wearing dark-rimmed glasses, like Zia's, and a checkered shirt done up to the top button. His smile is taking up half of his face. The girl is wearing dungarees, with an eye patch over her right eye. She looks like the happiest pirate ever.

The fire is burning actual logs and making that popping sound and I get the urge to throw something on it, just to watch it burn.

I picture Mum and Marc at home now, on our smaller sofa, getting ready to watch *Apollo 13* or something else that Mum's seen a hundred times and I feel OK. This feels OK. *You sure?*

"Sorry," Leia says, handing me a fat mug with a pattern that looks like a blueprint. "Two sugars, Mr Sweet-tooth."

"Thanks."

She's wearing tight stonewashed jeans and a loose black T-shirt with the sleeves rolled right up to her shoulders, her hair pushed back by a black band, like she just threw the outfit together and looks perfect by accident. I stare at the fire as she moves past me and smell something sweet and fresh. Is she wearing perfume? She sits on the other end of the deep leather sofa. My bag of rubbish snacks sits in between us. I should've dropped them in the bin.

"I'm sorry. About yesterday. I should've called or... I wanted to."

Leia's looking at me, like she's trying to work out whether I'm full of it or not. I deserve it. This is awkward. I turn back to the fire.

"He knows how to talk, doesn't he, your brother?" she says.

"Yeah." I watch strings of smoke snake up the chimney. "Ever since I can remember."

"Is this weird?" she says and I turn to look at her. The light from the fire on her face. *Don't let this go badly. Please.*

"I dunno. Is it?"

"What's my surname?" she says, and just stares at me. *You don't know her bloody surname?*

I hold her stare and say, "Roberts. Your name's Leia Roberts. It's in your email address. Next question?"

Leia narrows her eyes like a cat. "Not as dumb as you look, Skywalker." She pulls the box of cornflake cakes out of the carrier bag. "I love these!" she says, and I almost punch the air.

"So who's the *Star Wars* fan?" I say, pointing up at the poster above the fire.

Leia rolls her eyes. "My dad. He's obsessed. He did some camerawork on the prequel films and got to meet George Lucas."

"My dad loves *Star Wars* too."

She gives me the 'no shit, Sherlock' face. *You're sinking here.*

"Guess we should be happy they didn't name us Chewbacca, eh?" I say, and we both laugh like it's a joke we've heard fifty times before. *Lame.*

"Is your dad home?"

Leia takes a cake and eats it in one go. "No, he's working late." She points at the ceiling. "Toby's upstairs. Don't worry, he won't come down."

"I'm not worried." *Liar*. Her brother's upstairs. Her older brother.

Just be cool.

"You think we should've changed their names, for the script?" I say, reaching for a cake. Leia's hand goes for another, brushing mine and, for a second, I swear we both slow down, trying to prolong the moment. Then we both retreat like it didn't happen.

"I thought that at first," she says, "but I think it's OK. Your brother's called Marc. My brother's called Toby. We're making it up, but it's grounded in something real. I think it helps. Like it matters, you know?"

I want to touch all of her. "Yeah," I say. "I do." I'm imagining my hands on her face, through her hair. "Guess we can always change names later if it feels right?"

Leia points at me. "Exactly. Obi Wan and Darth, maybe?" And we're both smiling.

I'm watching her chew her cake, my fingers wanting to trace the line of her lips. I want to be closer. *Pull it together, you wuss.* But it's like every thought I have is undressing her, pulling her in. I'm suddenly aware that I'm really staring, and that I have no idea for how long. *Say something, you muppet.*

"Nice fire." *What?*

"What?"

I point at the fire. "Your fire. It's real. Ours is electric."

Nice fire? That's the best you can do?

"Yeah," she says. "It's pretty cool. Sometimes I just throw stuff on to watch it burn."

And I smile to myself as we both just watch the flames, a cushion apart, something unspoken and animal firing between us.

Then footsteps on the stairs. Toby's coming down.

"No," Leia says, straightening up in her seat. "What's he doing?"

And the way she moves says she might have been in the same thought that I was. I sit up too.

"Please ignore him, Luke, whatever he says." She's nervous. Her smile is hiding actual nerves and I'm still imagining her neck and naked shoulderblades and the valley of her spine and it's throwing me off and the footsteps are reaching the bottom of the stairs and my mouth is full of cornflake cake and…

"Who's this?"

He's not as skinny as I'd imagined. Nowhere near as big as Marc, but he's no featherweight. He's wearing a black T-shirt with the words 'Full Tilt Boogie' in white typewriter font.

He's looking at Leia, but pointing at me. I'm not sure where to look and I can smell weed.

"This is Luke," says Leia. "I told you he was coming over. Luke, this is Toby."

"Tobias," he says sternly. "You didn't say he was a boy."

There's something about how he's standing that's not right. Chest puffed, but like his legs don't really believe it. "Does Dad know?"

What's this guy's problem?

His voice is deep and there are shaving bumps on his neck. He's handsome. I mean, he looks like Leia's brother.

"What do you want, Toby?" says Leia, starting to lose her temper.

Toby looks at me. "How old are you?"

I look up at him. Then I notice his hands. They're balled into fists and this is just weird.

"I'm nearly seventeen," I say, my eyes moving from his face to his hands.

"Scorpio," he says, and his fingers spread and start to move like they're playing the piano against his thighs.

"Toby, can you leave us alone? You said you had work to do." Leia's sitting forward now.

Toby glances at her. "Scorpios are old souls. Resilient."

"What?" says Leia.

I point at his T-shirt. "I liked the film."

He glances down then looks back at me, eyes narrow like I just cracked his secret code or something. "What film?" he says, and he's trying to catch me out. *Full Tilt Boogie* is the behind the scenes documentary of the making of *From Dusk Till Dawn*. He doesn't want me to know that.

Something inside me smiles. "My favourite bit is the Harvey Keitel interview." And his face is confused frustration. "Is everything all right?" I say, leaning forward, and Toby actually stumbles backwards, like he's trying to avoid me. His eyes wide.

This guy's nuts.

"You OK, mate?" I go to stand up, but feel Leia's hand on my arm.

"Toby, please. Do you want a tea? The kettle's just boiled. Come on, I'll make you a tea."

And she's up and leading him out of the room. He's biting his fingernails and jabs a finger my way. "Good scar," he says, smiling a painfully fake smile. Then they're gone and I'm sitting on the edge of the sofa looking at the fire.

II.

INT. — NIGHT

Teaspoon stirs. Milk lightens the brown.

Cut to slender fingers, stroking thick dark hair.

Cut to four feet climbing stairs.

"Sorry," Leia says, easing the door closed behind her and sitting back down.

"Is he OK?" I feel a bit guilty. Like I wound him up.

She hesitates. "He's fine. Every now and then he likes to audition for protective older brother. Bad casting agent."

And it's one of those weak jokes that's just to let you know to change the subject. I offer a smile and picture Marc. Everybody has their baggage. *A bag full of the past.* Then she tips the last few cornflake cakes on to the sofa and holds up the empty plastic box. "Check it out."

She walks on her knees to the fire. "Come on."

I put my tea down and follow her on my knees. The heat cranks up as we get close and sit at the hearth.

"You know how they used to burn witches and stuff?" Leia says, and her eyes are dancing.

"Yeah?" I say, feeling the heat on my scar.

"So check this out…" And she drops the plastic box into the flames. There's a hissing sound and the plastic starts to curl up into itself, twisting and contorting. A dark circle forms in the middle of it, then spreads and ignites. I think of tech lessons and burning our names into the desks with soldering irons. The pair of us watch, hypnotised, until the whole thing is melted down to a small black lump.

"That's what happens to people," she says, and I look at her. The light from the fire shows just how smooth her skin is, and thoughts of touching her begin to grow again.

"What do you mean?" I say.

"When a person burns, all the water in your body evaporates and you twist up like that, before your skin melts and then you just shrivel up. Like plastic. My dad explained it to me at a bonfire one time."

Who is this girl?

"I reckon burning would be the worst, right?" She looks

at me, her face close enough to touch. The heat is raw on my skin. Leia doesn't seem to feel it. "I reckon with drowning, like if you were handcuffed to something heavy, trapping you underwater, it would be horrible, but I figure you'd still have a choice."

She's looking at me for agreement, but I'm lost in the image, so she carries on. "You could say to yourself, I'm screwed, this is it, and you just take your deepest breath and suck in as much water as you can to your lungs and then you'd drown. Right?"

I nod and shrug at the same time. Leia nods and slides back until she's leaning against the sofa. "And of course it would hurt. A lot. They say it feels like your insides bursting. But it couldn't last that long. From when you choose to give in to when you'd be dead, it would be pretty quick, I think. But with burning, you don't get that choice, do you? You can't just go, OK, I'll burn quicker now, thanks. It's not in your control. You just have to wait, in agony, until you completely melt, not knowing how long it will take."

I move back and sit next to her, both of us just staring forward, legs stretched out. I never expected to be talking about the best way to die, but I get what she means. Knowing it was inevitable, I'd just want it to be over too and I feel somehow closer to her. Close in the sense of knowing her more. I feel her elbow against mine and I notice how big my feet look next to hers.

"You ever get déjà vu?" The question comes out of my mouth as though I'm talking to myself and just hangs there.

"All the time," she says.

"Sometimes I feel like I'm remembering a dream," I say.

Leia nods. "My dad said Mum used to say it was a good sign. That it was your mind's way of letting you know you're where you're supposed to be."

And just like that, the urge to kiss her blossoms in the pit of my stomach. This girl is amazing. It feels right. I should do it. Now. I start to turn to her when she says, "I guess Mum never felt it."

And the moment is over. Just silence and fire.

I could ask more, but it feels like there's something in the way now, so I just sit, watching my right foot lean towards her left foot, and wait to see what she does. No kiss. Not yet. We sit for what feels like the length of a song.

Then she leaps up. "Let's watch a film."

Most films are better watched at night.

There's something about it being dark outside, and the glow from the screen that just makes it feel like the right time. Like the whole world is a cinema and you're sitting in the perfect spot. You curl up into your sofa or your bed and you get that crackle in your blood, like something amazing is about to happen. The studio logo comes up and you feel your eyes widen, ready to be shown something, something that might be magic.

12.

It's just gone midnight when the number 87 turns on to the high road. I'm standing up next to the driver, pretending that I'm surfing the bus, waiting for my stop. I feel like I just won something. Buzzing.

We watched *Grosse Point Blank*, which I've seen before, but not for a while, and Leia chose it. She could've chosen anything but she chose that. So good. Her dad's a cameraman. Her mum isn't around. Her brother's some kind of stoner oddball. And she loves chocolate cornflake cakes.

I didn't want Marc to come and get me and, even though he seemed a bit pissed off in the text, I wanted the time to myself. To think.

You should've kissed her.

No I shouldn't.

At least tried.

It wasn't the right time.

Chicken.

But I'm not listening. Nothing's gonna kill this buzz.

The doors open and as soon as my feet hit the pavement I breathe a different air.

Over here the air is thicker. Heavy with the weight of bad possibilities. I walk past the chicken shop. Drunk friends sit slumped, eating in silence. Two girls are dancing in front of the counter to a song nobody else can hear as the guy at the till just stares out like he's serving time.

I picture Leia on her front doorstep as I left.

"We should do this again, Skywalker." Me nodding. Backing up the pathway in my new Jordans, smiling, trying to make the coolest exit ever made.

There's no way I'm getting to sleep this charged.

I turn right by the bank so I can get milk from the petrol station. I'm gonna make tea and watch films all night.

It's quieter off the high road and there's less light. Do I text her? Say thanks? No, leave it. It's perfect. My phone's in my hand. I wanna do something, tell someone about her, but I can't think of who.

Then I hear the growl.

It's a blacked-out Ford Focus.

Headlights staring at me from further up the road. The

front bumper almost touches the floor and there's lead in the pit of my stomach.

That same growl.

My shoulder and chest muscles tense as I push my phone back into my pocket and the car's moving towards me, slowly, like an animal.

It gets level and stops. I can see my reflection in the gloss finish. The whir as the electric window slides down.

I already know it's him. He's smiling a smile that's cut into my memory. That lives next to blood and needles and torn flesh.

His sharp pasty face and dark eyes remind me there's a skull just underneath the skin. Craig Miller.

His left eyebrow slopes down over his eye and the cheek is misshapen, like a car door that's been hammered back out after a crash.

Echoes of what Marc did to him.

I think of Marc, just the length of a football pitch away, sitting in the corner chair, waiting up for me.

Craig pulls the cigarette from his mouth, turns down the music and lets his arm hang out of the window. It looks like a broken white tree branch against the black side of the car. My feet are twitching.

Don't you dare run.

"Well look at Little Luke Henry." His voice sounds like someone recorded him and then warped the tape, like his tongue is working hard to push words out. "Not so little any more, eh Lukey? Been lifting, have ya?" And I have to grip the seam of my jeans to stop my left hand coming up and touching my face. *Stand firm.*

I can't make out the face of who's driving next to him, and there's definitely at least one other person sitting in the back. I try to plant my feet into the pavement, pressing my toes into the soles of my trainers. *Don't you run.*

"Tryin to get big like Daddy, are ya?"

His high-pitched laugh is spider's legs running over my skin. He turns and looks into the dark back seat, like he's being passed something, and I get a flash of the drive-by scene from *Boyz n the Hood.*

Don't let him see you're scared.

Then, as Craig turns back to face me, whoever's driving revs the engine and I jump. They all laugh and my chest is shaking as I breathe.

Why don't you get out of the car, Craig? Just you.

Cold rolls down my spine.

"How's your brother?" says Craig, looking me up and down.

Say something, you idiot. Let him know.

"What do you want, Craig?" And his face is as shocked as I feel at the words coming out of my mouth, blunt and strong. *Good lad.*

I watch his bottom lip stick out, and he's nodding. "Well, look at the balls on him, lads. Big man now then, Lukey?"

His eyes don't leave me as his hand comes up to the left side of his face. "You look good," he says, and smiles like a snake.

Hit him. Dive forward and hit him.

And I could. I could be on him before he realised. Before they could react. But I don't move.

"Just saying hello, Lukey." He gives a little wave. "You take care, big man. And say hello to your brother for me."

Then he taps the outside of his door and his arm snakes back inside as the black window closes. I don't move. The engine growls and I make myself not look away as I watch the car drive towards the high road and turn out of sight.

The empty road. My heartbeat. That just happened. He's back.

My hand grips my keys, the silver front door one sticking out from my fist like a tiny knife.

Why is he back? I close my eyes.

It's OK.

My back teeth grinding. My heart pounding.

You didn't run. You stood your ground.

I squeeze my fingers tighter and feel the metal teeth of my keys digging into my palm. Marc's at home. In the dark.

And Craig Miller's back.

13.

Marc used to say we were quarters. Irish and Jamaican from Dad. English and French from Mum. He used to tell people like it was a superpower.

Dad said people didn't come in quarters, that people aren't cakes. He said we should think of it more like a mould in the shape of a person with the mixture poured in. Different blood blended inside us.

Marc told me Dad was wrong and we were like robots, constructed from pieces. I remember sleeping in the same room at Nan's and asking him which quarter was which. He said that he had English arms, a French body, Jamaican legs and an Irish head. I remember picturing the pieces of him being put together. He said that was why he was so fast and strong and stubborn, and that the French body was what made him good at cooking. I lay there, drinking it all in like gospel truth.

When I asked him if I was the same, he said he didn't know which bit was which for me yet because I was too young to tell, but that when I did find out everything would make sense. Before I fell asleep, I ran through every possible robot combination of body parts, trying to find the perfect model, and as I dropped off the best version I could come up with was exactly the same one as him.

```
INT. CAR — NIGHT
Dark dashboard like rhino skin. The sound of boys
breathing. Nervous fingers drum steering wheel.
```

"You have to tell him, Luke."

Me and Tommy are sitting in his car outside the flats.

It's nearly 2 a.m. My eyes ache. It happened, right?

"Marc needs to know, man."

Tommy's worried. I don't know what I'm thinking. It definitely happened. His twisted face. That voice. Me, stood, frozen. I didn't even move.

"Luke?" Tommy snaps me back to the car. "What did he say, exactly?"

I stare into my lap. The crack in my phone screen. *You should've fought him.*

"I dunno."

"Well, what did he look like? He look the same?"

"Yeah. I think so."

"You think so? You got a good look at him, right?"

"Yeah, I mean, it was dark."

"Chicken shit!" Tommy bangs the steering wheel with both hands. "Hasn't got the balls to show up in broad daylight. You know he'd never face Marc himself. I'm serious, man, let's go tell Marc and get Jamie right now and they'll drive round and—"

"And what, Tom? Kick his head in?"

Tommy nods. "Exactly."

"Then what, Tom? My brother who's just done two years gets done for assault?"

Tommy frowns. "Nobody would grass. Who'd grass? We can't just do nothing. Let's tell your dad. Your dad'll do something."

"No way."

Tommy growls. "If you're not gonna tell Marc, then I will."

"No, you won't."

We're looking at each other now and my eyes are hard. Tommy knows it's not his call.

"Don't tell anyone, understand?"

Tommy stares out of the window.

"I'm serious, man. Swear it."

"All right! I swear. Shit."

And I just want to break something. "I'm sorry, man. I'm such an idiot," I say.

"Easy, Lukey, you did nothing wrong. There was a car full of 'em, you said so. What the hell's he doing here, anyway? I thought he left, Scotland or whatever?"

"He did. My dad said." I stare at my phone. "Guess he's back."

I don't know what I'm gonna do when I see Marc.

"Miller won't do anything," Tommy says, lighting a cigarette. "He's just trying to shit you up."

I don't answer. Tommy winds down his window and exhales. "And if anybody sees him, he'll get a kicking just on principle."

I stare out at the empty playground. This is all familiar. The swings casting shadows with light from the flats, and Leia pops into my head. How different I was feeling just a few hours ago.

"You ever think about leaving, Tom?" I stay looking forward.

"What d'you mean?"

"I mean, leaving. Going somewhere else. Somewhere different."

"Where?"

"I dunno, anywhere?"

Tommy's looking at me. "What for?"

I squeeze the phone in my hand. "Just to be… not here." I look at him. "You know?"

And his blank expression is answer enough.

"Will you drop me home?"

"I thought you were stopping at mine?"

"I just wanna go home, man."

He nods, then reaches past me to the glove compartment and pulls something out. "Here."

It's a folding knife. Black handle about the same length as my palm. It looks proper.

"What the hell's that?"

"It's a knife."

"I know it's a knife, Tom. What the hell've you got it for?"

Tommy folds out the blade. Same length as the handle and curved slightly at the point. The matt metal catches the light from outside. "It was Dad's, from time ago. I found it in his tools." He scrapes the tip along the top edge of the steering wheel. "It's proper sharp."

"Why'd you need a knife, Tom?"

"I don't. Take it. Peace of mind." And he's holding it out to me.

"No."

"Why not?"

"Cos I don't need a knife, Tom."

I push his hand back.

"And what if he comes for you again?"

"He didn't come for me, did he?"

"Not this time he didn't. What's the problem? Just take it."

"I could have him you know, on his own, I could have him easy."

"Yeah, I know. Look, I'm not saying stab him, am I? I'm saying carry it when you feel to and, if you need to, pull it out and let him know. You flash it, scare 'em so they back off, then you run like a flipping emu."

"Emu?"

"I dunno, roadrunner, whatever, just fast, yeah? Take it."

And I do.

Tommy's smiling with the pride of feeling like he's helped.

It feels like a tool. Like you're holding something that only has one job. The weight of function. I tell myself I'll take it home, put it under my bed and leave it there.

Only people who can't fight need weapons.

I drop it into my inside jacket pocket and feel it against my chest and it's stupid and pointless cos I'm never gonna use it but, as Tommy starts the engine and the car hums into life, I'd be lying if I said it didn't feel kinda cool.

14.

Nan said: You are what people think you are. You make a reputation, then it makes you.

I ease the front door closed and tiptoe along the hall, expecting Marc to speak as I get to the living room door, but he doesn't. I turn on the light. The room's empty.

As I pull off my shoes, I feel the echo of pain in my foot. Craig Miller. Craig Miller. My eyes close as I climb the stairs. How many times have I trodden these steps?

I leave the landing light off and walk to my room with my back against the wall to avoid creaking any floorboards. As I reach my door I pat my chest and feel the knife, and I'm stupid. Stupid for taking it from Tommy. Stupid for telling him anything happened. But I saw Craig Miller and Marc needs to know.

I pass my room towards his. I'll wake him up and tell

him what happened. It's what I should do. He won't lose his temper. He won't go looking for Craig again. It's different now. But I'm not convincing myself.

Then a sound, coming from the other side of his door. It's like breathing, but more forced; not snoring, but regular. I lean so my ear is almost touching the wood. What, is he…? Wait, is he…?

He's crying.

I picture him on the edge of his bed, head in his hands, thinking Mum is asleep and I'm stopping at Tommy's so he's safe to let it out and my head is full of so many things.

I remember the first time the police brought him home. It was Christmas Eve and Uncle Chris was staying with us. I was in Year Eight. It was just before dinner and it had been snowing, but that crap snow that turns straight to slush. The copper who was with him looked about the same age, like they were two mates, one in fancy dress.

I got sent to my room. I remember lying flat on my floor, ear to the carpet, hearing Mum crying, Uncle Chris trying to calm her down while Dad just paced up and down.

Marc had been caught stealing from Boots. I pictured him sprinting through crowds of Christmas shoppers with electric toothbrushes under his arms, some poor overweight security guard trying to keep up with the county's under-sixteen's 800m champion. It didn't make any sense to me. Why would anyone rob Boots? That was the first time I heard the name Craig Miller.

Marc tried to argue back, then I remember hearing heavy steps coming upstairs and Mum calling after Dad. I opened my door a crack and watched Dad and Uncle Chris march Marc into the bathroom, Dad pulling off his belt. I buried my head under my arms as the whips started.

Him who can't hear, must feel.

That was the only time I ever heard Marc cry. Until now. Standing outside his bedroom door, a knife in my pocket, about to pile more crap on top of someone who's just come out of prison and trying to make sense of everything? I can't do that.

I back slowly away from his door and go to my room. Craig Miller. I close my door and take out the knife. Mattress? Too obvious. The weight of it in my hand. Where then? Wardrobe. Dad's old sheepskin jacket, hanging like a beige carcass. I used to put it on when I was little, just to get lost in it. The smell of the leather and the thick fleece collar.

I pull it out and slide it on. It's still too big, but I can see my hands. The comfort in its weight. Like another skin, thick and tough.

I slip the knife into the inside chest pocket and lie on top of my bed. The smell of Dad holding me. Craig Miller. I close my eyes and all I see is his face. That smile.

I fold up the collar and muffle my ears, blocking out the world, my head swimming and, as the tears come, I don't even put up a fight.

15.

Sitting in back seat of the parked car. Dad in the driver's seat, Mum in front of me.

I'm wearing my funeral suit. It's late morning bright. I can feel the glue from the dressing tightening the skin on my face. Nobody speaks. Every few seconds Mum sniffs.

Through the windscreen, the high brick wall of the courthouse is the colour of pumpkin.

I am heavy.

Staring at the back of their heads, it feels like I'm watching part of them die.

Dad sighs. "Well that's that then."

"You OK, Skywalker?" Leia says, as we walk towards class. She's wearing an old retro Adidas tracksuit top with the same skinny stonewashed jeans from the other night at hers.

Walking a couple of paces behind her, I can just make out the line of her knickers through the denim.

"Luke." She turns back and I look up quickly. "What's wrong?"

"Nothing."

She stares, scanning my face, trying to read me, then shrugs and walks in.

It's Tuesday. I spent most of Sunday in bed, avoiding Marc, and yesterday I skipped comms and english and stayed in my room pretending to work and doing press-ups. Everything since Friday feels like a dream.

I'm here today, right now, for film, and Leia. No sign of the blacked-out Ford Focus. Course not. Everything's fine.

Seeing Noah's gonna be awkward, though.

It really is. God knows what he's thinking.

My plan is to do what we've been raised to do, what my family have done to deal with embarrassment for generations. Ignore it and act like nothing happened. *A bag full of the past.*

I haven't told Leia anything about it, and if Noah's not a complete knob, he'll keep it to himself and we can just carry on.

I don't look at him as I head to my seat, but I can feel his eyes on me. Just let it go, Noah, yeah? You're from where I'm from and you've heard of my brother and it's kinda weird, but it'll all be just fine if we act like nothing happened and leave all that stuff on the other side of town.

And he does.

The lesson is all about shots and how big of a role a script should play in the director's choices. Noah says some people think a great script will have almost no shot description, just a few simple lines if they feel they're essential, while other people view it as a chance for descriptive poetry. He says there's no right or wrong, but that, to him, a strong script carries its clarity in the story and characters and the interpretation of what the camera does is left to the director. He asks us to think of ideas for an opening scene. A place to start.

"Remember," he says, "start where it matters."

He doesn't give me any eye contact. He understands. Course he does.

And the more me and Leia talk about our story, the more I relax.

She thinks we should start with Toby waiting outside of the prison for Marc, like he's been sent to pick him up. We see Toby sitting in the car, torn between excitement and disgust.

My idea is that we start with what put Marc in prison. A short violent scene that shows the dark side of Marc from the past, before we jump to present day.

"But then it's like we're just trying to shock or something," says Leia.

"No," I say. "It's like a punch in the face. A glimpse of what's possible, so that the violence is there underneath the whole time, you know?"

"Yeah, I see what you mean, I just… it just seems a bit…"

"A bit what?"

"A bit, boysy." She shrugs, making a face like she's smelling something bad. "I hate all that macho crap."

I feel the sting of my idea being undermined. "It's not macho. It's violent. I'm not celebrating it, I'm just… it's… I dunno, it's something solid. It's something clear."

I start to scribble like a sulky kid. Leia nudges my shoulder. "OK. If you think it'll work."

"Yeah?"

"Yeah. Just don't write any *Ill Manors* nonsense."

"Course not."

"I'm serious. If anybody uses the word 'gritty' or 'urban' I swear I'll throw up. That stuff is so lame."

"What about voiceover?" I say.

"What about it?"

"Well, some people think it's cheating."

"I dunno," says Leia. "What about *The Royal Tenenbaums*?"

"Or *Shawshank Redemption*?"

"Or *Taxi Driver*?" She smiles. "Some day a real rain will come…"

"…and wash all this scum off the streets."

"So you do know it!"

I smile. "OK, so we're saying a voiceover is a possibility."

"Let's ask Noah," Leia says, and starts to raise her hand.

"No!" I almost shout. Leia puts her hand down and looks at me, confused.

"Why not?"

"I just think that it should be our choice, not him choosing for us." My face wrinkles as I wait to see if she bought it.

"Agreed. You're thorough, aren't you?" *Who speaks like that?*

I nod back. "Do it properly, or not at all, my nan always said."

Now she's looking at me, head tilted.

"I'm still figuring you out, Luke Henry."

And my name out of her mouth is like hearing a happy memory.

"Some people are getting some food and meeting down behind the science block, you know that covered bit?" she says. "You could come? You don't have to…"

"I'll come."

Leia can't hide her smile, and I don't even try to hide mine.

We're almost the last ones out of the room and as we reach the door I'm ready to breathe out, happy that I haven't had to speak to Noah, when his voice stabs me in the back.

"Luke. Can I have a word, please?"

Leia looks back at me. I try to keep a straight face.

"I'll catch you up," I say. "Down behind the science block, yeah?"

"Yeah." She looks past me to Noah and then leaves. I turn to face him at his desk.

```
INT. CLASSROOM — DAY
Blocks of afternoon light slide across empty
tables and chairs. YOUNG MAN stands like a soldier
addressing a general.
```

"How's your foot?"

Noah points. I look down.

"Fine."

"Good."

I feel stupid.

"Listen, Luke, I just wanted to say—"

"You don't have to say anything." I don't look up.

"Yeah. I know," he says. "But I want to."

And the change in his voice makes me look at him. He's not quite smiling. "I know what it's like."

The phrase rings every lame alarm bell in me. I'm taken straight back to beige rooms with school counsellors after Marc got sent down. Old Mrs Martin with her young haircut and clothes. Me staring at her plastic cheese plant, as she stares at me, waiting for some *Good Will Hunting* moment. "It's OK, Luke. I understand what you're thinking. You can talk to me. I know what it's like."

No, I can't, Miss. I can't even talk to my own family, so how the hell am I gonna talk to you, some stranger with soft skin and a cotton-wool voice? You don't know anything.

I stare at Noah. I want him to be different. He's from the same place. Maybe he does know. Maybe he's got more of an idea than anybody. I want that to be true, I really do, but...

"Can I go now?"

Noah looks down at the papers on his desk. "Yeah. Course."

I turn to leave, grateful.

"Luke?"

I look back, and it feels like a scene from one of Dad's old westerns, the loner about to move on after helping the oppressed villagers.

Noah says, "I'll see you tomorrow."

What's my line? I'm Clint Eastwood, gimme a good line.

I guess you will.

I shrug. "I guess you will." Then I turn and walk out.

Perfect.

16.

Nan said: For every strength, a weakness; for every weakness, a strength.

I count six of them, sitting on the little wall and steps under the overhanging fibreglass roof behind the science block. It looks like the place where teachers would steal a quick smoke. Simeon, Jono, the ginger kid, Leia, the girl from film with the shaved side of her head and another girl with a jet-black bob, who I don't know, but have seen before. They look like the cast of *Skins* and I try not to hate them.

"Waterboy!" Simeon calls out, and everyone turns and watches me approach. I concentrate on lifting my feet as I walk so I don't trip. He's sitting with Jono and the ginger kid near the wall. Leia's slightly lower down the slope in between Shaved Head and the other girl.

You gonna let him call you that? In front of people?

I don't respond. Leia waves me over and I sit on the step down from hers. The girl with the bob is staring at my scar. Shaved Head is eyes down, in her phone.

"What did he want?" Leia says.

I shake my head. "Nothing."

"This is Luke," she says, pointing at me.

"Luke, this is Megan." Shaved Head gives the minimum acknowledgement it's possible to give, lifting her chin a millimetre. "And this is Michelle."

The girl with the bob holds out her hand and smiles. "We do English together. I've heard about you."

I shake Michelle's hand, trying to place her in English class. "Hi."

What's she heard?

"Come to hang with us then, Waterboy?" says Simeon, like I didn't hear him the first time.

I feel my arms tensing.

I don't look at him as I say, "My name's Luke," and I meant it strong, but not as aggressive as it came out. Nice. The girls watch. I try to neutralise it. "We've met, remember?"

I stare up at him. Jono and the ginger kid stare back.

Simeon smiles. "Sorry, man, just kidding. It's a pretty sick nickname though, right? I mean, as far as nicknames go.

Stupid film. Funny though. Ask Jono what they call him."

He slaps Jono's wide back and Jono looks embarrassed. I don't say anything. Simeon gives it a second then says, "Jugs."

Him and the ginger kid laugh. Jono looks at the floor, shifting his thick legs.

I look at Leia; she's avoiding my eyes.

Simeon shakes his head. "But I'm with you, Luke, let's leave the nicknames to the Rugby Club." Then he points at me with both hands like guns. "You can help us."

I look at Leia and Michelle. Both their faces are blank and I'm wondering who decided he was the leader.

"Six degrees of Kevin Bacon, but with different actors," Simeon says. "You any good at it?"

And he's not kidding. I can feel the sighs as Michelle and Megan roll their eyes. It feels like some kind of initiation test, but I like this game. I still play it with Dad sometimes; connect the actors via as few films as possible. I play it cool.

"Not really," I say.

"Course you are," he says. "Jonah Hill, to George Clooney. Go." And he stares at me, waiting. I do it in my head, the whole time acting like I'm not.

Then Leia cuts in. "Jonah Hill in *Moneyball* with Brad Pitt, Brad Pitt in *Ocean's Eleven* with George Clooney."

She leans back on her arms, pleased with herself, and I look down so I don't give away how sexy I just found that.

Simeon scoffs, "Too easy. Let's crank it up." And it hits me that I've never played this game with anyone my own age before and it feels good.

"OK," he says. "Erm, Jack Nicholson, to… let me see…"

Ginger kid leans forward. "Billy Crystal."

Everybody looks at him. Ginger kid closes his eyes and nods. Simeon nods too. "Sick. Good one, Max."

Come on then, Lukey boy. Do it.

This feels important. Everybody's staring into space, trying to make the steps in their heads.

"Got it," I say.

Leia smiles. Simeon frowns. "No way. Go on then."

I use my hand. "Jack Nicholson was in *The Pledge* with Robin Wright." I look at them for approval. Jono looks confused, so does Michelle, Max is nodding and so is Simeon. I carry on. "And Robin Wright was in *The Princess Bride* with Billy Crystal."

I spread my hands like I've just served them dinner.

"What the hell is *The Princess Bride*?" Simeon says, looking at me, then everyone else. Michelle and Leia shrug, so does Jono and my heart drops.

"I've seen that," says Max, and I have to fight to hide my smile.

"You kidding?" says Simeon.

Max shakes his head. "No. I watched it when I was little. My dad loves it. It's pretty old. With the six-fingered man and the giant called…"

"Andre," I chip in, then ride the wave of my win. "It's brilliant. Has no one else seen it?" I'm looking at Leia. She pouts and shakes her head. I give myself a lisp and say, "Inconceivable!"

Me and Max laugh at the in-joke.

"Fair play," says Simeon. "Come on then, your turn."

17.

Doesn't matter where you go. What you do. Where you end up.

You can't change where you're from.

It's nearly dark when I get off the bus. The quickest way home is the way I walked the other night, but I go the longer way round to stay on the better lit high road as long as possible, my front door key gripped between my fingers.

There's no car. *Of course there isn't*. But my ears are still pricked for any kind of engine and it's like a place I've known all my life now has an edge with my name on it.

I hear Eminem through the front door and I feel nine again.

Mum must be at work. I wonder where Dad is right now.

"Lukey!" Marc shouts over the music from upstairs.

I pretend I don't hear and go to the kitchen to make a tea.

She's never seen *The Princess Bride*. We could watch it together.

"What d'ya think?" He's standing in the doorway wearing the jeans and white shirt we bought on Saturday. He looks like a catalogue model, everything sharp and crisp and I can smell the Davidoff. His face scrunches up. "Too much?"

"Too much for what?" I fill the kettle.

"I knew it. Stupid. I look like I'm going on a blind date or something. Make us one too, will ya?"

I let the tap run for longer and notice a selection of vegetables I can't name next to the bread bin.

"Why you dressing up?" I say, clicking the kettle on.

"I'm meeting Donna." He pulls an exaggerated nervous smile. "I rung her."

"And she agreed to meet you?" I fetch mugs.

Marc sits down at the table and he seems young.

"Big mistake, probably. Haven't got a clue what to say to her." And he's talking to me, on a level, about Donna. Maybe that's how it goes. Maybe nobody tells you when you graduate in conversation, it just happens.

Act natural.

"I'd start with hello," I say, spooning sugars into the mugs.

"Yeah," says Marc. "I'll be fine. No big deal. You good?"

The water bubbles.

"Yeah."

Craig Miller.

"How'd it go with Leia the other night?"

Craig Miller.

The water boils. Forget it.

"Lukey? What's up?"

Click.

"Nothing. Where you meeting her?"

"At hers. Hopefully her mum and her sister aren't there."
His thumbs are drumming the table.

"And you're driving?" My hand wobbles as I pour the
water.

"Nah, I'm gonna walk. Build up some courage, plan my
lines." He forces a little laugh.

"Drive," I say, spilling hot water on the sideboard.

"Steady on, mate, I think it's full."

I grab the tea towel and mop up the spill. "You should take
the car. Did Mum leave it?"

"Yeah, but I'm gonna walk."

I fetch the milk. "Take the car, Marc." My voice sounds
wrong.

"What's the problem?" he says.

"Nothing." I pour the milk. "I just think it'd be better.

What if her mum's there? If you've got the car, you can go somewhere else, you've got the option, you know?" I stir, feeling his eyes on me.

"Jesus, who are you? Hitch?"

I put his mug in front of him on the table then lean against the side with mine. "I'm just saying. Be prepared, yeah? You don't wanna get stuck in their living room sitting with her mum and her sister, do ya?"

I sip my tea to hide.

Marc nods. "Pretty smart. Anybody'd think you were in college or something."

And relax.

"So come on then, Princess Leia, spill it." He leans back in his chair and for a second I picture jumping on him, trying to pin him down, whether I could do that, what would happen if we fought.

"Nothing to spill. She's a mate, we're in film studies together, she knows her stuff."

Sip again.

"Shut up, Luke! You kiss her yet?"

"It's not like that." I picture Leia, in the light of the open fire.

"Ha ha! You're thinking about her right now!"

"Piss off, Marc!"

"Nah, I'm just messing. That's a good thing, man. Feels good, right?"

And it does.

We both sip. Him thinking about Donna, me about Leia, and maybe I feel closer to him. In a different way.

"One thing I know, mate," he says, staring into his mug, "the stuff you think will impress them? It's all bullshit. They see straight through it."

He looks up at me. My brother. Do we get to have actual conversations now? Ones about things that matter?

"You know what I mean, big man?"

I nod. "Is that why you're wearing two litres of aftershave?"

We look at each other.

And we laugh.

When I was six Marc nearly killed me.

We were at Nan's house. He thought I was asleep.

The room was all night-grey light and I felt him creeping across the floor from his bed and his shadow slide on to me. Then his pillow was over my face.

I tried to scream through the fabric, but his older arms pinned my head to the mattress. I can remember the hot cotton in my mouth, the dry air seeping away as my body wriggled like a dog in a noose. I started to see white spots in the black and I couldn't tell whether my eyes were open or closed, I just felt the weight of him on top of me and knew it was pointless to fight.

So I stopped.

I let my body go limp and didn't try to breathe. My head swam in the hot dark as I felt the last drops of air scrape out from my throat.

I don't know how long he waited before he got off. I just remember my gasp as the cold hit my face and my lungs filling, pushing against my ribs.

I lay there, eyes open, still seeing spots, mouth gulping like a fish out of water, as he moved back to his bed without saying a word.

Years later he'd deny it. Laugh it off. Tell me I'd dreamt the whole thing, but I know it happened.

Don't get me wrong, I don't think he wanted me dead. I don't think murder was his plan.

I honestly think he just wanted to see what would happen.

18.

Dad's under a car, tongue out as he concentrates on unscrewing a nut.

Screen splits.

Mum's staring at a syringe as it fills with blood from an old man's arm.

Screen splits again.

Zia's in the staff toilets at the supermarket, practising a new joke.

Screen splits again.

Tommy's smacking the shit out of an old shed with a lump hammer while two older builders watch, smiling.

Screen splits again.

Noah's in the college staffroom, forcing a smile as an older woman tells him again about her husband's operation.

Screen splits again.

Donna's laughing, trying to wash up as Marc tickles her

in our kitchen.

All these films, happening now, at the same time. Always. All of them moving.

All of the

"What are you writing? More ideas?"

Leia's trying to read upside down. I close my notebook.

"Just stuff. We going?"

She nods and we're walking through campus at lunchtime and it feels different. Familiar. Like I've known her longer than three weeks.

Like we're already on disc two of the box set of our relationship. *Why do you talk like that?*

Then Michelle runs up.

"Did you ask him?" she says, and Leia looks everywhere, but at me.

Michelle clocks that she's put her foot in it and backs away. "Gotta go. I'm supposed to meet Megan. See you later, Luke." Her eyes flick to Leia, then she's gone.

"Ask me what?"

But Leia's already walking. I follow her. "What did she mean?"

I put my hand on her arm. Leia looks down at it. "Nothing."

I let go. "I'm sorry. What's wrong?"

"I said nothing."

And we walk, both feeling the weird air of an argument that should make absolutely no sense for two people who are just friends.

Then Noah's there.

He must've come out of the staffroom block. He's holding one of those padded yellow jiffy bags. He nods hello at Leia then holds the envelope out to me. I read my name and address in black marker.

"What's this?"

Noah shrugs. "I was gonna post it, didn't want to make a big deal of it in class, but you two are working together so…"

We both stare at the envelope. It's just a bit bigger than a DVD. I look at Leia. She shrugs. We both look at Noah.

"I'll see you Friday. For your eyes only, yeah?" he says and walks back inside. I look down at the envelope. The hand-written words.

"Open it," says Leia, but for some reason I don't want to. What if it's something about Marc? *Why the hell would it be?*

So I tear it open.

It is a DVD, called *Long Time Round*.

"I've never heard of it," I say.

Leia reads the title. "Me either."

I skim the blurb on the back and see the words 'Birmingham' and 'honest' and 'trouble' and 'perfect' and then I see his name.

Written by Noah Clarke.

"This is his film."

"What do you mean?" says Leia.

"He wrote it. This is the film he wrote."

"Noah wrote a film?"

"Yeah. This one." It suddenly feels important in my hand.

"No way!" Leia's face looks like mine feels. He's given me a copy of his film. *Why does it say Birmingham?*

Because Noah wrote a film about Birmingham.

"We have to watch it!" Leia says. "We have to watch it right now!"

And she's right. We do.

"You want to come to mine?" she says, both of us buzzing with excitement.

Then an idea, and I smile. "No."

I look at my watch and feel my skin tingling.

"I've got a place."

19.

It's not until we're climbing the dark narrow staircase to Dad's flat that I realise that it's probably gonna be a smelly mess. I'd only thought as far as the privacy it would give us. This was a bad idea. I'm bringing Leia to an art installation of my dad's pants and empty beer cans. What was I thinking? *Calm down. If a bit of mess scares her, she's not worth it anyway.*

I feel her behind me as we climb. Can't change my mind now. I start trying to come up with stories about whose place it is. Maybe it's not Dad's. Maybe it's a mate of Dad's, from work. Some grease monkey bachelor who lets me watch films at his place. Is that better?

Creepy, is what that is.

"Maybe we should go to yours," I say. Not turning round.

"Are you kidding?" says Leia. "We're here now. Come on. What's wrong?"

"Nothing."

Key in the door. Stomach knots.

"You OK, Skywalker?"

She's gonna run a mile.

"Fine."

Push door open. *What was I thinking?*

It's spotless.

Like he's hired somebody to come in and clean. It even smells fresh. The skylight's open and the light makes it feel like we're stepping into an old photograph. The bed is folded up, the carpet hoovered and the kitchen corner is gleaming. It's still tiny, but wow.

"It's perfect!" says Leia, walking in like she's viewing it to rent.

Thanks, Dad. I don't know how you knew, but thanks.

Leia drops her bag and takes off her hoodie. She's wearing a white T-shirt with a skull and crossbones on the back and no arms and I see the black of a bra strap. The dark edge of it against her skin.

"Whose is it?" She's straight down on the floor looking at the train of DVDs and videos.

"My dad's," I say, opening the fridge, and there's actual food, like steak and potato salad and coleslaw that looks homemade.

"Weird."

"What's weird?" Leia looks over.

"Nothing. You want some juice?"

She nods and I take out the full box of grape and pour two mugs.

"So he doesn't live with you then?" says Leia, as I hand her a mug and sit next to her on the sofa. It's nearly half three. Dad won't be home from work until seven at least.

"He moved out a couple years ago. I come here sometimes, to watch films." I sip the cold sweetness. Leia does the same, and we're alone, on a sofa that turns into a bed, in an attic, in the middle of the afternoon. *Nice work, big man.* And I didn't even plan it like that.

"It's good that you still see him," she says. "Last time I saw my mum I was four." She sips again.

"What happened?" I say, then regret it. "Sorry. None of my business."

"It's fine. She left. It happens."

"Yeah," I say.

"She was an actress, is an actress, I dunno. She lives in America somewhere."

I leave the space for her to carry on if she wants.

"My dad got her her first job, after she took time off to have me and Toby, some TV pilot thing over there he was working on. It was supposed to be her breakthrough role. We all lived in California for a year."

"No way."

Leia nods. "I was only two, Toby would've been five or six. Anyway, they make the pilot, the company likes it, says they'll make the actual show, everybody's excited, then, six months into filming, they pull the plug."

"Why?" I'm leaning forward for the story.

"God knows," says Leia. "Somebody changed their mind, I guess. We pack up and move back to England and then a couple of weeks later she leaves. Turned out she'd been having an affair with the director and he promised her a part in his new film, and boom, see you later, Mum."

"Wow, and you haven't seen her since?"

Leia shakes her head. "Nope. Guess we didn't fit into her career plans. She sent money when I turned eleven, but I made Dad send it back, so she stopped."

"Fair enough."

Leia looks at me, like that's not what she thought I would say.

And then it's quiet. Not awkward, just quiet.

Tell her about Dad's thing.

"My dad made a pilot. In America too. He was an alien."

Leia's looking at me. I smile. "He's big. It was ages ago.

236

They made him the Big Alien. It's kinda lame."

She doesn't say anything and it's clear she's half listening, half thinking about something else. I nudge her knee. "You OK?"

"I'm fine."

"What was Michelle talking about before?"

Leia shakes her head. "This place is so quiet," she says. "No interruptions. Just like it should be."

And out of nowhere, I can feel my blood. She's sipping her juice and I'm watching her and I wanna be the mug. I wanna be the mug she's holding. I want her lips.

"Come on then," she says, and I almost choke on my juice.

"What?"

"Noah's film? Let's watch it."

"Oh, yeah, course," I say, and I get down on my knees and load the DVD then go back to the sofa. Leia takes off her All Stars and curls her feet up. Her toes are millimetres away from my left thigh and I'm fighting the urge to touch them and the TV screen goes black and this is perfect.

Marc said: Great players make things happen.

I can't move.

Noah's file is amazing. *Long Time Round.*

It's actually set in Birmingham. A guy called Nathan gets a place away at university, which is his dream, but he's torn about leaving because it's just his dad looking after him and his younger brother, Jonah, who's already running with a gang led by this proper bad guy called Darren. His girlfriend, Sophia, doesn't want him to leave either, but Nathan makes his decision and does go and start his course in a new city. He meets all these uni people and feels well out of place, but excited.

Back at home, under Darren's influence, Jonah gets deeper and deeper in trouble and their dad can't handle it, so Nathan has to drop out of uni to come home. The second half of the film is the build-up to Jonah doing some big job, and Nathan's inevitable showdown with Darren to stop it happening, mixed in with him trying to patch things up with Sophia.

It's all building to this big climax, but then, just when things are going OK with Sophia and Nathan is ready to properly confront Darren, some other gang guy, who we don't even know, takes Nathan out.

It's proper sad.

And it's like watching my life. I recognise it all. Not the

238

story as such, but the details. The locations and the mood and the colours, the relationships and the way people speak to each other, make me feel like I'm actually in the film. Like my real world was on the screen. I feel like I know Noah. Like he knows me.

I feel like I just got hit in the stomach with a medicine ball.

"Wow," Leia says, as we both just stare at the end credits and listen to the slow plucking guitar soundtrack.

"You think that's based on his life?" she says.

I don't move.

"Luke, are you OK?"

That's when I realise I'm crying.

My lower jaw is shaking and I'm blowing out air to try and calm myself. Leia doesn't know where to look and I feel stupid and embarrassed, but it's all I can do to stay completely still in case I properly bawl like a baby.

Get it together.

I try to picture Noah, sitting at a computer, typing the script. Is that his life? It has to be. It was too real to be fake. It looked amazing. Like each scene was a photograph. No gimmicks, no sped-up drug scenes or slow-motion violence. It wasn't about gangs; it was about people who happen to be part of a world. It was about family and guilt and anger.

It was about love.

I wipe my eyes with the back of one hand. "Yeah, sorry. Stupid."

I look at her and try to smile. Leia's head tilts and she smiles back. Then she's on me. Straddling my lap, her knees either side of my hips, her hands on my chest. I look up at her, and my hands slide up her thighs to her waist. She's smiling, leaning forward. My hands curve round to the small of her back, her hands push into my chest, taking her weight, and we kiss, the places where our bodies are touching pressing against each other like they're hungry.

She's pulling at the back of my neck, I'm pushing her hips into mine and my hands are trying to tell her everything, to press out my whole story on to her body, to let her know me.

Then I hear Dad's laugh.

Leia bounces on to the sofa next to me as I spring up.

"What's wrong?" she says.

I look at my watch, it's only just gone five. What's he doing home?

His booming cackle climbing the stairs. Sounds like he's on the phone. I'm standing up. "It's... he's not supposed to... we need to... gimme a sec."

He's outside the door. The sound of keys. Then a woman,

laughing too. *He's not alone?* Nightmare. My body's trying to twist-up like plastic in a fire. They're both giggling. *New woman?* I'm looking at Leia, she's nervous and confused.

"Who is it, Luke?" She's straightening her hair, her face is flushed. Key in the door. I look at her and I freeze. Door opening, more giggling, *hold on, is that…?*

20.

Awkward times infinity.

Dad and Mum are in the doorway.

What the hell is this?

Dad forces a smile, his eyes dancing from me to Leia, then Mum, then back to me again. He's holding a bottle of something.

"What a surprise, son."

I look at Mum, she purses her lips and lifts her eyebrows. The silence is thick.

"What's going on?" I say, finally.

"Lukey," Mum goes to speak.

Dad cuts her off. "We just came here for a chat. Right, Ange? Talk things through, like. I didn't think, don't you have a class or something?"

The pair of them are squirming. *Yo, they've done this before!*

Then Mum takes control of the situation and steps forward,

cracking the tension. "You must be Leia!" she says, stepping past me. I turn and watch her shake Leia's hand. "It's lovely to meet you, I'm Angela."

My head hurts. "How do you...? Mum?"

Mum carries on shaking Leia's hand, but looks at me. "Your brother told me her name."

She's overdoing her smile. Leia doesn't know where to look and I watch her body trying to curl into itself. This is too much.

"I'll put the kettle on," says Dad, like we're gonna just sit and have a cup of tea together. Like this isn't some kind of freaky dream sequence.

"You've only got two mugs, Dad." He closes the door. I'm shaking my head. "I don't understand."

"It's all right," he says. "I've got another one somewhere."

"I don't mean about the mugs. I mean, what the hell?"

Mum sits down next to Leia. "So, Leia, you're at the college too?"

Leia glances at me, then nods.

I try to help her. "We have film studies together, Mum."

Mum's nodding. "Course, film. That's great. And how's it going?"

Leia still can't get words out.

"It's fine." I offer, "We're working on a script."

"A script?" calls Dad from the sink. "Fantastic! You didn't say anything, Lukey."

All eyes on me. I'm frozen.

"So Leia," says Dad, carrying on like I'm not even in the room. "Who's the Star Wars fan? Your mum or your dad?"

He fills the kettle. Leia checks with me. I shrug.

"My dad," she says, folding her hoodie in her lap.

Mum laughs to herself. "Luke and Leia, the movie romance."

"Mum!"

"What? I'm just saying. It's funny, eh?"

"It's fate," says Dad, not turning around from the sideboard. *Fate?* Who is this guy? And what's he done with my father?

"Actually, they were brother and sister," says Leia. "I mean, in the film. They weren't a couple."

Mum frowns. "But she kisses him. I remember it, Joe, they kiss, right?"

I want to die.

Dad turns round and winks at me. "They certainly did, Ange, but Leia's right. They were brother and sister. Vader's kids. You take sugar, Leia?"

Enough.

"We have to go," I say, reaching for my shoes. "We've got a thing to prepare, for tomorrow." I stare at Leia and she follows

244

my lead, pulling her shoes on.

"What about your teas?" says Dad and he smiles at Mum and I think I might throw up. I'm picking up both our bags, taking Leia's hand and leading her to the door.

"It was nice to meet you," Leia says.

"You too, sweetheart." Mum waves like the queen from the sofa and I'm opening the door. I let Leia step on to the stairs then look back at Mum, who pouts, then mimes the word "Lovely," and the last thing I see before I pull the door closed is her smiling and giving me the thumbs-up.

We used to test ourselves on long car journeys. Marc had a black Casio with a stopwatch on it and we'd time each other to see how long we could hold our breath. I'd stare out at the fields as we drove up north to see Uncle Chris, my cheeks puffed out to hold more air, my vision blurring as my head went faint. It always felt like an hour had gone by.

"Thirty-two seconds," Marc'd say, smiling at me. "Good try, Lukey." Then I'd hold the watch and time him, staring at the black digital numbers as they changed. I always loved the way eight became nine, just one piece disappearing to make a whole different number.

One minute fifty-four seconds.

And Marc would exhale like a horse. "I can do better," he'd say. "What's the world record for holding your breath, Dad?" Dad said there were divers who could go underwater for something like twenty minutes. I didn't believe him.

"Is that true, Mum?"

"If your dad says so."

Twenty minutes? That was a whole episode of *Ben 10*.

"Reset the watch, Lukey, I'm going for it," Marc said.

Dad laughed from the driver's seat. I watched the numbers, knowing he'd never once got to two minutes.

When we hit 1:30 Marc starts to grip the inside door handle. 1:40, and Marc's face is going red. 1:45. 1:50, I knew he'd burst soon. 1:55, I could see the cords in his neck and a vein in his temple. 1:58. 1:59.

"Mum, look at Marc."

Mum turning back and the shock on her face. "Marc, stop it! Marc!"

2:01. 2:02. He'd broken the two minutes.

"Joe! Stop the car. Pull over now!"

I don't know how long he was unconscious for. I didn't time that, but I remember sitting in the car, watching Mum rub his back, walking him up and down on the hard shoulder, thinking, my big brother is dangerous. Even to himself.

2I.

If humans evolve to achieve telepathy, will there still be awkward silences?

I'm staring forward. The sun's gone behind the tall houses and me and Leia are walking through shadows towards the high road. I'm embarrassed. I'm confused. I'm properly excited. That just happened. Man, she can kiss. How long have Mum and Dad been meeting up? What does it mean? Does Marc know? What would've happened if they hadn't showed up?

"Sorry."

"It's OK."

Leia's hands are in her hoodie as she walks next to me. It's getting cold.

"I didn't plan it, I mean, that, I just—"

"It was my fault," she says, "I shouldn't have..."

I see Mum and Dad in the doorway. "I don't even know

what that was. They've hardly spoken to each other for nearly two— Wait," I stop walking. "You shouldn't have?"

Leia carries on a few steps then stops too.

"I got carried away," she says, turning back. "Stupid."

Why would she say that?

"Why would you say that?"

She's looking at me like there's stuff she wants to say, frowning like she wishes I could just read her mind. I know how that feels. This could be rubbish. I have to save it.

"It didn't feel stupid." I don't look away. "It felt amazing."

She doesn't speak. *Say something else then*.

But I can't think of anything, so it's just the pair of us on the pavement. A backdrop of traffic sounds. Me, open. Her, frowning. *What is she scared of?*

I walk towards her. She doesn't back off, but she's shrinking into her hoodie.

"I wanted that to happen," I say. "Didn't you?"

Her frown flickers. I risk a hand out towards her.

"I think so," she says. I pull back my hand. *She thinks so?*

But then she smiles. Like she's not allowed to say the words, but wants me to know. I smile back.

"The bus stops down here." I point.

Her right hand comes out of her hoodie pocket and she

steps closer. I keep my eyes on hers as her hand moves up over my shoulder, to my neck and then my face. I fight the urge to flinch as her fingertips move to my scar. Her hand goes to pull away, but I hold her wrist, keeping her fingers against my face.

"How did this happen, Luke?" she says, following the line across my cheek. I see Craig, leaning out of the passenger window. I see Marc, standing in the kitchen doorway. I see Tommy handing me the knife.

"I wasn't ready."

I let go of her hand, but she keeps it there.

"Who did this to you?"

And I feel a tidal wave of everything swelling from my stomach, moving behind my ribs, heading for my throat. I don't want to cry again. I don't want to cry again. So I just step forward and hold her and she holds me back. Her arms around my middle, face against my neck. My arms criss-crossed round her bag, cheek resting on the top of her head. Right here. On the pavement. Like we're a life-size sculpture of what a real embrace is. As the street lights pop into life.

I breathe in the coconut of her shampoo and think to myself how all my favourite moments involve no talking at all.

22.

Mathilda: Is life always this hard, or is it just when you're a kid?
Leon: Always like this.

- Leon: The Professional, Luc Besson. 1994

Mum's waiting for me in the kitchen.

Her car wasn't outside so Marc must still be out. Did she tell him to stay out so she could speak to me? Does he know already? Did Dad want to be here as well?

I feel Leia's hand on my cheek. I see her head against the window as the bus pulls away. *Does this mean we're together?*

"Sit down, love." Mum's holding her mug in two hands and I wonder if it feels like a rehearsed scene to her as much as it does to me.

"I know you must have questions."

I sit down. Leia on top of me on Dad's sofa. The heat of

her mouth.

Does she regret it?

Mum's wrestling with her script; she thinks I'm gonna kick off. "See, adults, me and your dad, it's… sometimes you find comfort in what you know, the familiar… What's funny?"

"Nothing."

"So why the smile?"

I shrug.

"Listen, your dad and me… your brother doesn't know, see, it's complicated." She sips. *You're damn right it's complicated.*

"It doesn't mean that me and your dad are—"

"It's all right, Mum."

She looks at me, confused. "What do you mean?" *Yeah, what do you mean?*

"I mean it's OK. You don't have to explain yourself."

Mum's looking at me like she recognises me, but doesn't understand.

I imagine a cable car travelling between my head and hers, all the things we're not saying out loud travelling back and forth along the wire.

"You're getting big, Lukey," she says, after a while.

We sit on the sofa in lamplight, sipping cups of tea, and it feels good.

Like she's actually here. Like we could really talk.

"So, Leia seems lovely," Mum says, and I feel myself blush as I nod.

"Are you two an item then?" She's leaning forward a little. I shrug. "Dunno."

"Course, no need to rush these things, eh? You take your time, love." And as she reaches over and pats my knee I notice how small her hand is.

She gets up and goes to the dresser in the corner. "You know I was nineteen when I met your dad." She sits back down, holding the dark blue photo album.

"I know, Mum, I've heard the story. Big Alien fixes car."

"Nineteen. That's hardly older than you." She opens the album at their wedding shot. A younger her stands smiling, dwarfed by a beaming younger Dad.

"Look how young we were." I watch Mum stroke over herself and Dad with her finger, travelling back in time in her head. I don't tell her that even though they look younger, they still look a lot older than I feel. To Dad's left is Uncle Chris and Nan and an older, large white man I know was Granddad. Past him stands a crowd of smiling aunties and uncles and cousins. I see Mum look at the right side of the photo. She taps it with her finger.

I stare at the frozen moment. If Mum and Dad are the body, the spread of people looks like a butterfly with one wing. Dad's side is full, but on Mum's side there's only three other people present. Her stern-faced mum and dad, who I never met. They refused to have anything to do with her after the wedding because of Dad's heritage, then died before they could patch things up.

The other person is her younger sister, Kathy, who moved to Australia before I was born.

Mum sighs. "People are so silly, Luke," she says. "We live our choices."

And once again, I'm sitting next to someone as they take stock of their own life. Luke Henry, Best Supporting Actor.

Then the front door's opening and Mum snaps out of it. She quickly slides the photo album under the sofa as the door slams shut and gives me the look that says, 'please don't say anything'. I give her the 'don't worry' face in reply.

"What's this then?" says Marc from the doorway. There's a supermarket bag in his hand. "You two plotting something?" He still can't hide when he's pissed off. It can't have gone great with Donna.

Mum shakes her head dramatically. "Us, no, course not." She looks at me, I shake my head too.

"So how'd it go?" Mum asks him.

Marc's jaw tightens. "Not great."

I picture him standing outside Donna's mum's house, a tired bouquet of flowers in his hand as the front door slams in his face. Then I think of Leia, her lips on my cheek.

"What you so happy about?" He's looking at me.

I try to frown. "Nothing."

"I'll put the kettle back on," says Mum, getting up, slipping me a sly wink.

Marc puts the bag on the chair, takes off his jacket and drops it over the side. His T-shirt hugs his chest. "Gonna take some time I reckon, if I haven't burnt it already."

He shakes his head and he's genuinely unsure.

My big brother really doesn't know.

"What's in the bag?" says Mum.

"Ingredients. Thought I'd make crêpes. Take my mind off it. Yous want some? I've got lemon or Nutella. You still got my skinny pan, Mum?"

Mum puts her hand on his shoulder. "Yes, love. It's in the cupboard. Baby steps, eh? Give her time, you've been a long time round."

And it's like the ship of the room just hit an iceberg. I grip my mug. "What did you say?"

Mum and Marc look at me, confused. "What's wrong, Luke?" says Mum.

"You just said long time round."

"What's wrong with that?" says Marc, staring at me like I'm being stupid. My head fills up with images from Noah's film. How real it felt. How close to home.

"What does that mean, long time round?"

Mum and Marc look at each other like I'm some stranger in their house from a different country or something.

"It's just a saying, love," says Mum. "If you've been away for a while, you've been a long time round. You never heard that before?"

I stare at Mum and my brother, shaking my head, and it's like the two of them are on one side of the glass and I'm on the other.

Déjà vu.

INT. EMERGENCY ROOM — NIGHT

YOUNG MAN sits with head in hands. Muffled radio DJ voice. POLICEWOMAN sits next to him, leaning in, notepad ready. Clock above them says eleven forty.

POLICEWOMAN: I know this is hard.

She goes to rest her hand on YOUNG MAN'S arm. He flinches, she pulls back.

POLICEWOMAN: I need you to speak, Luke. You're brother's in a critical condition. They're fighting to save him.

YOUNG MAN lifts his head and looks at her. Confused.

POLICEWOMAN: I'm trying to help.

YOUNG MAN frowns. His mouth opens to speak.

Cut to black.

PART 3.
~~Changing~~
Breaking.

I.

Nobody's said the word 'boyfriend', or 'girlfriend'. Not once.

It's been just over two weeks.

We don't hold hands as we walk up the hill to college.

We never kiss on campus.

But, if there's some satellite in space, looking down, detecting the infrared and electromagnetic charges between people as they go about their daily lives, me and Leia are flagging up on that bad boy.

I feel animal. Like I'm in on some primitive secret.

As we sit in class and work on scene ideas for our story, it's like I'm split. Half of me is listening and talking to her, loving sharing ideas, and the other half is crackling with this need to just jump on her. In a good way.

    EXT. SUPERMARKET — DAY
    Dark blue supermarket fleece. Fingers play with

```
zip. Engine sound approaches. Fingers stop.
Crunch of loose grit as a car pulls up. Passenger
door opens.
```

Friday after film.

The autumn sun's properly out and we're sitting on the little wall and steps behind the science block. The same cast of *Skins*, but now I'm in it. The new guy. Trying to pull off the strong silent thing, once every five minutes trying to imagine Tommy or Zia fitting into this puzzle.

I should ring them. *Yeah, you should*.

"James Franco to Samuel L. Jackson," says Simeon. He's next to me on my right, wearing a tie-dye T-shirt that he said was ironic. Can clothes be ironic?

"I've got this one," says Max, opposite me.

Megan blows her nose louder than I've ever heard a girl do it before. "Don't you get sick of that stupid game?" She checks the contents of her tissue, like she's letting us know she doesn't care, before folding it up and stuffing it into the front pouch of her rucksack.

"Shut up, Sis," says Simeon. "Just cos you're crap at it."

Megan gives him the finger and lights a cigarette. I still can't believe nobody thought to tell me they were twins.

I look across at Leia, sat to Megan's left with Michelle. She's wearing a purple man's golf jumper that looks like a hand-me-down, but is somehow amazing on her, the edge of a white vest showing at the bottom of the V neck, highlighting her skin. *This girl.*

She's pretending not to look at me. Our secret. We actually have two secrets: us, and Noah's film. We haven't told anyone else we watched it, especially not Noah. I can't think of what to say to him that doesn't make it sound like I'm in awe. I've watched it four times now. *Awe?*

It's brilliant.

"Come on then," says Simeon to Max, winding time with his finger. "Franco to Jackson."

I make the steps in my head; James Franco with Robert De Niro in *City By The Sea*, Robert De Niro with Samuel L. Jackson in *Jackie Brown*. Easy.

I don't say it out loud. Max's thinking face looks like he's on the toilet. Jono doesn't speak or move.

"Your sister making that punch again?" says Megan, and it takes me a second to work out that she's talking to Michelle. Punch?

Michelle nods. "Yep. But maybe you shouldn't drink it this time, Meg?"

"Shut up!" Megan scoffs. "That's the main reason I'm coming."

What are they talking about?

That's when I notice Leia. She's squirming like somebody poured something down the back of her top. I try to catch her eye, but she won't let me.

"We should go, Luke," she says, starting to get up, but still not looking at me.

"Shame you're not into it, Lukey," says Simeon. "You'd make a perfect Bond villain."

What?

Leia cuts him a look. "Shut up, Sim." And she's standing up. *Sim?*

"What?" Simeon protests. "With the scar and everything. It's perfect!"

Everybody looks down, and I'm not even sure it's because of me. What's going on?

Are you gonna let him say that?

But I'm too confused to really react.

"Why do you even speak?" says Michelle, shaking her head at Simeon, and I get a flash of the history they all have together. The well-worn play that I have no part in.

"You coming?" Leia says to me, and I start to get up, feeling too embarrassed to call Simeon out. *What's wrong with you?*

What's wrong with me, is that I don't share their past.

"I've got it!" says Max, like he just discovered gravity. "James Franco in *This is The End* with Jonah Hill, Jonah Hill in *The Wolf of Wall Street* with Leonardo Di Caprio, Di Caprio with De Niro in that film about the kid and Sam Jackson with De Niro in *Jackie Brown*."

He points both hands forward like he's holding two guns.

"Hold on, hold on." Simeon's shaking his head. "What film about the kid?"

"The film about the kid, De Niro's his stepdad or something."

"It doesn't count if you don't know the name of it, Max."

Max screws up his face. I look at Leia. She glances at me, but for less than a blink.

"It was his first film," argues Max.

Leia slips her arms into her bag straps. "It's called *This Boy's Life*, and he's not his stepdad, he's his mum's new boyfriend."

She glances at me again. Max points at her. "See! *This Boy's Life*! Told you. How many steps is that?"

And him and Simeon start to argue as Leia walks off. I look at Michelle, who smiles sheepishly and then starts digging in her bag pretending to look for something.

I walk after Leia, hating that it feels like I'm being kept out of a secret.

2.

```
INT. CAR — DAY
The words AB-SOUL scroll across a jet-black
screen in electric blue digital letters. Red blocks
of a graphic equaliser as bass thumps. Fingers
drum on dashboard.
```

Me and Leia are walking past reception. I want to ask what the big secret is, or if there even is one, but the air between us is thick with that 'just leave it' feeling I know so well.

"So you'll finish your start scene tonight, yeah?" she finally says.

"Yeah, OK."

Our steps are out of synch as I count them.

"I didn't want you to feel like you had to," she says.

"Had to what?"

Then Megan pushes into the back of us. "You should just

hold hands." She mimes throwing up as Michelle catches up on the other side of Leia.

"Shut up," Leia says.

Megan links her arm to Leia's, but not mine and says, "It's like *West Side Story*."

Leia bumps Megan with her shoulder. "Shut up! Little Miss 'I only go for boy racers'."

They cut each other exaggerated death stares, then laugh. Michelle joins in and my outsider status gets underlined again.

Then a car horn sounds and everything stops.

"Lukaaaaaaaaaaay!"

Tommy's half hanging out of the window as he drives round the corner. I can hear a bass drum. I see Zia in the passenger seat. What the hell? I contemplate just turning round and walking back on to campus, but it's too late, the girls have already clocked him.

He spins the car round and pulls up so Zia's right next to us. He turns the music down. New stereo. Looks expensive.

"Yes, Lukey," says Zia, holding out his fist. We bump.

"Afternoon, ladies!" Tommy's leaning across him, he's eating something out of a Greggs bag and there's pastry crumbs on his cheeks. "What you saying?"

Words get stuck in my throat as I play head tennis between

my oldest friends and the girl I've been kissing. Zia sees me struggling. "We came to give you a lift."

"What do you... how come you're not at work?"

Tommy bites into his food. "It's Friday. I finish early."

Zia nods. "And my shifts have switched. I told you, remember?"

Tommy grins. "We haven't seen ya, man! Check out the system!"

Zia pushes him off. "You should answer your phone more. Who're your friends?"

I turn to the girls.

"I'm Michelle," says Michelle, holding up a hand before I can open my mouth.

"Hi." Zia's playing it well cool. He looks at Michelle.

Megan's checking out the car. Michelle speaks for her. "That's Megan."

Zia doesn't even look. "I'm Zia. It's nice to meet you, Michelle."

"I'm Leia." Leia holds her hand out. Zia shakes it, smiling.

"It's nice to finally meet you, Leia." The pair of them look at me.

"You're not Chinese," Tommy blurts out. Enough.

"OK," I say. "Let's go then. See you later." I reach to open

Zia's door.

"Is this your car?" says Megan out of nowhere. She's looking at Tommy through the windscreen. Tommy smiles a nod, his cheeks full of pastry. *Don't do it, Tom. Don't ask them.*

"You girls wanna lift?"

My earliest memory is snow.

It's Nan's back garden. I'm sitting in deep snow in a purple jumpsuit, watching Dad slowly stomp through the white to the back shed in his big sheepskin coat. He is a yeti.

Every sound seems dulled, like the air is muffled and there's some low musical score playing. Something with strings.

Dad wrestles the shed door and disappears inside. I look up at the dirty white sky and feel the delicate flakes touch my cheeks and dissolve.

Dad emerges, holding a shovel above his head like he's ready for battle. He strides back towards me, getting bigger with each step, until he's towering over me. He smiles.

I look down, and realise I'm actually sitting in one of his footprints.

3.

INT. CAR — DAY

Condensation on the inside of car window. One drop
of water runs down faster than the rest.

"You must never doubt the Dark Horse!"

Tommy bangs both hands on the steering wheel as we
drive back towards town. The car still smells like girls and the
windows are half steamed up from the body heat. We dropped
them home one by one. Michelle and Megan both live within
walking distance of Leia and I've now seen Simeon's house.
It's as big as I thought.

"Shut up, Tom." I'm in the back behind Zia, happy to be
able to finally stretch my legs. Four of us crammed into the
back wasn't even legal, but Leia on my lap for twenty minutes
wasn't exactly horrible and, to be honest, the whole journey
wasn't that bad. *Why would it be?*

Feels weird being the one in the back.

"Man just walks through college with a string of girls on his arm like flippin' what's his face, the old porno guy, with the smoking jacket."

"I said shut up, yeah?"

"Hugh Heffner," says Zia.

"That's him!" Tommy points at me in the rear-view mirror. "Hugh Heffberg!"

"Heffner," says Zia. "*Playboy*. And it's not a porno, it's a magazine. They used to have all the best comedians and journalists write articles. My cousin used to get it."

"Yeah, for the tits," laughs Tommy.

Zia stares out of the window. "You're a caveman."

"Well, I didn't hear you crack any jokes to them, Mr Funny. Captive audience and you flopped it."

The rain's heavier now and there's a mist around the tall buildings of town.

"So, Lukey, what time we gonna get there?" says Zia. He's holding up the flyer Michelle gave him. I grab it.

It's the size of a postcard. Quality paper. There's a detailed drawing of a skeleton done in fine black pen; it's really good.

I flip it over and read:

> ## Michelle's birthday party.
> You know the score.
>
> Come scary or not at all.
>
> My house.
>
> Saturday 19th Oct.
>
> 7 - late.
>
> r.s.v.p.
>
> **(No Harry Potter)**

Why didn't she tell me?

Because she doesn't want you there.

"Don't think I'm up for it, to be honest," I say.

"What?" Tommy turns back. "Are you kidding?"

We drive into the underpass and everything turns artificial light.

"Watch the road, man! I'm just… not that fussed. And it's fancy dress."

"I don't care if it's a 'wear-a-man-nappy' theme, we're going, Luke. You see how that girl was on me?"

"Her name was Megan, Tom. Can't we just hang out? I haven't seen yous much, have I?"

"Oh, now he cares," says Zia sarcastically. "I reckon Mr Dark Horse just wants to keep all the fun to himself, eh, Tom?"

I watch him draw an 'M' in the condensation on the glass next to his face.

"Yeah, stop being selfish, Lukey. We will be hanging out. With girls. She was fit. I mean, the shaved head thing's a bit weird, but still, I would. Is she your girlfriend now then, Leia?"

"No. What you talking about?"

The pair of them look at each other and exchange a smile, as if I can't see them.

We drive past the hospital, and I know I'm being tight, but she didn't tell me. *Why didn't she tell me?*

When Megan brought it up and Tommy and Zia got excited about it, Leia seemed pleased. I don't get it. Maybe she thought I'd think it was lame? Why would she think that? *Because it is lame.*

A party? With Leia? Dressed up? With these two there? Tommy and Zia with Simeon and them?

The two sides aren't supposed to mix.

"Come on," says Zia. "I can be out of work by eight. If you come get me, we can be there by half past. How long since we went to a party?"

"We should get the bus, so we can bring booze," says Tommy.

"I'm not drinking, man."

"I know *you're* not, that doesn't mean me and Lukey can't, eh, Luke? I could get Jamie to buy us something, swig it on the bus. What bus is it anyway?"

"We're not getting any drinks, Tom." The thought of him pissed up, mingling with the college lot, makes my gut turn. "And it's two buses."

Zia turns his head back. "So you're not in any actual lessons with Michelle?"

"No."

"Shame."

"Fine. They'll have drinks there anyways, eh, them posh kids?" says Tommy, clearly hyped. "I've never done fancy dress. I'm gonna be a zombie. What you gonna be, Lukey?"

"We're not going."

Zia reaches back and snatches the flyer. "Fine. You don't have to. I seem to remember them inviting us, Luke. We don't need a moody chaperone, right, Thomas?"

Tommy nods. "Right. But if Mr Moody Bollocks doesn't want us telling all his new posh mates embarrassing stuff about him, like the time he pissed himself on the coach to Drayton Manor, he might want to come along."

I stare out at the wet street. They both wait for me to say

something. I don't. I'm beaten.

"Sorted then," smiles Tommy. "I'll come knock for you 'bout seven, you can help me do my zombie, then we walk down and get him from the supermarket."

He holds out his hand for Zia to slap. Zia slaps it. And that's that. The Venn diagram of my life. The circle of college meets the circle of home, at the intersection of a fancy-dress house party. It'll be fine. It will. I mean, how bad could it be?

4.

The Brothers Different.

Opening Scene. Idea I.

Blinking cursor.

I just stare at the empty word document.

So far the only decision I've made is to write the title in courier font.

It's as close as I'm ever gonna get to an actual typewriter. Old school.

I know I want to write the scene that sends Marc to prison. I know I've imagined what he did to Craig a million times, but my hands won't type it. Maybe I should write in my notebook first.

It's half ten. Mum's at work. Marc's out. I told Leia I'd send my scene over before I went to sleep. Might be a late one.

I drop down and start some press-ups to help me think.

The man is down.

Nine. Ten. Eleven.

Leave it! He's done.

Don't.

Pump faster. Nineteen, twenty, twenty-one.

You weren't there.

My shoulders burn. Triceps on fire.

Teeth bared. Girl's voice screams.

I stop on the up. *It's not your story to tell.*

Elbows lock, hands pushing down into the floor, through the floor, trying to push the whole house down into the earth.

Then an engine growls outside and I freeze, ears pricked.

No music. Door opens. Craig Miller?

I go to my window, my arms hot and tight.

Marc's getting out of Jamie's car. Breathe out. *Stupid*.

He's holding a white carrier bag. They say bye and Marc swings the door shut. I duck back just before he looks up. My laptop pings with a new email alert. It's Leia. She's sent her scene.

I hear the front door as I sit back on my bed and open the attachment.

Hey,

Only first draft, so still rough. Hope you like it.

Sorry I didn't ask. Didn't think you'd want to come. Are you coming?

I'm wearing my costume right now. Just saying.

Send me your scene when you're done.

Lx

Toby idea. Scene I.

EXT. — LATE MORNING. SUNNY BUT CRISP

We see a high brick wall through a car windscreen.
A young man's fingers drum the steering wheel.
Set into the brick wall, large glass doors catch
the sun. We hear breathing. A white van pulls up,
waiting for a car to pass in the other direction,
obscuring our view.
It passes and we see a young man standing on the
pavement outside the doors across the road. He
wears a grey beanie hat, dark grey jacket, black
jeans and white trainers. An old red holdall hangs
from his right hand. He looks strong.
He looks up at the sky and shields his eyes from

the light.

The breathing inside the car gets louder.

Cut to shot from outside, through the windscreen.

Young man wearing thick black frames stares out.
His hair is wiry. Face fresh. Maybe twenty. He's
nervous. We watch him take a deep breath, then
push the horn.

Cut to a shot taken from over the other man's
shoulder, as he stares at the car from across
the road. The horn stops. We can make out the man
sitting in the driver's seat. He doesn't wave.
A red saloon car drives past.
Man starts across the road.

I read it again. And again.

It's good. I can really see it and it makes me think of the
start of *Buffalo '66*. I imagine opening credits in small letters
in the bottom right corner of the screen as the scene plays out.

The Brothers Different.

Now, what the hell do I write?

A knock. Marc's leaning on the frame of my door.

I didn't hear him climb the stairs.

"You're still up?" he says.

I close my laptop. "Marc, it's not even eleven."

He looks at his wrist. "Don't have a watch. Feels later. What you doing?"

"Nothing. Just trying to write something."

Marc nods from the doorway. "Cool."

"What's in the bag?" I point.

He looks down. "Nothing. Recipe books and that."

I watch him decide whether to say more. He doesn't. Instead, he scans my room. "So where's your weights then?"

"What weights?"

Marc frowns. "What, you go gym? How much you pay?"

"I don't go to any gym. Press-ups." I mime with my arms.

"Lukey, people don't get that big that fast just doing press-ups."

"Press-ups and puberty." I smile.

Marc gives a sarcastic nod. "Yeah. Right."

He's still annoying. Why's he think he knows everything? There's so much he doesn't know.

"OK, Lukey." And he goes. Just like he used to. Deciding the conversation is over, like he's the only one who can call 'cut'.

I stare at the empty doorway. The bars of the bannister.
Annoyed.

I open my laptop.

The Brothers Different.
Opening Scene. Idea I.

Black. Heavy breathing. Someone struggling.

Shot of young man being held back by two bodies.
His face like a dog, trying to attack.

MARC: Get off me!

MAN'S VOICE: Easy Marc, leave it! He's done.

MARC: No he's not. I said get the fuck off me!

He breaks free and runs forward.
Cut to man on the floor. Splayed out like he fell
from a building.
Narrow face. Sharp cheeks. His nose is broken.
Face bloodied.

His head moves, like he's just regaining consciousness.

Cut to shot of Marc, from the ground. He dives on to us. Teeth bared.

A girl screams.

MARC: I'll kill you! I swear to God I'll fucking kill you!

Swinging fists. He hits again. And again. The thuds of punches landing. Crack of bone. Screaming. Two bodies try to pull him off, but he is an animal. Sounds fade to silent. Marc still trying to fight as he's dragged off.

Cut to bright sunlight.

Sliding glass doors open and we step out into the crisp air.

Sound of near-distant traffic. A bird.

Deep breath. A car horn. Cut.

Yo.

Sorry it's late. Loved yours. Let me know what you think.

We're coming to the party. Can't wait to see your costume.

See you tomorrow. Skywalker x

My eyes are stinging. Attach File. Send.

5.

I open the front door to the worst zombie I've ever seen.

Tommy's standing on the front step wearing old jeans and a long-sleeved black T-shirt that's got rips and holes all over it. Around his eyes he's used what looks like eyeliner and he's tried to draw blood spots on his chin with what's clearly lipstick. It looks like a red goatee.

"Sick, right?" he says, spreading his arms, and I see his car parked across the road.

"Did you drive?"

"Course."

"It's like a minute walk, Tom."

"You think I'm walking the streets dressed like this?" He steps past me into the house.

I close the door. "We've still gotta walk and get Zia, you idiot. Two buses, remember?"

I watch the penny drop for him.

"No way. I'll drive. Forget the booze. Where's your costume?"

I shrug.

"Oh come on, Luke, you're kidding, right? Make an effort, man!"

"Make an effort with what?" Marc comes out of the kitchen in jeans and a black vest, tea towel over his shoulder. Tommy looks down.

"Easy, Tom. You good?" Marc leans on the wall, arms folded.

Tommy looks up.

Marc laughs. "Jesus, who are you? The Crow?"

Tommy shrugs. "Zombie."

"Right. You going clubbing?"

Tommy shakes his head. "House party. Fancy dress."

"Come on." I start up the stairs. Tommy follows me like a naughty dog.

"Yous wanna eat something before you go?" Marc looks up. "I've made kofte. Fresh mint and yoghurt."

I shake my head. "We're good, thanks. Smells good though."

INT. KITCHEN — NIGHT

Clear juices drip as sizzling meat turns from raw to ready.

"Kofte?" says Tommy, checking his face in my wardrobe mirror.

"They'll be good, too," I say, checking my laptop again for any new messages. Still no reply from Leia about the scene. I'll see her later.

"So he's back into the cooking and that?"

I close the laptop. "Proper. It's like flipping *Masterchef* in this house. Is that your mum's make-up?"

Tommy turns round. "Course it is! Is it rubbish?"

I laugh.

"Piss off, Luke. At least I made an effort. You turn up normal, that's just lame."

And he's right. If we're going, I've gotta do something.

Tommy opens my wardrobe. "What's this?" He pulls out Dad's sheepskin. "Yo, wear this. This is heavy!"

"Literally," I say, waiting for him to acknowledge the pun. He doesn't. Then his face lights up.

"I've got something!" He drops the coat and runs out of my room, down the stairs. I hear the front door open. Then my phone beeps. Leia. Please be Leia.

U cumin pub later? Dodx

I picture him in his flat, on the sofa typing the text, and realise I haven't seen him since the awkward afternoon with Leia.

Then I see Mum there, next to him, curled up, her hand rubbing his shoulder, stroking his arm and… *CUT! You're sick.*

Going party with Tom and Zia. See you in week?

I throw my phone back on to my bed. Why hasn't Leia replied? Did she hate it? She hated it. She thinks I'm just trying to shock. *Will you shut up?*

Tommy's standing in my bedroom doorway holding something grey.

"What's that?"

He scoops up Dad's coat. "You got a black vest?"

"What? Why?"

He drops the coat on to my bed, his eyes dancing. "Yo, your brother was wearing one. Borrow that one."

"No, what for? What is that?"

Tommy sighs. "For God's sake, Luke, work with me, yeah?"

I don't move.

"Fine. I'll get it." He flicks me the V's and walks out again. I stare at Dad's coat and listen to the mumbled voices coming from the kitchen.

Beep. *Please be her. Please.*

No poblem. Hav fun. B careful. x

"Put that on." Tommy throws me Marc's black vest.

"What's going on, Tom? Did he just give it you?"

"Course he gave it me, he's got vision. Just put it on, will ya?"

So I do. And it fits. More or less.

"Perfect. I wouldn't fight ya," says Tommy, picking up Dad's coat. "This too."

I slide my arms into the coat and feel the weight.

Tommy's almost giddy. "Right, now hold still," he says as he moves behind me. I stare into the mirror and see a grey dust mask come over my head on to my face, the elastic straps cut across my cheeks behind my ears. Tommy's grinning reflection peers over my shoulder. He points straight into the mirror. "Bane!"

And I can't lie, it feels wicked.

"Do the voice," Tommy says.

I stare into the mirror. "I am Gotham's reckoning."

It's crap. Tommy laughs. "I'd go with the silent, dangerous flex instead."

I fold my arms and frown. Dressing up is all right. Then I feel the knife.

I pull it out of the inside pocket. "Take this back." I hold it out.

"Why?" Tommy says.

"Because I don't need it, that's why."

"What about Miller?"

I look down. There's been no sign of Craig Miller since that night.

"Just take it, Tom." I push it into his hand just as Marc comes up the stairs. Tommy quickly sticks it into his jeans pocket.

"Here you go, lads." Marc's topless. He looks like a shopping channel model, holding a plate of meat skewers with fresh mint and a little bowl of yoghurt. It smells amazing.

He puts it on my bed.

"Even Bane and a zombie need grub before a big night." He looks me up and down. "Suits ya."

I pull off the dust mask. "Thanks. For the food, I mean."

"No problem. You driving, Tom?"

Tommy nods, stuffing his face with kebab.

"So no drinking, eh?"

"Course not, Marc. This is beautiful."

Marc points at him. "I'm serious." Tommy's genuinely scared, in that silent contained way you can be of family.

"You stopping in?" I say, taking a kebab.

Marc smiles, shaking his head. "Going The Goose. With Dad. Maybe try and surprise a certain barmaid, eh?" He actually winks. "Have a good one, boys."

```
INT. HOUSE — NIGHT
London Grammar 'Hey Now' plays as a girl's hand
stirs a bowl of red liquid with a wooden spoon,
adding vodka as she goes.
```

We pull round the back of the supermarket under the one floodlight. I stare up at the dark wall and see the security camera.

Tommy lights a cigarette.

We stare at the door, waiting for Zia to pop out.

"He wants to hurry up, man. Emma'll be missing me."

"Her name's Megan, Tom. You might wanna start with

getting her name right."

Tommy pouts and nods. "Course. All good, Lukey." He rubs his hands together. In this light his face looks like a skull.

"Promise me, man," I say.

"Promise you what?"

"That you won't do anything dumb. Promise me that."

"Shut up. What am I gonna do? Why you gotta be like that?"

"Because I know you."

Tommy wiggles his fingers like he's casting a spell. "Don't worry, Luke, I won't embarrass you in front of your posh mates."

"I'm serious, Tom."

I stare at him like a parent stares at a child they know is lying. Tommy cracks. "All right, fine, I promise. Whatever. Happy? It's not even one of them ones, is it? We're not fighting. Tonight's about the ladies." He gropes imaginary breasts in front of him. My oldest friend.

"Do you even hear yourself when you're speaking?"

"Chill out, Lukey. Yo, reach in the glovebox. I nicked Jamie's Kano CD."

Then Zia walks out of the dark in a full pin-stripe suit and shoes. He's carrying a rucksack. Tommy looks at me. "What the hell?"

I pull on my mask and get out to let Zia in.

"Bane!" He says straight away and I take a bow.

"Who's he supposed to be?" Zia's pointing through at Tommy.

"Shut up! I'm a zombie, man. *The Walking Dead* and that." Tommy does his zombie groan.

"And who are you, James Bond?" I pat Zia's suited shoulder.

His face lights up. "Check it. Close your eyes, both of you."

We do. I hear a zip and the bag fall on the floor. "One sec, hold on…" His voice is muffled. "OK."

I open my eyes and it's Chewbacca. In a suit. He's got the full head mask and hands. It looks brilliant.

"Where'd you get that?"

Chewbacca shrugs. "Got it online ages ago. Couldn't afford the whole suit. This is my first chance to wear it out."

"I don't get it," says Tommy.

Chewbacca's head tilts and from inside Zia says, "The Wookie of Wall Street, ready to party!"

6.

```
EXT. — NIGHT
Moving Car. Through windscreen. Kano's 'Ps & Qs'
plays.
Bane, The Wookie of Wall Street and a crap zombie
nod along in time to the track as they drive
through town.
```

I pause before ringing the bell.

Michelle's front door has stained glass panels in it, like Leia's. The kick drum and muffled chatter of a party from inside. I can smell the plastic of the mask and, stupid as it sounds, in my costume, in Dad's jacket, I feel powerful.

"Remember, yeah?" I hold my hand up like a platoon commander. "Together."

I feel the two of them sigh behind me.

"OK, Captain Bane," says Tommy. "We get it."

"What did I say, Tom?"

Zia speaks for him. "We know, Lukey. Kitchen is the base. We go off, do what we want, and if anything happens, we find each other first. Relax, yeah? Nothing's gonna happen."

"Not nothing," smirks Tommy, and I know he's grinding the air behind me.

"Can we ring the bell now?"

A furry hand reaches past me for the door. I block it off.

"Just remember, yeah, some of them talk different. Mouthy. Doesn't mean they're startin'." I picture Simeon. "Just stay cool."

"OK, Lukey." Zia pats my back. "You don't have to be so dramatic."

"Yeah," adds Tommy. "Stop being such a drama king, Baaaaaaaaaaannnnneee."

And then the front door opens and it's Stewie from *Family Guy*.


```
INT. PARTY — NIGHT
Muffled music. The glint of a metal cannister. The
hiss of gas. A balloon inflates.
```

The layout of the house is the same as Leia's.

I can see Tommy taking it in like it's *MTV Cribs* as Michelle leads us back past the two rooms to the kitchen. Her Stewie costume looks expensive and has a full head mask like Zia's. I don't recognise the music in the back room. It's some glitchy obscure electronica and there's already a bunch of people dancing.

The kitchen is massive. The fridge is one of those big curved American ones and has the ice cube dispenser thing built into the door.

There's maybe fifteen people standing around and more outside on the patio, through the French doors. I see Frankenstein, a couple of glittery vampires, Iron Man and the Joker. Down one sideboard there's a buffet that looks like it's straight out of a Marks & Spencer advert. This isn't just any fancy dress party, this is—

"What do you want to drink?" Stewie Griffin points to a crowd of spirit and beer bottles next to the sink. "Help yourselves."

"Is that punch?" says Tommy, pointing to a big glass bowl of red liquid.

"We're driving, Tom," I say.

"Yeah," says Michelle. "My sister made it."

Tommy's already spooning himself a plastic cupful of the

punch. He feels me staring. "What? Just one. Then I'll drink pop, I promise."

"I love your costume," Zia says to Michelle. "I love *Family Guy*."

"Me too!" she says a bit too excitedly. "Yours is great! Chewbacca on his wedding day, right?"

Chewbacca glances at me and Tommy. "Yeah."

Stewie nods. "I got a bit nervous about mine; thought somebody else might choose it. There's a Brian and a Meg here somewhere too."

"Megan?" says Tommy, scanning the characters.

Stewie points up. "I think she's upstairs. She's Hit-Girl."

"Who?" Tommy looks at me.

"Purple hair and a Zorro mask," I say. Tommy just stares blankly. "Just look for the girl who looks like she could kick your arse."

He shrugs and smiles. "In a bit, boys." He walks back into the hall.

"Leia's not here yet, Luke," Michelle says, taking Zia's hand. "I have to show you to Clare, she loves Wookies." She gestures to the French doors and the two of them walk off without looking back, leaving me, standing in the big kitchen, on my own, dressed as Bane.

The best ducks can swim in any pond.

The back room's all standing. People in costumes are shuffling more than dancing, like it's a packed train carriage full of imaginary friends.

I'm separate, leaning against the wall behind the door to seem smaller.

The punch is strong. I can't tell with what, but whatever it is, I can smell it inside my mask every time I put it back down after a swig. I need something to do with my hands. It's only been an hour, but I'm proper conscious that I'm an outsider.

There's one of those disco ball lamps, projecting dots of colour all over everyone and the book-filled shelves, making the scene dreamlike. I watch the bunny from *Donnie Darko* trade moves with Willy Wonka, the Johnny Depp version. I don't recognise anyone and I'm glad that the mask is covering half of my face. There's no sign of Leia or Simeon or the others and there's something in the air that I can't put my finger on. It's a kind of familiarity, like they do this a lot. Like this is completely normal for everyone here but me.

It's safety.

That's it.

That's what it is. You can feel it, on the walls, in the way people move. Everyone here feels safe. Nobody's waiting for things to go wrong. Their muscles aren't coiled ready for some attack. There's no need. All's good. *Weird*.

I like it.

I picture Marc and Dad in The Goose. Marc's at the bar, trying to play it cool as Donna serves some old boy. I see him leaning forward to get her attention, Dad in the background sipping a Guinness.

Then she's there.

Stepping into the room, like somebody just called 'action', and it's perfect. She's Natalie Portman as Mathilda from *Leon*. Light-green bomber jacket, black vest, striped cut-off shorts, Doc Martins. She's even got the little black velvet choker with the pendant round her neck and the red beanie she wears when he takes her for target practice on the roof. Amazing.

"Who you hiding from?" she says, like she's been looking for me. I stand up straight and instantly feel bigger than everyone in the room.

"Bane," I say, and dramatically crush my plastic cup in my fist.

Are you drunk?

Leia leads me out into the hall.

"You look great," I tell her, feeling the blood in my legs.

You're drunk off one punch?

"It's strong," I say. Leia looks confused.

"The punch. The punch is strong."

She's just looking at me. Something's wrong.

"You OK?" I ask.

She nods. I lift up my mask and smile. "It's my first fancy dress."

I follow her through the kitchen. Zia's in front of a horseshoe of laughing superheroes and villains. His mask is off and he's doing an impression of his dad. Michelle is watching him, eating from a paper plate. He sees me and gives me the 'this is amazing' smile. I picture a spotlight on him, in his little corner by the sink, a microphone clutched in a furry Chewbacca hand.

Leia's leading me into the garden where the cold air hits me and I feel the blood in my face. We cut through an argument between *The Little Mermaid* and *Hell Boy*.

"Your mates don't mess about with the fancy dress, do they?" I say as we step on to the dark grass.

Leia sits down on a bench halfway up the garden and it takes me a second to realise that the smooth black ground to the side of it is actually a pond. Light from the kitchen stretches out along the thin lawn, past us towards a greenhouse.

"You might need to rescue Megan from a crap zombie." I smile as I sit down. "Tommy can be pretty persistent."

"Megan's fine. She can handle herself."

She's playing with her amber ring. *What did I do? What did I forget?*

"I read your scene," she says.

The cold snakes its way up my sleeve under the jacket on to the bare skin of my arms. My head is warm.

"Yeah? Yours is great, I had this idea about combining them, you know? Like a flashback type thing?"

"Is that what happened, Luke?"

She seems almost worried.

"What do you mean?"

"What you wrote. Is that what happened, to you?"

I reach for her knee. She flinches. My heart cracks.

"No."

"But it seems… so real."

And underneath my fear and confusion, my brain acknowledges that as a compliment.

"Thanks," I say. "Is that why you're being funny?"

She stares into her lap. I don't understand.

"I don't understand. Did you not like it?"

And her silence is her answer. Gutted.

But she said it felt real. Surely that's the point?

"Leia." I risk going for her hand and she lets me take it. "Are you OK?"

I realise the mask is still on my head and take it off, watching her wrestling with something.

"I just…" She looks at me, unsure. Like she can't remember her lines.

"Yo. It's cool," I say. "It's all right. Should I leave?"

She shakes her head, popping my question and I breathe out with relief.

"Whatever the problem is, we can sort it, yeah? Maybe it's not the right scene for the beginning, you know? Maybe it's too much."

Why you being soft? You wrote it how you wanted it. If she can't handle it, that's her problem. Shut up.

"Marc," I say.

She waits.

"It was Marc." And his name coming out of my mouth feels different. I'm not talking about a character now. I'm talking about my brother.

Leia squeezes my hand. "He did that?"

I nod.

"That's why he went to prison?"

I nod again and it feels like a part of me falls out and it's just there, on the dark grass in front of us.

Then she kisses me.

7.

I don't get it. She hates that kind of thing, but she's kissing me. And she means it. Her lips pressing into mine, like she's explaining something, and the punch buzz and the fresh air and the background music and my body's growling.

Then two figures stumble out of the greenhouse, cackling like hyenas.

Leia pulls away. I pull away. The air between us charged with confusion.

"Yes, Waterboy!"

Simeon's standing arm in arm with Max in front of us, still giggling. They're both wearing blue convict overalls and Simeon's right ankle is chained to Max's left with oversized shackles that look plastic. Even in the dark garden I can see their pupils are wider than they should be. Jono walks out of the greenhouse holding what looks like a silver whipped cream can. He's dressed like a chunky Captain America.

"Look at them," Simeon says, swaying. "Beauty and the Beast." *What?*

He smiles and points at Leia. "Course, if anyone else calls you Beast, I'll rip their lungs out."

It's a Joker quote from Tim Burton's *Batman*. *I don't care where it's from. Knock this prick out right now.*

Jono stands behind them, straight-faced.

"I thought you promised Megan, Sim," Leia says.

Simeon over-emphasises a shrug. "Whoops. Don't tell on me, Leia, pleeeaaase?" More laughing.

My hands make fists. *That's it. Tell him.*

Max sticks up his thumb to me. "You want a balloon, Lukey?"

I don't reply.

"What about you, Leia? For old times?"

The pair of them laugh. I stare at Jono. He should've dressed as a sidekick.

"You look good together," says Simeon, pretending to take a photograph with his hands. "Same cloth." *What did he just say?*

I lean forward. Jono puts a hand on Simeon's shoulder, looking at me as he does.

"We're just talking here, actually, if you don't mind," I say.

Simeon's face drops. I feel Leia's eyes on me. The boys stare. My eyes tell them I'm not playing.

"Course!" Simeon shrugs off Jono's hand and throws an arm round Max's neck. "Let's leave the lovebirds to it. There's punch! Take it easy, Waterboy, and make sure you've got room for the family baggage."

Then him and Max three-legged walk to the house, Jono following silently behind. *Family baggage?* I wait until they disappear behind bodies into the kitchen, then turn to Leia.

"And you went out with him?"

Leia shrugs. I don't move.

"What?" she says. "You never made a mistake?"

I pretend like I'm trying to sneak away.

Leia whacks my arm. "Shut up! I bet there's a couple of rude girls in your back catalogue."

What's that mean?

"What's that mean?"

"It means, everybody's done stuff, Skywalker. Simeon's an idiot, but he's not a threat."

"Damn right he's not. I could break him with one arm." *Better.*

But even as the words leave my mouth I can taste my mistake.

Leia's face says it all.

"Is that how you think?" She's serious. I've messed up.
Need to save it. Come on. Come on. Light bulb. I pull the
mask back on.

"It is how I think," shit Bane voice, "I would break him like a
twig," stand up for effect, "For I. AM. BAAAAAAAAAANE!"

Hold maniacal pose for effect. Pray she bought it. It was
all a joke. I was in character. Look at her. She's smiling. It
worked. Thank you.

Sit down. Mask off. Ride the wave. "You ever kissed a
supervillain?"

```
INT. CAR — NIGHT
The sounds of kissing. Close-up: dark edges of
fabric against skin. The squeak of a trainer
against dashboard. A masked girl. A fly unzipping.
```

We're in the attic.

Not sure how long we've been up here, lost track of time.
We had to use some of those fold-down steps. Leia's insider
knowledge. Our only light is through the skylight, which is
about four times bigger than the one at Dad's place. I can smell
new carpet.

There's not enough room to stand up, which is fine, because we're lying down and we can't fully make out facial features, which is fine, because we're using our hands. Side by side, my left arm under her body, her left leg over my hips. Dad's jacket behind me, her bomber jacket and beanie behind her. This is happening.

I'm not sure whether I'm hearing or feeling the music through the floor, but either way we're moving in time to it. She's holding my head as we kiss. My fingertips are skating round the top of her thigh at the edge of her shorts.

This is really happening. This is what I want. Is it what she wants? *Course it is, why would you think that?* But what if it isn't?

"What's wrong?" Leia says, sensing it.

"Nothing, sorry, I just… This is really happening. I'm not dreaming it."

Leia touches my face and I flinch.

"Sorry," she says. "Does it hurt?"

"No. It's static."

She smiles and we kiss and I want her. All of her. I'm not dreaming this. I pull my head back to look at her face and be sure. I can make out the darkness of her curved lips, her tongue. I want to say something perfect.

"What did he mean, baggage?" And the second I hear my own words I want to take them back.

Leia's smile disappears and her hand slips away from my face. *Why did I say that?*

"Sorry. It's none of my business."

The song downstairs changes.

"It's OK. It's the past. Doesn't have to determine now, does it?"

Phew. Her hand comes back and she runs her finger along my cheek, crossing the river of my scar down to my chin. "Stupid boys," she says. Kiss. "Doing stupid boy stuff." Kiss. "Like your brother."

And the film skips.

All of me freezes. "What d'you say?"

Leia's confused. "What he did. How stupid it was."

What?

I sit up. "What you talking about?"

Is that why she kissed you outside? Because she felt sorry for you?

"What's wrong, Luke?"

"Don't call my brother stupid."

She sits up too. "Luke, I didn't... I wasn't calling your brother stupid. I meant the violence, what he did."

"What do you know about what he did, or why he did it?"

It's like my body is leading my mouth while my mind watches. "You don't know anything."

She reaches her hand out. I shrug it off.

"Luke, I didn't mean to upset you." She's shaking her head.

"Upset me? You didn't upset me. How you gonna upset me?" *Tell her.* "You haven't got a clue."

She leans forward. "Maybe I have got a clue, maybe I know, maybe—"

"Maybe you should shut your mouth."

Killer. She wasn't expecting that. I wasn't either. I'm sorry. *No you're not.* I'm reaching for Dad's jacket. I don't want to. *Yes you do.* But I am.

"Luke, please, let's not fight." Her eyes are pleading, trying to understand.

I stare at her. "This isn't fighting. This is leaving."

And I'm opening the trap door thing, folding down the steps. The crack of metal as they snap open too quickly.

"Luke, please."

Don't look at her. Princess.

I don't look at her.

I pull on Dad's jacket as I move along the hall. My heavy armour. I can feel my blood.

"Yo!" Zia's running up the stairs. "There you are!"

Michelle's with him. Scared. His face says trouble. "Come. Now!"

8.

EXT. — NIGHT

Out of focus streetlight. Girl shouting. A jar of
honey hitting the floor.

We're outside the house. Jono's holding Simeon back near the front step. Max is on the floor, leaning against the bottom of the bay window, hand over the front of his face, blood running between his fingers, the shackles between them broken.

Tommy's standing next to the gate, his T-shirt almost completely ripped off, his fists up. Megan is behind him wearing a tartan mini-skirt over purple leggings and just a black bra. Her hair's a mess.

"Get off me!" Simeon's voice is slurred. "I'll kill him!"

Jono doesn't let him go. I get in between them.

"What's going on?"

"Ask this prick," says Tommy, pointing at Simeon. "We

were just having a bit of fun and then he's kicking my car, giving it the big un."

"Get away from my sister! Get off me, Jono!"

Jono holds firm, nodding at me.

"You OK, Max?" I say. "Why'd you hit him, Tom?"

"He asked for it," says Tommy, staring at Simeon. "That one went to hit her, Lukey. Like, actually hit her. Then this one got involved." He points down at Max.

"She's my sister!" Simeon's voice cracks. "You're dead!"

"Shut up, posh boy!" Tommy spits.

"He hit me," says Max from the floor, still processing whatever happened.

"That's what you get!" Megan says, jabbing her finger from behind Tommy. Her eyes are wide. She's enjoying this.

"Shut your mouth, you slut!" Simeon shouts. At his own sister.

Hit him.

"Yo, we're leaving," I say. I gesture to Zia. "Come on."

Zia nods and exchanges a look with Michelle. She can't make herself smile.

"Why we gotta leave? It's his fault." Tommy's still charged. "You want more, you dickhead?"

Simeon breaks free from Jono and rushes Tommy. I stop

him with my right arm. He's got some strength, but I've got him. *Hit him.*

"Just me and you!" shouts Simeon. There's drool on his chin as he reaches for Tommy. Then Tommy's flashing something. Tommy's flashing the knife.

"Yeah? You want some of this, big man? Come on then! Let him go, Lukey, I'll have him!" He holds it out in front of him like a torch.

"What you doing, you idiot! Put it away!" I put my hand on Tommy's chest, so I'm holding them both with one arm each. "What's wrong with you?" I push Simeon back towards Jono, who catches him, then turn back to Tommy. "Tom! Look at me! Put the fucking knife away!"

I push him out of the gate. His eyes are glazed and I see how wrong this could all go. Megan pulls on Tommy's arm. "Stay! It's their fault."

I cut her a look. She tries to deflect it, but when I step towards her, she lets go of Tommy and steps back. Zia follows us. "Jesus, Tom." Tommy folds the knife back up and puts it into his pocket. We're on the pavement.

"Yeah, take your scabby friend and fuck off!" shouts Simeon.

I turn back to him. He's puffing his chest up, but Jono's still holding him. My arms are tight. *Do it.*

I shake my head. "Just go back inside and do some more balloons, yeah?"

"Fuck you, Scarface!"

And the word goes through my chest like a metal spike. *Do it. You have to.* And I want to. I feel it. For everything. For me. For his own good. For things that have absolutely nothing to do with him. For things not being fair.

But I close my eyes and turn away. "We're going."

Then I hear him break free of Jono. I feel him move towards me. I feel him mean it. My eyes open and he's standing there, in my face, jaw clenched, pupils wide as fifty pees. *Hit him.* I don't blink. Leia.

Hit him! I could kill you, Simeon. I could end you right here. Do it. Leia. I don't move. I don't want her to see this. To see me. Leia. *Do it!* For what? What will it prove? *You have to do it!*

She steps out on to the path and moves in between Simeon and me.

"Move, Leia," Simeon spits, and the blood in me rises.

Leia holds her hand up. "Please, Luke. Don't." And her face. Her eyes.

Simeon jabs his hand past her. "Should've told you,

Waterboy, it's a Chav-free party." *What?*

Leia turns to him. "Enough, Simeon, go inside."

Simeon leans into her. "Shut up, bitch. Another charity case for you to look after." And he pushes her, hard.

She falls to my left, hitting the floor, and something inside me snaps.

```
Black.
Shouts. A punch connects. Scream. Then another.
A grunt.
```

I'm on top of him, the collar of his jumpsuit twisted in my left fist. *Again.* My right swings and I feel his head rock to the side. Pain shoots through my knuckles up my arm. Good pain. *Again.*

Jono tries to pull me off, but only manages to block my next punch. I can't see. But I can feel. They can't stop me. *Nobody can.*

Somebody screams again. Blood. A voice. Luke. Her voice. "Luke!"

I fall back. *What are you doing?*

Jono's cradling Simeon in his arms. Blood on his face and chest.

Simeon coughs.

Leia's trying to reach past Michelle, who's holding her back, in front of a crowd of everyone else, scared to step outside. Staring.

I look at Leia, my chest heaving. She's looking at me, into me and I know the look. It's fear.

"Come on." Zia's pulling at my collar. "Luke, enough."

I'm up on my feet. My eyes on Leia the whole time. I feel the bridge between us burning.

"Lukey! Come on!" Zia's pulling harder.

I walk backwards, out of the scene, eyes on her, flames between us, watching her fear subside, and disappointment take over.

INT. — NIGHT

Black.

The beep of a heart monitor.

A sigh.

Cut.

PART 4.

~~Him who can't hear,~~
~~must feel.~~
Idiot vs Maker.

I.

```
INT. CAR — NIGHT
Close-up: Fingertips trace the bloodied knuckles
of a fist.
YOUNG MAN fights to control his breathing.


Cut to open dual carriageway through windscreen,
carpet of amber light. Dark sky.
```

"Stop the car."

Neither of them respond. None of us has spoken since we pulled off. The air thick with mistakes. The hot throb of my knuckles.

"I said stop the car, Tom." My gut's churning. We're not in town yet.

Tommy pulls over in front of what looks like a care home. The forecourt security light clicks on as I open the passenger door, lean out and puke.

"Jesus, Lukey!" says Tommy. "How much d'you drink?"

I could tell him a lot. I could say I had more punch than I can remember. Maybe that'd make this better. Easier. But I've never felt this sober.

"There's a petrol station in a bit," says Zia from the back seat. "We can get some water."

"I'm fine," I say, wiping my mouth, staring at the puddle of chunky red on the pavement. That just happened. What are they doing now? Is Simeon OK? What about Leia?

"That was so stupid," I say, closing my eyes, squeezing my eyelids together until I see white. Then I can see her face.

"We showed 'em, eh, Lukey?"

"Shut up, Tom." I sit back in my seat, the door still open. The tone of her voice.

Tommy carries on. "Pricks. You see that ginger kid's face?" He's almost laughing. I think of Marc. Would he have gone so far if Donna had been there that night? If he'd heard her voice? Seen her face?

"I said shut up, Tom."

"What?" He genuinely doesn't get it. I look at him. My oldest friend.

"You're an idiot." I make every syllable of the sentence clear and I know Zia's watching from behind us. *Don't blame Tommy.*

Tommy frowns. "What you talking 'bout? He started on me, Luke. He was gonna hit her."

"No he wasn't."

"Yeah, he was. He was off his face." He takes out his cigarettes. "You sorted him anyways, eh?" He goes to pat my knee.

I block him. "They're twins. He was just looking out for her." I can taste sick.

"Whose side you on?" Tommy says, sparking up. "She was fit though. I swear we were gonna do it, right in the car."

I get out.

"Where you going?"

I start walking. Dual carriageway stretches out. Oncoming headlights.

"Lukey?" Tommy's opening his door. "What you doing?" He leans between the door and the roof. I stop, but don't turn round.

"You pulled a knife, Tom."

I can hear him exhaling smoke. I turn round. He laughs it off. "Shut up. I wasn't gonna use it, was I? Just wanted to shit him up."

"You shouldn't have pulled the knife."

"He's right." Zia gets out through the passenger side. The three of us are a triangle with the car in the middle, lit by the stark floodlight.

"Calm down, will ya? Both of ya. Nothing happened!" says Tommy.

"Is that what you think?" I step towards him. "Nothing happened?"

I'm picturing Leia's face. I think I might throw up again.

"Look," says Tommy, "we had a laugh, it went a bit funny and we sorted it out. End of. Now, can we go please, it's cold." He folds his torn T-shirt to cover his bare chest.

"Why d'you have to ruin everything?" I stare straight at him.

Tommy's confused. "Me?"

"You couldn't just leave it, could ya? You couldn't just take it easy and not cause some kinda fuckin' scene."

Tommy looks at Zia, then me. "Don't blame me, Lukey. It's not my fault if your new mates are all dickheads."

"I knew you'd mess it up."

Why you blaming him?

"Shut up, Luke. You sticking up for them over me?"

"I'm sticking up for anyone over a dickhead."

"What d'you call me?"

"You heard, Thomas."

"Easy, man." Zia's arms are out. "Let's just get back in the car, yeah? Go get some food or something. Who's hungry? I'm starving."

"Nah, Zia, let him speak. Let him get his little speech off his chest. You've got a little speech coming, right, Lukey? Sitting there planning it in your head, were ya? Something tragic?"

My shoulders tense. He knows what he's doing.

"Leave it, Tom." Zia's shaking his head.

"You leave it." Tommy's blood's up. "You said it yourself, he's not fussed about us any more. Blanking calls and that."

I look at Zia. Zia shrugs. "That's not what I said, Luke, I just... we haven't seen you much. Shut up, Tom!"

"You shut up! Ooh, big Lukey, running with the posh kids, doesn't wanna be seen with his proper mates any more. Thinking he's the leader. 'Just stay cool, boys. Don't embarrass me in front of the Princess'."

I step towards the car bonnet. Tommy closes the driver door.

"What? You want it with me now, Lukey? Finally got some balls off slapping a rich kid and now you want it with somebody real?"

Closer.

"Fuck you, Tom."

Closer.

"No, Luke, fuck you!"

We're toe to toe. I'm bigger. I'm stronger. He knows it. He doesn't care. Tommy doesn't care. *Tommy's real.*

"Stop being pricks!" Zia's trying to break us up, crow barring his arms in between us. My hands are fists. I wanna hurt him. I really wanna hurt him. It's all gone wrong.

Tommy's shark eyes don't leave me. "Why don't you run back to your new mates? Snuggle up and watch a film?"

Then I say it.

"You're nothing, Tom."

Three words that cut to the heart. That slice through the bravado and the anger and the hype, just like they did from the teachers at school. His eyes soften, and something in my gut snaps. I look at Zia. Confusion. *Why would you say that?*

And I walk away.

Not looking back, as everything behind me blurs out of focus.

2.

Nan said: It's hard to hate what you know well.

Nan said a lot of things. Growing up, everybody did. All the time. Spewing pearls of wisdom.

Pretending to listen.

I don't know what happened. Things got out of control.

Send.

It wasn't my fault. I was trying to stop them

Send. Re-read. Regret.

It was my fault. I don't know. I'm sorry x

Send. Wait.

Please say something

Send.

By the time I reach the high road, it's just after one.

No reply from Leia.

I've spun the same ideas in the roundabout of my head the whole walk back and now I'm dizzy. I turn down towards the petrol station. He pushed her. I had to do something. *Exactly.* I couldn't just stand there. *Course not.* I went too far. *No, you didn't.* Yeah, I did. I messed up. She thinks I'm a thug. I hurt Tommy. *He's an idiot.* I'm an idiot. *She called Marc stupid.* No, she said violence was stupid. I am violence. I am stupid. I should call. *Don't you dare call.* It's burned. I burned it. She burned it. My hand hurts. Her face. Shit.

I look right. Empty road. I look left. And I see the car.

It's turning in from the high road, slowly.

It's him. It's Craig Miller.

If he's come to me again he wants something. This is bad.

I feel my stomach trying to climb up into my chest.

And I run.

The engine growls behind me and I reach the other side of the road and dart straight on to the petrol station concourse.

Dad's coat is heavy and I get a flash of a broad figure in the glass, as I dart past the kiosk and jump up on to the fence, hearing the car mount the kerb and the screech of a skid.

I pull myself up, swing my legs over and drop down into a garden. A knife of pain stabs through my foot as I look up at the dark house. I hear car doors opening and slamming as I hobble to the front gate.

"Luuukeeeeey!"

He's shouting after me, his voice snaking round corners into my ears. My whole body has a pulse as I'm up and over the locked gate, trying to lower myself but still feeling like my foot is broken. The car screeches. They must be driving round to head me off.

I cut across the road almost dragging my leg, looking for people, anyone, but it's empty. Then the car headlights are on me and the engine growls again and I'm in front of the flats and panting. The coat feels like I'm carrying someone. I look back across the road and see Craig climbing over the gate. He lands and just stares at me, smiling that smile.

Focus. Just get home. Get to Marc.

I try to sprint down the alley, but my foot's killing, and I'm not fast enough. I can feel him behind me. I look back and he's there, not running, just walking, like he knows he's got me. I need to get on to the road, but then the growl, and the car's there, blocking me off. I'm reaching for my phone. My hand's shaking as I try to push buttons and scroll through, and it's like my fingers are asleep and then I drop it. I watch it hit the floor, but don't hear any sound, just the thump of my heart against my ribs and the throbbing in my foot and they're getting out of the car.

There's three of them and I don't recognise any of their faces. My jaw's clenched. I picture Marc, sitting in the dark, staring out of the window. I'm sorry. I'm sorry. *Shut up. Focus.*

And the three men are walking towards me and it's like my feet are sinking into the concrete. *Focus, Luke!* Craig Miller's getting closer. *Keep your chin down, and punch from the middle. You hear me?* I try to move, but I'm stuck. *No, you're not!*

Then his voice curls round my neck. "Why you running for?"

I'm sorry, Marc.

Craig circles round so he's in front of me. The other three stand spitting distance behind him. The cold sweat on the back of my neck. I look down at my hands. Remember the blood. My blood. I can't move.

"That's better."

He's kind of swaying from side to side, even more like a

snake, a cobra. He's not bigger than me, but there's four of them. I ball my hands into fists and pain shoots up the back of my hand into my wrist.

"Been scrapping, have ya?"

He's pointing at my hands, smiling. I look at the others behind him. None of them look familiar. Have they been following me? Have I not noticed? *Breathe, big man. Set yourself, and if it's on, you make sure you take him with you.*

So I do. I lift my chest and my chin and I look him in the eye and I breathe. If this is where I get a kicking, then so be it. I deserve it. I don't care. Right now, I honestly don't give a shit.

Then he's shaking his head, grinning and blinking slowly.

"No no no, big man. We're not fighting."

He shakes his finger and smiles at the others. I don't get it.

"So what do you want?" I ask, hoping my voice doesn't crack.

Craig calmly folds his arms.

"Nothing."

3.

I stand in the hall with my head in my hands.

I'm exhausted. No sounds, and I can smell the kofte Marc cooked earlier.

Craig's face. His boys behind him. Me just standing there confused.

Then they left. No threats. Just messing with me.

Me bending down to pick up my phone. The head-light beams cutting across as they reversed away.

What do I do? Somebody tell me what to do.

My phone beeps and I almost fall over. I sit on the second stair and open the message.

Is that what you are?

Read it again. Imagine her face as she sent it. Slump forward. Re-read it. Again. Again. Feel the question digging between my ribs. *Is that what I am?* No. I don't know.

My foot throbs as I creep upstairs. Mum's at work and the landing's dark, but there's a crack of light cutting through at the bottom of Marc's door. He's still up.

I have to tell him.

I walk to his door. Seven steps. It used to be thirteen. I hear the sound. Maybe the same sound from the other night. Is he crying again? Should I leave him? No. Now's the right time. I tap the door. No response, so I push it open.

He's not crying.

He's doing press-ups, with his feet up on his bed to increase the angle, make it harder. Breathing deep, arms pumping up and down, like pistons on a machine.

"Marc."

He stops.

"Lukey." He's up on his feet in one controlled movement, like a gymnast. "You OK? Good night?"

I look round the room. It feels lived in. No more museum. There's a new printer still in its box.

"What's that for?"

He follows my eyes. "Printing. Recipes and applications and that."

"Applications?"

He starts stretching out, rolling his shoulders. "How'd the costume go down?"

I shrug. *Is that what you are?*

He sits on his bed and motions for me to join him. So I do, a flicker book of the whole night playing in my head.

"Yo! What happened to your hand?" He reaches for me. I pull my hand back and slide it into the jacket pocket.

"Did you fight? Who was it? You hurt?"

His voice is definite. Heroic.

"I'm fine. Just some stupidness."

"Let me see you." He grabs my chin and lifts my head, taking me in like a sculpture he's just finished moulding.

I shrug him off. "I said I'm fine. Leave it."

"What happened, man?" He crosses his legs on the bed next to me.

I shake my head.

"Tommy got into a bit of trouble." *Liar.* "So I sorted it."

You sorted it all right.

"And you didn't get hit?"

"No." I look at him. He's smiling. "Fair play."

"No, Marc, not fair play. Stupid. It wasn't even a fair fight, geezer was off his face and I could've had him anyway."

Tell me I'm stupid. Please. Shout at me. Tell me I should learn from your lesson. Call me out. Do something!

Marc just shrugs. "Well, if you had to hit him, I'm sure he had it coming."

My stomach turns. "You don't know anything about it! How can you say that?"

"Lukey. I trust your judgment. It's not nice, but if you thought you had to fight, then you did. You didn't go overboard, right?"

I picture Jono, cradling Simeon, and I stand up. I don't want to tell him anything else. I just want to be on my own.

"Luke, wait," he says. "I need to talk to you."

I scan the floor, avoiding his eyes, wait.

"Are they prospectuses?" I point to the floor near the TV.

"That's what I wanted to talk to you about. Sit down, will ya?"

He reaches down and grabs the chunky pamphlets as I sit back on to the bed. The covers show photographs of smug looking students smiling on the front steps of glass buildings.

"What are they for?"

"I'm thinking of going to college." His face is hopeful, a bit embarrassed even.

"To do what?" My voice is a bit too cutting, but instead of reacting, he gets more sheepish. "Food," he says. "Nutrition. Catering and that."

Then he waits for my response. I don't know why I don't like the idea.

Yes you do.

"Aren't you gonna say something?" he says.

"That's great. Good for you."

"Don't sound too positive, will ya?"

It's my turn to nod like I'm happy. "It's brilliant, Marc. Where you thinking?" Don't say my college. Don't say my college. He smiles.

"Leeds."

And the whole house shakes.

"Luke, what's wrong?" He stands up after me. "What's the matter?"

"No," I say. Punching the word out from my throat.

Marc's oblivious. "No what? Luke?"

"You don't get to leave."

I start out the room. He grabs my arm. "Hold on, man, what's that mean?"

I look down at his hand on me, and we both know the look.

Looks can be acts of aggression.

"What's your problem?" he says.

"Let go of me, now." I tense my arm and he feels it.

"What the hell's wrong with ya?" But he does let go.

"Leeds?" I say, feeling my voice breaking.

"I dunno. Maybe. I thought it might be good, you know, to get away?"

"Get away? You? Few weeks too much for you, is it?"

His face hardens. "Easy, Luke."

"What a joke." I turn to go again. He grabs me again.

"I said get the fuck off me!" I throw him off violently enough that his shoulder rocks his body back.

"What d'you think you're doing?" he says, setting himself. He can feel it in the air. We both can.

"You leave us here for two years? In your mess? The stink of you in the walls? And now you think you can just fly off again?"

"My mess? You call it my mess?"

I watch his body tighten. The muscles between his neck and shoulders. What the hell's happening? Are we gonna fight?

"Walk away, little brother." His eyes are stones. "Remember who you're speaking to. We'll talk tomorrow."

But I don't move. I want this. I wanna feel this. This is everything poured into a moment. He's older. He's stronger. I set myself.

"I said walk away." He pushes me in the chest and he's strong. He's so strong. But I don't care.

I push him back. He can't believe it. He hardly moves, but I can tell he felt it. He's shaking his head, his teeth bared, and I know it's wrong.

I know I'm stupid, but as he comes for me, I swear I feel myself smile.

There's a thousand different types of laughter.

Multiple variations on what a laugh means. The nuances and motivations behind and inside an expression that's universal to humans.

There are only two types of crying.

Think what you want. I don't know you, or where you're from, but where we're from, there's two kinds of tears.

There's the tears that come for someone else. Tears you cry because you're watching something bad happen to somebody you love, or something coming to an end. Those tears come quickly. They start right in the moment – usually a goodbye, for a while or forever – and they belong to whoever's leaving.

They are the feeling that colours the picture that person gets to take with them.

That's one kind.

The other kind are the ones that come for yourself.

They take longer.

Tears that come when a moment cracks the dam of you, who you are, the wall that you've built and kept up since you can remember and when that wall cracks, and the pressure's released, the tears that come carry everything. Every mistake. Every promise. Every lie. Every cold shoulder. Every bite. Every tiny death that you've ever felt floods out, over you. Through you.

The tidal wave crashes and the edges blur as you fall to the floor, feeling the power of what you've started and can't control.

And when they're done, those tears, when you come up for air, your clothes sodden, and the waves have soaked into the floor and the walls and all the rubble they've left, you slowly lift your head, and the whole world is different.

4.

INT. KITCHEN — NIGHT

`Bloodied water snakes down a silver plughole.`

We're in our kitchen.

The kettle's boiling. I'm holding frozen peas against my face. My ears are ringing. My bottom lip's split. My jaw aches, throat scratched from crying. The muscles in my chest and stomach and arms all tender, but I feel better. I feel real.

Marc's sitting at the table, dabbing his left cheek with a damp tea towel. His eye socket's already swollen.

I look at him. He smiles.

"Lucky shot."

I smile back.

"Yeah. Course."

And we sit with our teas. The hot liquid stings my lip, but everything's warm. Everything's messed up, but everything makes sense at the same time. A definite mess.

I just fought Marc Henry. I just held my own with my big brother.

"You should call her." He nods as he sips.

I shake my head. "I can't."

"Fair enough. Give her a bit of time then. That's what people always need." I watch him picture Donna. "I hope."

I see Leia's face. Her disappointment.

My mind zooms out to her standing on the doorstep, Michelle behind her. Other faces too. The light behind them. Zoom out further, to Jono cradling Simeon while Max sits to the side holding his face. Zoom out to the street. The back of me. Bane. Thick shoulders heaving as I walk off.

The fire in my gut.

"Ask me," Marc says, and I'm back in our kitchen.

"Ask you what?"

"Whatever question you keep trying to swallow."

"Were you trying to kill him?"


```
Close-up.
Tendons flex under the skin of raw knuckles.
```

Marc stares across at the sink for what feels like a long time before he speaks.

"When I was about fourteen, he used to come over to the football pitches when we were playing, trying to sell us weed and that. Nothing hardcore. He had this done-up white Golf. Used to rev the engine when he showed up." Marc shakes his head at the memory. "He starts offering us money to do stuff, like dares, he says, throw this brick through so and so's window, slash this guy's tyres, or whatever. We were bored and it was dough, so we just did it, no biggy. All through till we left school, people were scared of us and I suppose we liked it.

"He used to make little digs, all the time, take the piss out of us, talking himself up, making sure we always thought he was the man. A few of the others bought it, but me and Jay always just nodded along.

"Then he started on the shops. Getting us to nick proper stuff. We knew it was stupid, but –" he shrugs – "lot of stuff's stupid, eh?" He sips his tea. "That's when it got a bit more serious, and that's when Dad found out."

He looks at me. He knows I remember.

"That's when I stopped running with him, and he didn't like it. Used to try and embarrass me, threaten me in front of people, say he was gonna do stuff. He never did, cos he knew I could kick the shit out of him and he'd have to live that down, big Craig Miller, battered by a kid four years younger. So he starts sniffing round Donna, following her home and that. I warn him off, and we have this proper row outside The Goose, it was just after my eighteenth, I remember it clear as anything. He pulled a knife. Prick. Who pulls a knife?"

I shrug and avoid his eyes, picturing Tommy standing with his torn top, holding the knife out.

"A chicken who can't fight, that's who. So I told him. In front of all his little henchmen, that if he went near Donna again, I'd kill him, giving it the big one myself, like. And that's when he says I'd better watch it, that my family'd better watch it."

I've never heard him talk about this. I watch his jaw tensing, his eyes darting from his hands to the sink, to the floor. Everywhere but me.

"I've thought about it so much, Lukey." He's fighting tears. "He was all talk. He was always all talk. I never thought…"

Then he makes this sound. It's like wood cracking. Like a heavy chair scraping against a hard floor. And I want to help, to make this better, but the words just walk out of my mouth.

"He's back," I say.

Marc wipes his face with his hand and stares at his mug. Why did I say that? Why did I have to make it worse? Why isn't he reacting?

"Did you hear me, Marc?"

He looks at me and it's like a slap in my face. He already knows.

I go to get up. "No, Lukey, stop." His arms are out towards me.

"Are you kidding me, Marc? You knew?"

"It's all right. Don't worry. Nothing's gonna happen."

I'm up now. Looking down at him. "What are you talking about? It's Craig Miller!"

"Easy," he says. "It's fine. I've spoken to him."

"You what?!"

My head's spinning again. Craig's crooked face.

"Sit down, Luke. It's all good."

I sit, and my head falls into my hands.

"Nothing's gonna happen," Marc says. "It's all the past. Time to move on."

I look at him and he looks like he believes what he's saying. Like it's not for my benefit and I don't get it. Craig Miller.

"It's different now, Lukey. I'm different."

He smiles. "New chapter. I'm all about the food now. Making a go of it. Something proper."

"With Donna?"

He shrugs, and skates his fingertip round the lip of his

mug. "If she'll have me, yeah."

"He told me to say hi."

Marc sits bolt upright. "He came to you?"

And the anger's right back in his eyes.

I shake my head. "No. Kind of. He passed by in a car."

"Where?" And the bite in his voice is scary. I can't tell him everything.

"Near town. I was walking back. It was last week."

"Why didn't you tell me?" And then he clocks what he said and what we've just been talking about and he slumps back into his chair.

"What's he want, Marc?"

"You don't have to worry. Not about him. He's just trying to save face, let us know he's not scared. He's not gonna do anything."

"How do you know?" I say, leaning on my elbows.

Then Marc runs his fingers over his knuckles and smiles a smile that he stole from Dad.

"Because it'd be a mistake."

5.

Boy stares out of moving bus window, his head against the glass

Boy sits in back corner seat of moving bus next to old lady, trying not to look at her as she just stares up at the side of his face, like she's trying to read his story.

```
INT. CLASSROOM — DAY
YOUNG MAN sits drawing concentric circles on
lined paper. Lost in thought.
```

I'm in comms. Louise asked everyone to come up with one law they would implement if they were in charge of the country. I stare at my doodle, trying not to look over at Max.

I had a quick glance as we came in and that felt awkward enough. What am I gonna say to him? What am I gonna say to Simeon in film later? To Leia? *Relax. What's done is done.*

My eyes hit Max's just as he looks up. His face isn't marked. Tommy must've just popped his nose, not broken it. I make myself hold his gaze, give him the chance to be in charge, cut me a look, anything. He just stares back blankly. I try and say sorry with my eyes. Then the lesson ends.

I've rehearsed different versions of what I'll say to her. But she probably doesn't even want to see me. Let alone talk to me.

Is that what you are?

Her text is tattooed on the inside of my eyelids.

I've decided the worst thing I can do is say sorry. An apology is pointless. Apologies are for when you forget something. Or bump into somebody. Apologies are for accidents. You can't apologise for something you chose to do. That's like apologising for being you.

I can say I wish I hadn't done it. That's different. I wish I hadn't done it, Leia. I wish I hadn't done any of it.

Yeah, cos that's not pointless.

She doesn't come to film.

Neither does Simeon. The empty seats next to me and Jono scream 'guilt' the whole lesson. I try and make eye contact with Jono a couple of times, but he's having none of it. Megan doesn't acknowledge me either.

We're supposed to share our opening scenes with everyone. Read them out to see how they feel. How am I gonna do that? How am I gonna read out a scene about a guy beating the crap out of someone after what I did?

Noah's working his way round the horseshoe from my left. I saw him notice my face. The fading marks from Marc's fist still colouring my cheek. Maybe he's put two and two together, the empty seats, people missing, me bruised.

Where is she?

Maybe they're together. Maybe Leia's round at Simeon's house right now, sitting on his big sofa. No. He pushed her. He called her…

But I bet he's apologised and she's let him off. And now they're watching a film. Something old. And as it plays it all feels familiar to them, and before long they're sitting closer, her leaning against his shoulder, his arm round her, just for comfort, nothing said out loud, but both of them feeling the warmth of their own memories of when they were together. That's what's happening. Right now.

"I gotta go toilet."

I'm standing up. The boy reading out his scene stops. Everyone looks at me. Megan's giving me evils.

"Sorry. I feel a bit sick. I better go."

I start packing my stuff.

"Do you need that?" says Noah.

"What?" I actually do feel queasy.

"Your stuff. Do you need to take it to the toilet?"

I'm blushing, but still packing. "Dunno how long I'll be. Feels pretty bad." And I leave, feeling every eye in the room watching me go.

I walk off campus, down the hill, not thinking anything. No memories, no scenes, no details, just a blank, grey screen.

A projection of empty.

6.

Reflection of strip light in the tiles of the underpass.

Dad said, we go back to what we know. The same flavour pizza, the same shampoo, the same song, the same people. We make things our own and we stick with them. Creatures of habit.

I sit on the same bench in the graveyard.

A breeze runs between the gravestones and I think about Nan's funeral. Watching Dad and Uncle Chris carry her coffin from the long black car to the crematorium. How small the wooden box looked high up on their dark-suited shoulders. I remember thinking about how weird it is that children get bigger than their parents. How people make new people and those people grow past them. Mum saying, *we all outgrow who we came from* and me thinking, if that's true, surely we should all be giants by now?

"Don't you have a lesson now?"

Max stands, keeping his distance, fiddling with the strap of his rucksack, his black hood half on his head.

I shrug. "Didn't feel well."

Then nothing.

I picture the wide shot of us, him standing, me sitting, dirty gravestones, the shade of the church and trees. Me looking at him.

And subtitles appear at the bottom of the screen:

```
LUKE: I'm sorry you got hit.

MAX: I'm all right. What happened to you?

LUKE: Doesn't matter.

MAX: Can I sit down?
```

All that, said in one look. I shuffle across to make space for him on my right. He's waiting for me to speak, I can feel it, and I want to, but my throat feels tight. So I just wait too, wondering whether a passer-by would think we were mates or strangers.

"Pretty messed up, right?" Max says, his eyes staying

forward.

"Yep," I say. "Pretty much."

"He gets like that sometimes, Sim. With Megan, I mean."

I don't understand. Is he blaming Simeon? I make myself stay silent. Max scuffs the floor in front of us with his foot. "Nobody's hit him before though." He looks at me. "Ever."

And there's something in his face, something that's not anger or disgust.

"Ever?" I say.

Max shakes his head and allows the corner of his mouth to crack a smile. I feel to smile too, but I don't.

"Is he OK?" I say.

"He's fine. Split lip and a bit of a bruise. He was so out of it he probably doesn't remember much."

For a second I feel a pang of disappointment, before allowing the relief to flow. "He wasn't in today, I thought, I dunno…"

"Luke, when you're Simeon Mckenzie, getting battered in front of everyone you know might take a while to get over, you know? Nothing even remotely like that's ever happened before."

And now the look on his face is clearer. I think he's grateful.

I allow myself to smile. "I guess."

"I reckon he'll wait a while, let the marks fade."

We could be friends. Me and Max. In a different life.

He's staring up at the church. I look down at my hands. Her name runs up and down my throat.

"What about Leia?" I say, finally.

Max's mouth tightens as he shakes his head. "I dunno, man, that's different."

I nod like I already knew that.

"After what happened to her brother and stuff." *What?*

"What happened to her brother?"

"Oh," he says.

"What happened?"

Pause.

"I shouldn't have said anything."

He stands up.

"Max? What happened to him?"

Pause.

"They put him in a coma. About a year and a half ago." He swings his bag over his shoulder. "He was at a cash point. It really messed him up. Her too."

"Who did it?" I say. It feels like there's a ball bearing in my throat. Max shrugs. "Just some guys."

And looking up at him, we both know it doesn't matter who.

Just like it doesn't matter when, or why.

All that matters is that she saw it in me.

Toby got put in a coma. That's why he doesn't go out. That's why he was so awkward. And that's what Leia thinks I am. Somebody capable of that. The pit of my mistake just dropped to the core of the earth.

7.

Walking through crowded shopping street. Sound
muted. Bright windows and blurred faces.

I know it's stupid.

But I just wanna feel near her.

I ride the slow escalators up between the floors, standing
statue-still as the scene moves around me.

I get tea and sit in the same place we sat together. It's a little
later than it was that day, but the scattered cast of afternoon
old people are all here.

I take out my notebook and my pen and I scan the room,
watching eyes staring into space, lost in memories.

Over by the window I recognise the old mixed-race lady
from the retired spy couple I saw last time. She's alone, staring
out of the window, one pot of tea on her table. Where's her

partner? My pen taps the page.

He died. He died a couple of weeks ago in his sleep and now she's on her own. Name?

~~Rose~~

~~Charmaine~~

She's here, sitting where they used to sit, remembering him.

I'm sure of it. That's her story.

She'll come here every day now, sit at the same table, in memory of him, until she fades away herself.

I should speak to her. I should go over, ask to sit down and speak to her. Give her some company.

What makes you think she wants company?

Cos her husband just died. The love of her life.

I stand up, take my tea and start to walk over.

Nobody's looking, but it feels like I'm watching myself.

She's still staring out of the window. Her hair's back in a bun. She's wearing a cream cardigan and there's a thin gold chain against the skin of her neck. She looks like an older Leia.

"Excuse me, young man."

I step back as her partner moves in between me and their table holding a tray with two plates covered with silver lids. He's not dead.

"Thank you. Here you go, princess." He lays the tray delicately down, places her plate in front of her and sits. His dark brown pinstripe suit is immaculate and he smells like soap.

She smiles at him and I'm standing too close to their table for a stranger. They both look up at me.

"Are you OK, son?" says the lady, her voice silky and calm. I'm gripping my cup tightly.

"Sorry," I say, backing away from them. "I was just… checking the view."

We're walking back from football. Me, Marc and Dad. I reckon I'm nine, in my coat and woolly hat. Marc's got his jacket on, over his muddy black shorts, socks pulled up, carrying his boot bag. Him and Dad are talking about the game. Marc got Man of the Match. Again.

We're waiting to cross the road on the corner. There's a big silver car trying to park next to us, on my side. I watch the red brake lights go on and off. Dad and Marc are busy talking and don't see it and, as we step out, the car reverses right towards me. I freeze.

Then Dad jumps in the way. The car jerks to a stop. I look up at Dad. His face goes hard, then he smacks both his hands down on the boot of the car. It sounds like a fridge falling over and the whole car bounces. The driver's door opens and a man who looks like a teacher gets out and he's like, "What the hell are you doing?!"

Dad moves me back on to the kerb next to Marc. "Wait here," he says, and walks round to the front. Next thing, he's pinned the guy against the side of his car and he's saying. "You could've killed my boy! Why don't you use the eyes that God gave you?" and his voice is full of thunder, but he's not shouting and I'm scared, for the guy and myself, for what might happen. Dad grips the guy's head and turns it so he's looking at me and I'm embarrassed and excited and Dad says, "Apologise to him."

The guy looks confused and my stomach drops, cos it feels wrong, but part of me's buzzing, and the guy says, "I'm sorry. I didn't see you." Dad holds him there for a second, then lets him go, walks back round to us, grabs both our hands and leads us across the road. His eyes look straight ahead the whole time.

I turn around and the guy's just standing there, shaking. I look up at Dad and he must feel it, cos he says, "Some people don't understand anything else, son."

I try to work out what he means as we walk. I look at Marc and he's staring up at Dad, like he's looking at the coolest man in the world.

```
INT — AFTERNOON
Three men sit in a living room, like Russian dolls,
watching the TV.
```

"Quality," Marc says, as Russell Crowe floats through tall grass into the afterlife. "Father to a murdered son."

"Are you not entertained!" shouts Dad, holding his arms out to the packed coliseum. They both look at me like it's my turn to say something.

But I just check my phone, again. Nothing.

Marc and Dad are exchanging looks.

"What?" I say.

They give synchronised shrugs and pull their best oblivious expressions.

"She can't stay mad forever," says Marc, like it's a line from the big brother comfort handbook.

"Who can't?" says Dad. Nice one, big mouth.

"Leia," he says. "Luke's girl, he upset her the other night."

And just like that, I'm on stage, like it's *Jeremy Kyle* or something. Marc's hosting. He explains his version of my version of what happened. Dad's the relationship expert, nodding along, murmuring his approval.

"She might need some time," he says. "Time's your best friend." I look at Marc. He's not even smiling. They're both completely deadpan.

"I smacked her ex-boyfriend in front of her, Dad. He was wasted and couldn't even really defend himself. She hates violence, like properly. Everybody saw it." I see Leia's face. I don't mention Toby. "I messed up."

Dad actually rubs his chin like he's contemplating the best course of action. Marc mimics him.

"Why are we even talking about this?" I reach for the remote control.

"Easy, Lukey," says Dad, patting the air in front of him.

Marc gets up. "Time for steak. Joseph, medium-well?"

Dad nods.

"Cassanova?"

He's trying to make me laugh. I'm having none of it.

"Calm down. We'll sort it," he says. "And in plenty of time for your birthday."

And that's when it hits me.

I'm seventeen in a week and a half.

8.

INT. KITCHEN — NIGHT

Girl finishes drying a plate. She checks her phone
on the sideboard, shakes her head and leaves the
kitchen.

"Stop bloody thinking, will ya?" Dad says, as I hand him the wet frying pan. He's drying, Marc's putting away. His steak was amazing.

"I told you, give her some time." The pan looks small as he rubs the tea towel over it.

"Can we just leave the relationship advice, Dad, please?" I dig into the hot soapy water for cutlery. "Does Mum even know you're here?"

Dad shrugs too dramatically. "Of course she does. I told her I was popping over to see you both. She's fine with it."

"I bet she was."

I feels his eyes burning me.

"What's that mean?" says Marc. I stare into the dark glass of the window and see the three of us. We look like weight lifters on the podium. Dad's gold in the middle, me and Marc look the same height, though, so who's silver?

"Nothing," I say, pulling the plug out.

"Unexpected gift at an unexpected time," says Marc, closing the cupboard.

Me and Dad look at him. He shrugs. "I'm telling ya."

"Where's that from?" says Dad, racking his brains.

I've heard it before too, but I can't place it. Marc's beaming. "The key to a woman's heart, is an unexpected gift at an unexpected time. Remember? The one with Sean Connery. He's the old writer geezer and the basketball kid breaks into his house and that."

Dad's still trying to figure out what it is as he fills the kettle.

"*Finding Forrester*," I say.

"That's it!" says Marc. "Remember, Dad?"

Dad clicks the kettle on and shrugs. "Nope. Getting old." He taps his temple. "Sounds like good advice though."

"But what gift?" I say.

Marc takes mugs out. "That's on you, mate. Great players make things happen, Lukey." He spoons two sugars into all three. "Something personal."

Dad brings the milk from the fridge. "Something from when you first met. Best gifts are the ones you make," he says, sitting down opposite me. "I used to make tapes for your mum, back in the day." He smiles at the memory.

"What's she into, Lukey?" asks Marc. "What's something that'll feel special?"

We sit with our teas. Three boys, thinking about three girls.

I see Leia's face in the light from her fire as we sat in front of it. The heat. Stealing looks at her as we watched the film on her sofa. How much do I really know her? I feel like I got closer to her than any other girl ever, but what does that really mean? I didn't know about Toby. What else don't I know? Probably loads more than I do. I didn't even have time to find out important stuff, and now I've blown it.

"Well?" says Marc.

I shake my head. "I haven't got a clue."

I never saw anybody nervous.

Growing up as Big Joe Henry's son, little brother of Marc Henry, what's to be nervous about?

They've got everything under control. Nothing rattles them. That's what you think.

That's what I thought.

What's gonna happen?

Relax, Lukey, what's the problem?

Like all you need to do is highlight the problem to deal with it. Like it's all under your control.

Decide what the problem is, then either hit it or walk away. Job done. Problem solved.

Nerves don't even come into it.

9.

Five days since I saw Leia. Five days since her question. Five days of me not replying. How many minutes staring at my phone?

Max and Jono are walking out of the refectory as I approach it.

No Simeon. I keep my head up. They both blank me as we pass.

I watch them walk away. They look kind of awkward without their leader. Like they're not even speaking to each other.

Max turns back and sees me looking. I shrug. He nods. And I know it means that Leia's here today.

Mum said: Nothing's ever as bad as you imagined it, but nothing's ever as good either.

She sits next to Jono.

Everyone else just gets on with their work, oblivious to Leia clearly avoiding me, even though it feels like the loudest statement to me. Her hair's out. I've never seen it like that before. It's gorgeous. She's wearing a man's cotton checked shirt with the sleeves rolled up and she looks like the fittest dancer from a music video.

She won't even look at me.

Gutted.

Noah's definitely noticed. I'm not sure what I'm supposed to do. Our idea seems dead without her. It's dead anyway, thanks to me. *Is that what you are?*

Forget her. Just do your own thing.

And what's that?

I feel to leave, to walk out, but I don't want her to see me do that.

I pretend to write in my notebook for the first half of the lesson. Leia seems to be writing loads. What's she writing? *Just forget her.*

A phone beeps and people look up. Leia too. Everyone checks their phone. I stay staring at her. The phone beeps again. Everyone's looking at me. It's my phone. Noah's frowning. I force a smile, then check under the desk as everyone goes back to working.

Yo. Football tomorrow night. Come. Let's squash this. Z

I picture Zia in the freezer behind the milk display, sneakily typing the text. I haven't spoken to him or Tommy since the weekend. Does Tommy know he's asked me?

"I generally prefer mobiles to be switched off." Noah's standing in front of my desk. I scan the room; nobody's watching us.

"Sorry," I say, pushing my phone into my hip pocket.

"No worries," he says. "How's it going?"

He's looking at my face. The bruises are fading, but they're still there. He points at my notebook. "With your story?"

"Oh." I stare at my page of doodles and notice I've drawn a pattern of knives. "Yeah." I look up at him. His beard's almost full now. He looks older. "I might have to re-think," I say.

Noah nods. "I see. Well maybe we should talk it out, help you get it clear?"

I nod back.

"I thought we'd watch a film tomorrow," he says. I frown.

"In class, I mean. Inspired by you. I thought we'd watch *Leon*."

And as he says the word, that's when I sense her watching, past him, from the other side of the room. I don't look over, but I know her eyes are on me, I can feel them, and not in the way that I want.

The feeling rolls over me, like a tractor wheel.

It's done.

10.

A deep plastic bowl full of coarsely cut homemade
coleslaw is placed on to a fridge shelf. The sound
of a man whistling, happy in his work.

Mum's coming down the stairs in her work clothes, tying her hair back.

I close the front door.

"What happened, love?" She stands there, looking into me.

"Nothing." I drop my bag next to the phone. "I'm fine."

Mum smiles. "You need a cup of tea."

She's right. I do. I need a cup of tea and to talk about what's happened with someone who isn't gonna quote Sean Connery. Can I smell cake?

"I saw Zia at the supermarket," she says, straightening her collar.

"Did you speak to him?"

"Not really." She checks herself in the mirror. "Just a quick hello. You should play football tomorrow night."

I picture her and Zia chatting in the cereal aisle and shrug. Mum turns to me. "You should. It's important to make time for your mates too, you know. All work and no play and all that."

She smiling, and there's something different about her, the way she's moving. Something lighter.

"I'm on all night, but your brother said he'd be back later." She takes her jacket off the banister. She's going.

"Where's he gone?"

"Somewhere with Donna. He mentioned cooking for your birthday, you all right with that? He's been practising. You could ask your mates over?"

"What about my cup of tea?"

"Kettle's just boiled, love. You can sort yourself, right? There's fish fingers in the freezer and Marc made bread and lovely coleslaw."

She brushes past me to the door.

"See you tomorrow." A blown kiss, then a frown. "Phone your mates. Sort it out."

And she's gone. Just me in an empty house.

I don't bother with the tea and go up to my room. Lie

down. Open my laptop. *Long Time Round* still inside. I stare at the 'The Brothers Different' folder I created on my desktop. Guess I need to start again.

Shit.

Click DVD player. Menu. Play.

Everything's black and white.

I'm on top of him. My knees either side of his chest. My fists swinging, hitting his head. His face is pale. His eyes are closed. Blood dark as tar.

The thud of each impact shooting up my arms. Growling.

Hands reaching from all around me, pulling at me, trying to stop me hitting him. His face is broken.

The side of it caved in.

I keep hitting, the whole time feeling this sharp stabbing in my throat, in my chest.

Like I've swallowed a kitchen knife. Simeon. Simeon.

His eyes creak open. Not Simeon.

Her bloody mouth moves. Craig. Craig.

But it's not Craig.

Her mouth.

It's Leia.

Battered. Staring. "Is that what you are?"

I sit up, chest heaving, sheen of sweat on my back. It's a dream.

I was dreaming.

Is that what you are?

Guilt in my skin.

My room's all dark and silver edges. Like those pictures where you scratch off the black to reveal the image.

I feel my face.

Everything's quiet. Just the thump in my chest.

I need a tea.


```
INT. — NIGHT
Duvet stirs at the edge. A foot, an ankle, a girl's
leg. Painted toes reach for the floor.
```


The smallest sounds seem louder in the middle of the night.

Unscrewing the lid on the milk. The rollers on the cutlery drawer. Even the tea bag landing in the mug, like a heavy snowflake.

The oven clock says 03:33. I stand waiting next to the sink. My foot doesn't hurt any more.

In the dark window I see myself. I am getting big. The clear outline of my chest muscles. My upper arms thick and starting to define. The ridges above my hips cutting inwards, then down behind my jogging bottoms.

I look strong.

As the kettle boils I hold my hands out in front of me, balling fists and tensing every muscle in my upper body, lifting my chin.

"Looking good, Lukey."

I almost fall over. It's Donna. She's standing in the kitchen doorway wearing one of Marc's T-shirts and nothing else. It only comes halfway to her knees. My eyes go straight down to the floor and I see her red toenails.

I'm half naked. *What did she say?*

"Can't sleep either?" Her voice is soft enough to not need to whisper and I have to grip the seams of my jogging bottoms to stop my hands coming up to cover my body.

"Make us one too, will ya?" She nods at my mug on the side and I spin round to get another from the cupboard. Donna's here and I'm half naked.

You're just topless. No, I'm half naked.

I hear her pull out a chair behind me. I didn't even hear them come in. If she's staying over, things must be going well.

"Is Marc asleep?" I say, pouring the water, seeing her reflection in the window.

"Like a baby," she says. "A baby who snores like a lorry and sleeps in a star jump."

And I can feel her smile.

"Sugar?"

"No, thanks, but you got any biscuits?"

I reach into the bread bin and pull out the half packet of ginger nuts. "Only these," I say, holding them up, still not turning round.

"Perfect," she says, and I'm ten years old, trying not to stare at her bra. I hand her the mug and the biscuits, then take my mug and go to leave.

"Sit with me, Lukey? For a minute?"

So I do. I sit opposite her, elbows on the table to hide more of my body. The difference between topless and half naked is who else is in the room.

Donna bends her knees and puts her feet up on the chair and all I see are the edges of T-shirt against the skin of her thighs, her arms, her neck.

What you looking at?

I grip my mug with two hands and stare at my thumbs.

"So how's college?" she says, and I try to make her my big sister. Having a big sister would be brilliant. Somebody who knows more, but doesn't make you feel like you're a rubbish version of them.

"It's all right," I say.

The crack of a ginger nut. Her fingertips brushing crumbs from the side of her lips. Marc's asleep. Me and Donna are John Travolta and Uma Thurman in the diner scene from *Pulp Fiction*.

"So yous two are getting along?" Sip.

Donna shrugs. "Yeah." She dunks half of her biscuit and bites it. "He feels different."

What does that mean?

I don't say anything.

Donna takes another ginger nut. "Who knows, Lukey, eh?"

She offers the packet. I shake my head. She puts it down and speaks through a full mouth. "My dad used to say to us, if things don't alter, they'll stay as they are."

I repeat the words in my head. Whoever's writing this script is giving all the best lines to everyone else.

"What about you?" she says. "Did you sort it out with your girl?" She smiles. "Your brother told me."

And it should feel awkward. It should've cranked the embarrassment up another notch, but it doesn't. There's no point feeling embarrassed about something that's broken.

"She's not my girl," I say.

Donna leans forward. "But you'd like her to be?"

Leia's face in the doorway. Disappointment. My blank phone screen.

I'm biting the inside of my cheek. "No chance of that now. It's been made pretty clear. I messed up."

"And that's it?" Her voice is slightly harder. I look at her. Donna from the pub. Marc's girl.

"What do you mean?" I say.

Donna takes out another biscuit and points at me with it. "I mean, handsome, if you really like her, if you actually like her, it's not done."

"It's complicated, Donna."

"Course it is. Everything's complicated, Lukey. Listen, look at me."

I do.

"What do you see?"

I don't know what to say and I want so badly to say something amazing.

"A girl, right?" she says. I still have nothing.

"A girl who fell in love with an idiot. A brilliant idiot, but still an idiot. Agreed?"

Don't you nod. I nod.

"Right, so if that's what I did, does that mean I'm an idiot?"

I'm not sure what I'm supposed to say. No?

"No."

Donna shakes her head. "Of course I'm an idiot. I should be the one in control. The one who says no, you see?" She doesn't give me time to answer. "But that's the thing, I'm not in control, am I?"

She puts another biscuit in her mouth and crunches.

"But what about choice?" I say.

Donna thinks as she chews. "You can't choose a feeling. You can only choose how to act on it."

And I'm trying to figure out whether what she's saying completely goes against what I've always been told, or whether she's kind of saying the same thing in different words. Either way, it feels like it's helping. I don't feel like a little kid.

"So why would you choose to be with an idiot?" I say.

Donna finishes her tea.

"Because nobody's one thing, Lukey. You make a person one thing, and you'll miss out on everything else that they are. That they could be." She points at me. "And they'll always let you down."

She stands up and puts her mug in the sink, then walks back over to me. "If you've ever had a moment where you felt her feel good with you, like, really felt it, then it's still a choice.

Just give her some time to make it."

I'm about to ask more, to get her to explain, be more specific, but before I can, she leans down, kisses me on the top of my head, walks to the door, then stops and turns back. She looks like a film poster.

"Nothing before its time, handsome." A smile. Then she's gone.

My fingertips trace the top of my head where her lips were as I picture her tiptoeing up our stairs, along our landing, easing the bedroom door open, crossing the room and slipping under the duvet of the single bed, next to my sleeping lucky idiot older brother.

II.

INT. CLASSROOM — DAY

A squared horseshoe of faces. Light flickering in
a darkened room.

The sound of gunshots through a silencer.

Noah's face as he stares at the empty seat.

Cut to time lapse of clouds moving above high city
buildings as the sun rolls down the curve of the
sky.

EXT. — NIGHT

The burnt halo of a floodlight.

Laces pulled tight. The sliding metal of a gate
unlocking.

Shouts of boys.

I don't know who picked the teams, but I'm with Zia and Tommy's on the other side. His cousin Aaron and his workmates make up the rest. Tommy didn't even look at me as everyone laced up. Now he's standing in the centre circle of the five-a-side Astroturf pitch, the ball under his foot, looking like a Spartan in an Aston Villa kit. I look across at Zia, he just shrugs and then we're off.

Straight away I feel slow. I haven't played in a while and these lot are used to playing with each other, pinging it around the damp ground, like a pinball. They're all older and shout constantly, telling each other where to go, what to do. I'm just concentrating on holding my position, guarding the space. Then Tommy's on the ball and heading straight for me. His feet dance. Step over. Drawing me in. Drag back. I lunge, he skips past, leaving me cold. I feel like a tree. By the time I turn round, the ball's in the back of the net and he's slapping the hands of his team mates.

"One nil," he says, as he jogs past me, moving back into position.

And that's how it goes.

Every time Tommy gets the ball he attacks me, running through other people just to take me on. I lose track of the score after they've got fifteen. It's like he's floating. That feeling of watching somebody sing. The music of talent.

Nobody says anything, but it's obvious. This is my lesson.

When they call time, I can feel my lungs, and I get it. I deserve it. Yeah, he pulled a knife, but he would never use it.

What he did was stupid. What I said was mean.

Everyone moves off the pitch to let the next game start. People are swigging from bottles of sports drinks, patting each other on the back, shaking hands. I work my way round the other team, pressing sweaty palm after palm. I can feel Zia watching as I approach Tommy, my hand out.

"Good game, Tom."

He gives me the briefest shake possible. "Guess strong's not the same as fit, eh, Lukey?"

I can feel him ready to bite back at anything I say. So I just nod. "Guess not."

He almost looks disappointed as he turns and walks off towards the car park. I roll my socks down to my ankles and feel the cold on my calves.

"I'll speak to him," says Zia, patting my back.

The two of us watch Tommy drive off, then start walking towards the bus stop.

"I wanted to ask you something," Zia says, looking at his phone.

"What?"

Things get darker as we move away from the floodlights.

"Michelle texted me."

It takes me a second to place the name, then I see it, the two of them in the kitchen, her looking at him.

"I just wanted to… you think… is it cool to text her back?"

He puts his phone away and looks at me like he just stole something.

"Course it is, you idiot," I say, and his face lights up.

"Yeah? I mean, I didn't wanna, you know?"

I bump his shoulder with mine. "Do what you like, man. You're not the one who messed up."

I2.

Smart phone vibrates on the arm of a suede sofa.
A girl with black bobbed hair opens the message
and smiles.

I hear explosions.

Donna and Marc are curled up on the sofa watching *Rush Hour*, I can't tell which one.

"Where's Mum?"

Marc doesn't look up from the screen. "She's with Dad. Think they're talking birthday plans for you."

Yeah. Right.

Donna looks up at me. "You OK?"

Her expression says she means about Leia, like, have I done anything to try and sort it out? My mouth says, "Yeah." The rest of me tells her I haven't done a thing.

"You wanna come sit with us?" she says, patting the sofa next to her. I pull at my sodden T-shirt.

"Thanks, but I need a shower."

"I made casserole," says Marc. "It's in the pot in the oven."

Chris Tucker swings Jackie Chan round like a rag doll to kick a bad guy in the face.

```
INT. — NIGHT
Condensation on a mirror. Running water. The edge
of a hand.
An arm curved around a knee. Naked thighs.
A body folded in half, lying down in the shower.
```

You're taller in the morning. That's just science.

The decompression of your vertebrae and cartilage as you sleep.

The chance for your body to recover. To grow. Fact.

The best time for your body is when you're unconscious.

Doing nothing allows space, and in that space, you take the steps to move forward. Sometimes, doing nothing is the best thing you can do. Right?

*

Everybody's dead.

Except Arnie, of course. And his daughter. And the pretty lady from the airport, who just happened to get dragged into the chaos.

The end credits of *Commando* roll up the screen, but I'm not really watching. I can't remember when Saturday mornings switched from SpongeBob to Schwarzenegger, I just remember enjoying Marc letting me be part of it.

Him and Donna are still in bed. I'm guessing Mum is too. She wasn't back when I went to bed. I bring up Leia's number on my phone and stare at the numbers behind the fracture in the screen.

What's she doing right now? *Really? Again? What's the point?*

Fine, what's Tommy doing? *It's Saturday morning. Tommy's asleep.*

Dad? *Asleep.*

What's Zia doing? *Are you gonna go through every single person you know?*

He's probably texting Michelle, trying on different outfits for when he meets her later.

I click off the TV and just sit, in the corner chair, staring out through the net curtains. My eyes close and I'm on the street.

I'm driving and I can see the flats to my right. I pass the

petrol station, pass City Road and hit the dual carriageway. The sun's doing its best to bleed through clouds and the roads are still Saturday-morning empty. I'm on my college bus route, the scenery moving past me like familiar photographs. I approach the cricket ground and, instead of going straight on, I turn left towards Cannon Hill Park.

The houses get bigger and the colours seem to deepen and the roads have more trees. Red and brown leaves pasted on to the floor by the damp. I take a left and slow down, rolling to a stop outside her house. I move up the front path, then up, past the door, above the ground-floor bay window and red bricks, to the bedroom, through the glass, and there she is. She's sitting on top of her duvet, propped up by thick pillows, her notebook resting on her thighs as she writes. Dark T-shirt. Stonewashed jeans. Hair in a bun. Perfect.

She looks up, like she heard something.

Then I'm there. Standing at the end of her bed. She doesn't even look shocked.

"Took your time, Skywalker." She's smiling, and I can feel myself filling up with calm.

Cut.

Empty living room. Just me. Staring at my cracked phone screen. Luke Henry. The idiot who thought he could be different to those who came before him. Who wanted to be. Pretended he was, pulling a rug over the fact that he's exactly the same.

Push button. Delete contact? Yes/No.

Why did I have to break everything?

I don't deserve her. Yes.

Contact deleted.

13.

INT. SUPERMARKET — DAY

Bearded man holds a shampoo bottle in each hand.
One expensive designer. One own brand. He weighs
them like he's checking fruit.

I'm pushing a trolley.

As I lean on the back, the front wheels lift up and I'm thinking I could probably lift this thing clean off the ground and how far could I throw it?

Marc gave me a list of stuff to get and I was happy to get out of the house. The supermarket's full of old people taking six hours to choose a melon. I could push off and plough these lot down like dusty skittles.

Courgettes.

I see Pete, the manager, near the deli counter. He's giving some blonde girl a lecture about how to arrange the cooked meats. Dickhead.

I doubt he'd recognise me even if I walked right up to him, but I turn back down the fruit and veg aisle and loop round to avoid him.

Brown rice.

I think about Simeon. Is his face marked? His perfect skin? Has he been working out in the mirror, telling himself he's gonna kill me when he sees me?

Sesame oil.

Then I see Noah.

I hang back, so I don't catch him up. Last thing I want is some strained conversation about missing the lesson yesterday, or even worse, questions about Leia.

A young mum passes the end of the aisle, pushing her trolley with one hand, dragging her sobbing toddler behind her with the other. Zia's probably somewhere with Michelle, giggling and sharing a milkshake, avoiding saying my name in case it kills the mood.

"Afternoon."

He came up behind me. For a split second I consider pretending I didn't hear him and just walking away.

"All right?" I say.

"I'm all right, how about you? Missed you again yesterday."

"Yeah. Sorry."

I look past him towards the tills.

"I spoke to Leia." Please don't ask anything. Please just leave it.

"I guess you'll be working by yourself now?"

My stomach's twisting. Read my face, Noah. Leave me alone.

I take a can off the shelf. It's coconut milk.

"If it'd help to talk, I'm happy to," he says, and I picture swinging the can round into his face. Would he be quick enough to block it?

"I'm fine, thanks." I drop the can into my trolley. "I'll see you later, Noah."

"Luke." He puts his hand on my arm. I look at it. Then at him. He's smiling. "Sometimes, when things don't work out, it's good to go back to the start, to what you know."

"Like you did?" I watch his face change at the tone in my voice. I'm facing him now. He's like, half an inch taller.

"I'm sorry?" he says, staying calm, but I can feel him setting himself.

I shake my head. "Doesn't matter."

"No." He stares at me. "What did you mean?"

Really, Noah? Here? In the supermarket? Fine.

"I mean, is that what you did? Was that coming back to the start?"

My hand squeezes my trolley bar like I'm trying to break it off.

Noah shakes his head. "I still don't get you. You might need to break it down for me, sensei."

He wants it. I can feel my pulse.

"What happened?" I say. "You write this film, you get out, move away, probably get all kinds of chances to do more films, and yet here you are, back here, teaching a bunch of snotty kids in a Portakabin. Shopping on your own on a Saturday afternoon."

"You're shopping on your own on Saturday afternoon."

"That's not the point! What happened? Why'd you flop it?"

"I didn't flop anything."

"So why then?"

"Luke, easy." He reaches his hand out, I smack it off.

"Don't touch me!"

"Calm yourself, mate." His voice drops a tone.

"Answer the question!"

People are looking. Eyes on us. My arms are twitching.

Noah nods. "I think I'll go now."

And he starts to walk away. *Yeah, walk away.*

"What's the point, Noah?" I shout after him. "If it all goes to shit anyway?"

He doesn't look back, and I'm left, breathing through my nose, with an audience of pensioners.

14.

Nan said: Nothing teaches like a mistake.

I step through the sliding glass doors feeling stupid.

The sun's cutting through clouds and as I walk towards the supermarket car park. Rays hit my face like an idiot spotlight. Ladies and gentlemen, Luke Henry, the Bridge Burner!

The Fiat almost runs me over.

"Watch where you're going, you knob!"

The driver door opens. It's Noah.

"Get in."

He points to the passenger side. I don't move. Noah bangs the roof of the car. "I'm not playing, Luke. Let's go."

    EXT. — DAY
    Dull jagged letters scratched into wood. L + T.

He drives us to the woods.

Through the edge of trees I can see the grass sloping down to the brook and up the other side. We pull into the little car park and stop next to a Land Rover.

Noah turns the engine off.

"What's going on?"

"Get out," he says, stepping out himself.

I follow him around the wood-chip path, past the old white stone fountain that we used to drink from before it got turned off. The row of massive pine trees is still there. I get a flash of running down the slope, arms stretched out either side of me, pretending to be a kite. Noah's walking with purpose towards the bushes and, looking over my shoulders, I can't see a single other person.

This is well dodgy.

I stop walking. "Where we going?"

"We're not there yet." And he carries on.

I take another look round. Why is it so empty? Noah disappears between two trees. I could just leave. Walk home, right now. But I don't. I step through the trees.

He's sitting on the chocolate-coloured roots. Loose strands of the bark are frayed like horse hair. I stand just under the dark canopy.

"This is where we sat," he says, patting the ground next to

him. "I was here, she was on this side and we just sat, staring out between the trees, not speaking. Year Nine, we were."

What's he talking about?

But I do the calculation. "I was one and a half."

For some reason I smile as I say it. Noah smiles too.

"Mad, right? I'm sitting under here getting my first kiss and you're five minutes over that way chewing the remote control." He points in the direction of our house.

"First kiss?" I say, taking a step closer to him.

He nods, grinning like he just tasted something amazing and I feel myself sitting down on the twigs and fallen leaves.

"Who was she?" I say.

I picture some kind of Super 8 footage of a boy and a girl standing in front of a tree, looking awkward, but happy.

"I haven't been here for years," he says, "but sitting here I can still see us."

"We used to climb the trees back there." I point. "Gave 'em names and everything." And I get a flash of looking down through the branches at a ten-year-old Tommy. Him daring me to climb higher and carve our initials into the bark.

"Noah, listen, about just now…"

"Cut," he says, standing up. "You're giving too much weight to the wrong things, Luke. Come on. Your turn." He's looking down at me. I shrug.

"Fine," he says, "I'll go again."

EXT. — DAY

A crushed can of Relentless drops in the wet bus-
stop bin.

We pull up outside Sandhu's.

Rusty metal mesh over the windows. Flaking maroon paint on the sign.

Noah turns off the engine.

"Right. So I'm on the wall there." He points. "Matho's next to me on my right, and Pete's placing an empty can of Tennant's Super three paces in front of us. Yeah?" He looks at me. I nod. "So, the bet is that he can't climb up on to the wall, jump off and crush the can perfectly flat in one stomp. If he does, me and Matho owe him a quid each. If not, he owes us. Zoom in on the can."

He makes a frame with his thumbs and index fingers.

"And?" I say.

"That's it. Can you picture it?"

"Yeah, but did he do it? Did he win the bet?"

Noah smiles. "Broke his leg. Still walks funny now. We let

him off the two quid."

He starts the engine. I get the game.

"So?" he says.

I nod. "OK. I've got one."

EXT. — DAY

Charred bubbles in burnt plastic. The remains of
something burned on the fire.

The bus stop outside The Bear Tavern.

We park in the little side road and walk round.

"OK, so you're Tommy." I shepherd him on to the metal
seat. "Zia's next to you here, and I'm standing here near the
kerb. We're waiting for the bus."

"Where are we going?"

"Nowhere. It's nearly half four and we know that the Girls'
School bus'll be coming soon. We just want them to see us."

Noah's smiling. "How old?"

"Thirteen." I stare up the road. "So we see it coming and
we're all leaning, acting casual, but what we don't see is the
massive puddle." I point down to the gutter. "Like proper
deep. Bus pulls in, boom! Total wipeout, watched by a bus full
of laughing girls."

"Perfect!" says Noah.

"You mean painful."

"That too." He folds his arms like he's actually waiting for a bus.

"So was that before or after the scar?"

And I freeze.

EXT. — DAY

Shadows of tall trees cut across grass towards the skate park. Car pulls up. Engine off. Quiet.

The ramp looks the same. Covered in tags and graffiti.

The sun's going down and the cold moves through me.

"We didn't even skate," I say. "We just used to hang around here cos that's what everyone did."

I stare across the tarmac to the empty little kid's playground and I can hear muffled shouts.

"I was this side, with Tommy. Zia was way over there talking to some girls. Then people are just running."

Noah sits down on the edge of the ramp. "What happened?"

"Nothing," I say. "Somebody said Craig Miller was here with his gang, but we couldn't see anyone. There were too many people."

"And did you run?"

"Not at first."

I watch two BMXs roll down into the bowl of the tarmac and loop back up the other side like marbles.

"Tommy saw someone he knew, one of Craig's lot. That's when we ran. Up that way." I can feel Noah watching me, and I'm imagining the camera circling round, taking in the park from every angle.

"We knew who he was. Everybody did. So we knew it was best not to stick around." I scuff the floor with the sole of my shoe. "Maybe if we hadn't've run." Craig's boney face. "If we hadn't got split up. I dunno."

Looking down at my hands. The blood.

We don't speak. I've got no idea what Noah's seeing in his mind, what he's thinking, but I've never spoken about that day to anyone before.

Not like this.

"It didn't hurt," I say, looking at Noah. "But it should've."

The streetlights flicker on past the metal railings behind me.

"Then what happened?" says Noah.

"I went to hospital. Mum stitched me up."

"Mum?"

I nod. "She's a nurse. She wouldn't let anyone else touch me."

Noah's eyes narrow. "That must've been tough."

"Yeah. Then she phoned my brother."

Marc's eyes when he saw me, my sliced face. How he looked at Mum.

How she looked at him and how, even though I knew it would end badly, I felt the fire of pride in my gut as he took her keys and stormed out.

"I didn't see it happen."

Dark sky.

"But I've pictured it. I've pictured it a million times."

Fading light.

"We all did," Noah says and offers a smile.

He's heard the story. Course he has. My hands go into my pockets and I look at him. "I loved your film."

And I watch the words flow out of my mouth, snaking through the air towards him. Words I really mean. About the past and right now.

He opens his hands and we both watch them curl round into a snail-shell spiral across his palms. The story of my scar. Never told to anyone who wasn't there. How I feel. Now in his care.

He closes his hands like a book and they disappear.

15.

We pull up right behind Mum's car. The front room light is on.

"Thanks," Noah says. "That was good."

"Yeah."

I thread my fingers through the carrier bag handles between my legs.

"Ideas, Luke. There's nothing like the buzz of a good one."

I don't look at him, but I know what he means. I've felt it. In class. On the bus. With Leia.

"I messed up," I say, still staring into my lap.

Noah taps my elbow with his fist. "Yeah. You did."

I turn to him.

Noah Clarke. Boy from Bearwood who wrote a film.

Then he points past me out of my window.

"Two streets that way. Richard Dwyer's house."

I look out.

"In Year Seven, he chased me round the whole school twice, then gave me a kicking in front of everyone."

"Why?"

"God knows. He felt threatened, or he had stuff going on at home and was lashing out, or he was just a nasty piece of work. That and a thousand other shitty things. It doesn't matter." He mimes pouring from jugs with both hands.

"It all goes into the pot, Luke. Along with the first kisses and the broken bones and the packed bags and train journeys and the late night phone calls and funeral speeches. All of it. Stuff just happens. Nobody knows why. I didn't know that I would come back home, but I did. Not because I failed, because I chose to. That's what matters. That's what happens in my story, and I'm fine with it. I get to play with ideas and help other people do the same every single day. Maybe one day I'll write another film. Maybe I won't. Who knows?

"I love what I do. I love where I'm from and that I found my thing. Not everybody does." He balls his fists. "And that's fine. It is what it is. But if you do find your thing, something that makes your blood crackle, you better damn well do it."

He looks at me with sharp eyes. "You messed up, Luke, no denying it. But you're a maker, not a destroyer. You're a builder of ideas. I can see it."

He points right at me and I don't know what to say.

"Is film your thing?" he says, lifting his chin.

"I think so."

"So make, then! Stop wallowing in what you think you've broken and make something instead! Build something with Leia, or do it on your own, but do it."

"It's not that easy," I say.

"Who said anything about easy?" He sticks up two fingers. "Throwing that at the whole world is easy. Any idiot can do that. But making something that matters? Something that hits home? Only a handful of people can do that."

I can feel the energy coming off him.

"You just make sure you tell your story and nobody else's, yeah? Say what you want to say."

He bangs his chest with his fist.

"You do that, Luke, and you might even find out who you are."

16.

Tommy tearing the plasterboard from a partition wall with his hands.

Zia in Selfridges surrounded by orange fake-tan faces, accidentally spraying aftershave in his own eyes.

Marc wiping his eyes with the back of his hand as he chops onions.

Donna looking at flats online.

Mum signing a patient's cast with an 'X'.

Dad waiting in the Argos queue, blocking an old lady's view of the screen.

People talk about 'the zone'.

Marc used to speak about it when he was still running in races. That place where you almost feel like you're outside yourself. Like some higher power is passing through you and you're watching your own body performing what you were born to do.

Tommy on the football pitch.

Marc on the track.

I dunno if this is the same thing, but I know I can't stop.

I'm on my laptop. It feels right for this. Cutting and pasting.

Arranging lines in place.

If I'm not typing, I'm combing through my notebooks, finding bits. Scenes and thoughts. Memories and lines. Scribbling words. If I'm not doing that, I'm pacing my room, speaking ideas out loud, chunks of dialogue.

Or doing press-ups while picturing camera shots, trying to piece scenes and moments together.

Marc brings me bits of whatever food he's experimenting with.

Tahini and falafel. Chorizo and couscous.

Sunday comes and goes.

Monday night I pass out on my laptop keyboard.

Tuesday morning I wake up with my legs literally under a blanket of paper. My eyes sting, but every bone in me has a charge. I can't stop.

I won't stop. Not until it's finished.

I work all day. Donna comes over. Her and Marc invite me to watch a film with them. I tell them I don't have time. I run a bath, then forget I did. Piece by piece I build up my story. I use Marc's printer and make a physical pile, printed sheets mixed with notebook pages. Whole passages get crossed out, then rewritten. Typed-up, deleted, typed again.

My life is my scrapbook. Scribbled on. And full.

Balls of scrunched-up paper dot the room like graffitied snowballs.

I drink enough tea to fill a skip.

Noah said: Stuff just happens. Nobody knows why.

I can hear birds. It's early, but I've been awake for over an hour. I'm holding my most recent notebook.

I read the line: Life isn't a film.

And I laugh out loud, sitting on my bedroom floor, a bombsite of ideas.

I'm Tom Hanks in Castaway. I'm Edward Scissorhands. I'm that other guy, from that film—

"Lukey?"

Mum opens my door and I watch her eyes take in what must look like carnage to her.

"You OK, love?"

She's in her uniform. It's Wednesday morning.

"I'm all right," I say, and speaking the words feels like my brain slows down a little bit. "Just working on something."

"That's great, sweetheart. Can I open your window a bit?"

I nod. She tiptoes over notes and opens the window. The birdsong gets louder.

"You look tired, Luke." She's nodding the 'nurse' nod.

"I am tired, Mum. I'm knackered."

She looks worried.

"Don't worry," I say. "I'll be finished soon, then I'll rest."

Mum smiles. "You always were your own man."

"Pardon?"

She waves her finger like a wand over the whole floor. "All this, you and your ideas. Something would just set you off, and whoosh!"

She's picturing something from the past, something she's never told me about before.

"Never needed stroking," she says. "Not like your brother, and God knows your dad did. Still does. You were always different. Always seemed like you were just gonna do what you wanted off your own back."

I look up at her. It's like I'm listening to her talk about someone else.

She sees my face and smiles. "Nobody pushed you and you

found your way." She tiptoes back to the door and stands on the landing. "You do your thing, Lukey. I'll see you later."

And she goes. I hear the front door open and close, then through my open window her steps to her car, the door opening and swinging shut, the engine as she pulls away. I grab my pen and the nearest notebook.

Black.

Hum of a strip light and radio static as a dial tries to find a station.

Fade up to a face.

Noah never mentioned endings.

"Start where it matters," he said. "Start with a question."

Does that mean you should end with an answer? What does that even mean?

```
INT. — DAY
A pile of papers like crumpled A4 leaves full of
words, some typed, some handwritten.
```

I tidy my room.

I shower.

I feel like I just climbed a mountain. All ache and satisfaction.

It's Thursday afternoon.

I did it.

Marc's made pad thai from scratch. I'm eating my second bowl in front of the telly watching a man deciding which red, numbered box to open.

I think of Noah. I want to tell him what I did. Show him.

But first I have to get it to her.

I reach for my phone. Contacts. Tommy. New message.

Yo. I need your help. L

Send.

The game-show host asks the question, "Deal or no deal?"

I stare at my phone and wait.

17.

EXT. — NIGHT

Nearly midnight. Dark windows. A silent front
door.

I am a maker. I am a builder of ideas.

Tommy's messing with the stereo as I get back into the car.

"Done?" he says.

"Done."

"So what now?"

"Now I sleep."

And we drive back towards town from the other side. The
night-time road gets blurry in the distance.

"Thanks, man," I say, fighting to keep my eyes open.

"No worries. Let's hope she likes it."

I picture Leia opening the door in the morning, looking
down, reading her name.

"You excited about tomorrow? Big one seven, man."

"I guess. Marc's making chicken like my nan used to do, with the rice and peas and gravy."

"Banging. I'll come straight from work."

He presses a button and an acoustic guitar starts. A deep voice like a lullaby.

"Who's this?" I say, frowning.

"Shut up. What? I can't like a bit of acoustic stuff sometimes? It's good thinking music."

I smile. Even my oldest friend has stuff he doesn't show.

"So what was in it then, the story?" he says.

I lean my head against the cool window.

"Everything."

```
EXT. — NIGHT
A thick brown A4 envelope rests against a front
door.
No address, just a name in block capitals. LEIA.
```

I'm lying on my back. There's a light in my eyes. I can see spots. Big saucer-shaped blobs of hot white and there's a voice. A female voice.

Then it's dark. I blink and there's no difference with my eyes open or closed. I can hear water dripping, maybe into a metal sink. The drips almost sound electronic.

Now I'm running. It's afternoon and I'm running home. I look down at my feet and my strides are long. I'm bounding like a gazelle or something and then blood is dripping. Thick drops of it hitting the pavement in front of me. I feel my nose and it's flat. Like it's been pressed into my face.

I'm sitting in a snowy footprint.

I'm outside the head master's office.

I'm kissing Leia in the street. Her hot mouth pressed against mine.

I'm behind bars.

I'm sliding a wad of paper into an envelope.

I'm standing outside our house, with Chewbacca and a zombie, giving the thumbs-up.

I'm hugging Marc. He's hugging me. His arms are strong and I feel safe and then he's squeezing me tighter. And tighter. I try to break free but he just keeps squeezing and I can't breathe. I'm trying to scream but my mouth is full of cotton and he just keeps squeezing.

18.

"Yo!"

His voice comes through my bedroom door.

"Wake up, Lukey! Birthday breakfast!"

I roll over. Check my phone. Nothing. My head hurts. Starved of sleep.

The smell of a fry-up. Notebooks stacked in a pile.

Happy birthday to me.

They're all sitting at the table. Dad in his old place in between Mum and Marc. They start to clap as I walk in.

"Finally!" says Dad.

"Don't you have work?" I say, rubbing my eyes.

"Don't be daft, big man. My boy turns seventeen? I think that's a day-off type situation. Come and sit down."

Mum gets up as I sit and brings a plate from the side full with fry-up.

"Hold on, Ange," says Dad and pulls something out of the

chest pocket on his shirt.

"There." It's a candle, sticking straight up out of the sausage on my plate.

"Hold still, Mum," says Marc, leaning in and striking a match.

Mum lays the plate down in front of me as all three of them sing the song.

"Don't forget your wish, love."

I stare at the little flame.

"Isn't he a bit old for that?" says Marc.

Dad points at him like a judge. "You better just shut your mouth, Marc Henry."

And the pair of them smile.

Leia's face.

I close my eyes. The curves of her lips.

Eyes open. Blow.

"Right," says Dad, clapping his hands. "Let's nyam!"

Four terrible jokes. Three cups of tea. Two embarrassing stories. One Darth Vader impression.

A lot of laughing.

I look across at Dad as Marc eats. Dad shrugs and holds up

crossed fingers. I do the same. Two boys hoping to win the girl back.

My body feels heavy.

"Here you go, love." Mum hands me a box wrapped in Christmas paper. It's a bit smaller than a shoebox, so it's not trainers.

"It's not trainers," says Marc, and his eyes are dancing.

"Thanks, Mum," I say.

Mum shakes her head. "It's from all of us." The three of them beam smiles.

I put on a posh voice. "Thank you, All of Us."

"Open it, then!" says Dad. So I do.

Stunned.

"The geezer in the shop said it's a good one," Marc says as I pull off the last of the paper. It's a brand new camcorder. My throat itches.

They've got me my own HD camcorder. I look up.

"Is it all right?" says Mum, and she looks genuinely concerned.

"It's amazing," I say. "Thank you."

I watch her hand reach for Dad's and their fingers intertwine, and I have to whistle to stop myself crying.

"Smethwick's Scorsese." Marc eats a sausage with his fingers and the walls feel like they're smiling and I want to press pause on everything to stretch the moment out.

Yo! Happy Birthday man! Coming later with Tom. Z

Me and Dad watch *Big Trouble in Little China* while Mum and Marc go shopping for things for dinner later. Dad does his audio commentary the whole way through.

"You know, Kurt Russell was offered the Superman role before Christopher Reeve and turned it down?"

I pretend he hasn't told me that one, and all the others, a hundred times before and just sit, half watching, half drifting off, my new camcorder in my lap the whole time.

"You can do test shots for your script," Dad says, as the bad guy's face expands like a balloon on the screen. "Let me know if you need a suave father-figure character."

He pulls his James Bond face, but keeps his eyes on the telly. The bad guy explodes.

I stare at my phone. Nothing.

"There's definitely a role for Big Alien Pilot," I say. "You look like you'd be perfect."

Mum and Marc get back in time for lunch and Donna's with them.

Her and Marc make everyone sandwiches and start prepping for dinner.

Dad turns off the TV.

"We should play dominoes!"

"I'm all right, Dad," I say.

"Shut up, killjoy. Ange! Where's the dominoes?"

Mum comes into the living room holding a card. "They're where they always were, Joe, why don't you get up and fetch them? Here, Lukey, this was on the mat."

She hands me a yellow envelope with just my name written on it, no address. My stomach flips as I take it. No address. Does she know where I live? Could she have found out?

It's a postcard showing a still from *Reservoir Dogs*. Harvey Keitel leaning over Steve Buscemi, both of them pointing their guns at each other. I turn it over.

Write YOUR story.
Noah.

"Who's it from, love?"

Mum sits down on the sofa.

I stare at the picture and smile. "Just a mate."

By the time Zia and Tommy show up, I've played enough dominoes to last me until I'm as old as you're supposed to be to play them in the first place. Marc and Donna are still in the kitchen. Mum's curled up on the sofa.

"Yo!" says Zia, pointing at the camcorder box. "That's high-end, man."

I look at Mum, smiling like a cat.

Tommy sits down next to her. "You filmed anything yet? Hi, Mrs Henry."

I shake my head.

"Hello, Tom. How's your dad?" Mum says.

"Good, yeah, thanks."

"We got you this." Zia holds out the present. "It's a notebook."

I take it.

"For all them ideas, Lukey." Tommy smiles.

I smile back. "Thanks man."

"We need music!" says Dad and disappears.

Then Donna shouts, "Food's ready!"

It's incredible.

The gravy tastes just like Nan's. Dad found one of his old

dancehall CDs upstairs and that's our soundtrack as people catch up in between licking their fingers and asking for more. Tommy keeps looking at Donna, then pretending not to when Marc catches him. Zia can't help staring at Dad, like he always used to, and Dad and Mum keep stealing looks at each other. I just watch it all playing out, present, but conscious of the missing character in the scene, never once letting my phone out of sight.

    EXT. — NIGHT
    A man with a broken face steps onto the petrol
    station forecourt. He looks both ways, smiling to
    himself as he unwraps a packet of cigarettes.

"Will you do the apple trick please, Mr Henry?" says Zia, looking at Dad like a puppy waiting for his walk. Dad's busy trying to get rid of the subtitles he accidentally set up on the TV. Everyone's stuffed.

    "My name's Joe, son, and I haven't done that for years."

    "Oh, go on, Joe," says Donna, egging him on. Marc goes to the kitchen and fetches an apple.

    "Go on, old man." He throws it across the room to Dad. "Do your trick."

Dad holds the apple up in his hand like it's some ancient relic. "By jungle law, I call forth the power of ten tigers. Drum roll, please!"

Everyone drums their knees. Dad closes his eyes, takes a deep breath, then crushes the apple in his fist. Bits of pulp shoot out either side and into his lap. Zia actually cheers.

"We going to the pub, then?" says Marc from the doorway.

Donna starts to get up. Dad's still brushing himself down. "You kids go. Me and your mum'll stay here."

Marc looks at Mum. Mum nods. "He's right, you don't need us cramping your style. Go and have some fun, but be careful."

"Yes, Ma'am. Come on, people."

```
EXT. — NIGHT
Boney fingers tap the ash from a cigarette as a
car prowls city streets.
```

Marc's staring at me from across the little table.

"Cheer up then, birthday boy!"

He raises what's left of his Guinness. I do the same. Zia's playing *Who Wants To Be A Millionaire?* on the machine. The pub's Friday-night busy and Donna's helping behind the bar, winking over at us in between serving regulars. Tommy's outside smoking. No word from Leia.

"I'm just gonna grab some air." I rub my stomach. "I'm still stuffed."

Marc nods, his eyes on Donna the whole time.

19.

Cigarette smoke snakes out through the crack of a
blacked out car window.

The two of us stand, backs against the outside wall. "So Marc
and Donna are back on then?" says Tommy.

"Looks like it. They're talking about moving."

He takes a drag of his cigarette. "Where to?"

"Leeds."

Exhale.

"Leeds?"

"I know."

It feels like we're on stage. A director watching us from the
darkness.

"Stuff's changing, eh, Lukey?"

I slide my hands into my pockets. "Guess so."

419

The pub door swings open and light from inside stretches towards the kerb.

"Yous two alright?" Marc steps outside. Me and Tommy nod.

"Have you phoned her yet, Lukey?"

"Nah. I haven't got her number." They both look at me.

"I deleted it."

"Why would you do that?" says Marc.

"Because. I dunno. Are we going back in?"

"Oh, for God's sake, Lukey, let's go." Marc steps towards the kerb.

"What?"

He turns back. "You obviously can't stop thinking about her, so come on, I'll drop you over there now." He steps into the quiet road. Mum's car's parked a bit further down on the other side.

"Leave it, Marc. I'll cheer up, I promise."

"No, come on. Let's do it. Life's too short, man. Tell her how you feel, whatever you did, talk it out. Make her see."

Then the engine growls.

Marc's walking backwards with his arms out. "Come on, little brother. Now or never."

That same growl. *No. Please No.* A million volts pulse through me, making my blood scream.

"Marc!"

I rush forward. Marc's face drops, looking confused. "What?"

And it's coming.

The black car.

Craig Miller.

No.

I'm stretching to get to him. My brother. Everything I owe him. All the love in me. Pushing my legs forward. Please, no. Marc turns. He sees the car, but the headlights are blinding him. He can't react. He's frozen. My big brother. I'm almost there.

"Marc!"

Tommy screams, "Lukey!"

Marc's face. Panic. The light in his eyes.

The black bonnet inches away. *Please.*

I throw myself at him. *Please.*

Black.

`Screeching tyres.`

`The thud of a body.`

`The crunch of metal on metal.`

`A boy screams.`

INT. EMERGENCY ROOM — NIGHT

YOUNG MAN sits, mouth open, ready to speak.

Hiss of sliding doors. YOUNG MAN's face drops. His
mouth closes.

GIANT MAN and PETITE LADY stand in entrance.

PETITE LADY runs over. POLICEWOMAN looks up.

YOUNG MAN looks down.   Clock says eleven fifty.

PETITE LADY: What happened? Where is he?

YOUNG MAN doesn't look up.

POLICEWOMAN: Mrs Henry? He's in theatre now. They're
operating.

PETITE LADY: God. I need to see him. I'm a nurse.

Crying. GIANT MAN holds PETITE LADY. YOUNG MAN
looks up.

GIANT MAN: What happened son?

YOUNG MAN: I don't, he was, I didn't...

422

GIANT MAN: Tell me what happened.

POLICEWOMAN: I've been trying to ascertain the details, sir.

GIANT MAN: Stay out of it. Son, look at me. What happened?

YOUNG MAN: I'm sorry, Dad.

PETITE LADY: How is this happening?

She tugs at her hair. GIANT MAN pulls her closer.

POLICEWOMAN: With all due respect, sir, Marc's in intensive care. As I was just explaining to Luke, here, a hit and run is a very serious crime. The sooner I can establish the details, the sooner I can get to work.

GIANT MAN and PETITE LADY stare at POLICEWOMAN. YOUNG MAN looks down.

GIANT MAN: That's not Luke. That's Marc.

~~Part 5.~~
~~Part I. Beginning.~~
EPILOGUE?

I used to pretend I was asleep when we drove home at night. Part of it was so that Dad would have to carry me inside, but mostly I loved listening. People say the best stuff when they think you're sleeping.

    The cold beep of machines.
    Swinging doors. Latex gloves peeled off.
    The sounds of humans fighting death.

I feel broken.

I am broken. My right leg in two places. My ankle. Four ribs. Eleven stitches in the side of my head. Serious abdominal bruising. And my pelvis is cracked.

The doctor told Mum I should've died. That the only reason I'm not dead is because I didn't get dragged under the car when it hit me, and the only reason that didn't happen is because of my size.

Not so little, Luke Henry.

    A thick brown A4 envelope on a bedroom floor.

"Let me come back to the house."

"I don't think so, Joe."

"I want to be there, Ange. I can help."

"It'll just confuse things. He needs to rest."

"He needs to feel safe."

"Keep your voice down. Look, I think he's stirring."

Blurred edges.

Mum's sitting next to my bed, leaning forward, holding my hand, her head on her arm. Dad's asleep in the chair next to the door. I can tell by the light outside that it's early.

The thick trunk of my white cast slopes up away from me. My naked toes sticking out at the top look like skiers waiting to come down a slope.

I squeeze Mum's hand and her head is straight up.

"Lukey? What is it, love?"

My throat is sore as I swallow.

"Where's Marc?"

A beige plastic cup in a robotic claw. Black liquid and steam.

"You look tired," I say.

Marc's standing next to Mum's empty chair. Her and Dad went to get coffee.

"You wanna sit down?"

He does. And the way he's moving is wrong, like somebody's controlling his body remotely.

"How you doing?" he says.

"I'm OK. Look at this." I press the hand controller and the bed lifts me up. The pain shoots up from my waist. I wince.

"Be careful, Luke."

He takes the controls and lowers me back down. I stare at the ceiling. The potted polystyrene panels look like giant graph paper. The lines blurring. Like it's a dream sequence. My mouth is dry.

He sits quietly. Watching me as I drift off.

I'm in front of the whole school.

More than a hundred faces staring at me as I stand next to Miss Cooper. I'm in Year Two.

I look down at my feet. My black school shoes are now a battered grey. The sheen on the parquet floor.

I've got butterflies.

"Amazing story, Luke," Miss Cooper says, and she hands me a signed certificate for 'outstanding achievement in literacy' and a two finger KitKat. I look up at her smiling face and feel her hand on the back of my neck, as the whole hall gives me a round of

applause. My throat is dry as I scan the crowd.

The oldest kids are at the back on the PE benches. Marc's right in the middle. The coolest boy in Year Six. He's staring right at me as he claps.

I squeeze the chocolate in my hand and smile at him.

The applause finishes and everything goes quiet. Miss Cooper points to the front row for me to sit back down, then Marc shouts out:

"That's my little brother!"

And the hall erupts into a football chant.

LU-KEY, LU-KEY, LU-KEY!

I look at my big brother and feel my chest rising.

Marc does a thumbs-up and smiles.

He's still there when I wake up.

Sitting upright, hands in his lap.

"Morning," he says, and forces a smile. "I told them to go and eat. You hungry?"

I shake my head. "What day is it?"

"Sunday."

I run my tongue around my dry mouth. "It feels like a Sunday."

I can smell soap.

"I'm so sorry, Luke."

I look at him. He looks young.

He leans forward. "I'm so sorry."

And he cries.

Leia on my lap. Her hands pushing my chest. My hands on her hips.

"You need anything?"

Zia's standing at the bottom of my bed next to Tommy. They look like they're auditioning for a cop buddy movie.

"I'm good," I say.

"No." Tommy moves round and sits down. "You're a mess."

"Thanks, man."

They look at each other.

"What is it?"

They look at me.

"They got him, Luke," says Tommy. "They got Craig Miller."

And the name goes through me.

"Who got him?"

I see Dad and Marc in the car, not speaking as they drive, looking for Craig. What did they do?

"The police," says Tommy. And I breathe out.

"They found the car all smashed up and someone tipped 'em off. He's going down."

"How do you know?"

"You kidding? You know how many people are willing to say they saw what happened?" Tommy smiles.

INT. — NIGHT

A pub full of weathered faces turn to look at camera.

"I saw," says Tommy. "It was mental. Proper *Die Hard*."

He rugby tackles Zia in slow motion. "Rammed him, you did. Just in time. Maaaaaaaaaaaaaarc!"

Zia stumbles under Tommy's weight and the pair of them fall down, hitting the wall.

"Get off me, man," says Zia, getting up.

"Sorry." Tommy stands up and dusts himself off. "I'm just saying. It was sick. You're a hero, Lukey."

"Shut up," I say.

"He's serious," Zia says, moving to the chair. "It's true. You saved Marc. You properly saved his life."

He's smiling. Tommy's smiling. "You did it, Lukey."

What is this feeling? I don't know it.

Leia.

I turn my head to the side. "My phone. It's dead. You got a charger?"

Zia frowns. "Forget about your phone, you idiot. Get better."

"I've got one in the car," says Tommy. "Shall I get it?"

I nod. "Please." Then I turn to Zia. "Can you get Leia's number from Michelle?"

A dark rucksack upzips. A notebook slipped inside.

There's seventeen missed calls from Mum. Five from Dad.

No new text messages.

Nothing from Leia.

Has she read the script? My story? I don't know.

I stare at the cracked screen. Broken, but still here.

And my thumb is my pen.

I don't know if you got it, but I did it for you. For us. I'm not what you saw. I'm more than my past.

Send.

A girl rides the department store escalator. Lost
in thought. A phone beeps.

No reply.

My phone is on my chest as I try to stay awake.

A nurse brings me dinner. The room darkens. I hear a baby
giggling.

The nurse takes the full plate away. I try to stay awake.

Why won't she reply?

Eyes closing. Fighting it.

Then black.

I feel her.

Like the memory of a dream. An echo of what I could of
had.

I open my eyes and the chair is empty.

Of course it is.

We live our choices.

YOUNG MAN sleeps. Wounded. His leg in traction.
His face bruised. His fingers wrapped tightly
around his phone.

I open my eyes and see her.

In the chair.

I see her.

Hair back in that same bun. Her lips. Her eyes. Perfect.

The girl I lost. I could cry.

Deep breath as I close my eyes.

I hold them shut, then open them to pop the dream.

She's still there.

"Leia."

My voice is croaky.

Her hair is back in a bun. Her sweater's navy blue. She's still there.

"You came."

She tries to smile, then pulls her feet up on to the chair, bringing her knees to her chest. Like she's hiding from what's happened to me.

I go to sit up, but the pain shoots up my spine and I drop back on to my pillow.

"Careful!" She stands up. I watch her eyes take me in.

"Look at you," she says.

And there's something in her face that I haven't seen. She's trying not to cry.

I hold out my hand. "I'm sorry."

She takes a hesitant step toward me, then shakes her head. "This wasn't supposed to happen."

My hand is still out. Please take my hand. Please take my hand.

She looks down, "You're not supposed to die."

"I'm alive," I say, smiling up at her, "And you're here."

Then she's leaning down, coming to me, her hand brushing mine as it moves to my face. Her touch on my skin closes my eyes and she kisses me. Her lips soft and slow, a flutter in her breath and I can feel her tears on my cheek.

Stay with me, Leia. Let me show you more.

She stands up and wipes her eyes with her sleeve. "How dramatic is this?"

And we both smile, as sunlight fights through the blinds.

"I sent you a message," I say, holding up my phone.

Leia's eyes widen, then she moves back to the chair, reaches down into her bag and pulls out the envelope.

"You really did."

She sits down and I feel every single muscle in me wake up.

She slides out the script. "You've been busy, Skywalker."

"You're really here," I say, and now I'm welling up. But I don't care.

This is real.

Her fingers stroke the title of my story.

I watch her read the words, "*It's About Love*."

Hearing her say it out loud feels like she's inside my head. Like she knows what I mean.

"You were right," I say. "Underneath everything else. The ugly. And the stupid. Under the bad choices... That's what it's about. All of it. Even the people who mess everything up. They're blunt and coarse and stupid and wrong, but what they do comes from love. Marc. My dad. Me."

That's what I mean. I said what I mean.

Leia nods. "I know."

And I don't need anything else.

She leans forward, reaching out for my hand. Her slender fingers around mine, and it's like something bonds. Something solid. The kind of thing we'll never have to explain. The kind of thing that makes you want to be brilliant.

"So what'd you think?" I say.

Leia exaggerates a pout. "Yeah. Pretty good," her head tilts, "for a first draft."

She leans back and picks up her notebook.

"Pretty good?"

She smiles. "I think we could do better, I mean, if you're up to it?"

I smile. She takes out her pen.

We are makers.

"We should start where it matters," I say.

We are the builders of ideas.

She's looking at me. The fire in her eyes.

"I guess we start with right now then."

Acknowledgments

Again, massive thanks to Nick, Sam, Hannah
and everyone at HarperCollins Children's Books.
The more I learn, the happier I am to be with you.

Mary, our chats mean a lot.

Lily, your work helped so much.

Thank you, Cathryn and Siobhan,
for making things feel easy.

Thank you, Lenny, Andrew, Nathan, Chrissy,
Tuffy, Jenny, Marcello, Sandro, David,
Aaron, Simon, Janet, Donna, Sian, Michael
and Richard, for too many jokes and golden moments.

It's About Love was inspired by where I'm from
and what I was shown.

Thank you, Glen, Mr Hogan and Nan — the only
role models I've ever needed.

Thank you, Yael, Sol and Dylan — my best friends.

And, finally, when I was seventeen, a boy from the year above
said something in a classroom that I doubt he'll even remember
saying, but it genuinely changed the way I looked at the world.
Wherever you are, Paul Evans, thank you.

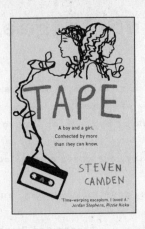

HELLO? IS IT ON?
I'M JUST GOING TO SAY IT...

2013

Things happen for a reason. That's what Ameliah tells herself. The universe has a plan. Right? Why else would it take her parents? Then she finds an old tape, with a boy's voice on it – a voice that seems to be speaking to her.

1993

Ryan is lost. Mum gone, new stepmum, evil stepbrother. Why would this happen? He records a diary on a tape, for his mum, about a girl he just met, who he can't get out of his head.

Ameliah and Ryan are linked by more than just a tape.
This is their story.

Read an extract from TAPE...

Hello? Is it on? Yeah, I can see the light. It's on. I'm starting again. I'm recording.

That just happened. That actually just happened and the crazy thing is it didn't even feel weird. I think I get it now, Dad. I think I understand.

It's probably best not to think about it too much, right?

The universe and everything.

I'm here. That's what matters. I'm here doing this and it happened. Just like you said, so I guess the universe is happy.

Was it always meant to be now? Sorry, I'll leave it alone.

Everything happens when it should.

This is what you did, sitting down and pressing record, and now it's gonna be what I do.

I'm talking into the speaker — how does that even work?

Everybody always said, 'It's important to get stuff out, Ameliah, put it down, it's part of moving on.' I never really listened.

I guess I just didn't want to do it their way. Maybe I wasn't ready, I dunno.

This feels different. This feels right.

So much has happened. There's so much to say, so I'm gonna say it.

It's half twelve now and I'm recording my voice on to this tape.

Just like you.

Ryan wiped the condensation from the small circular bathroom mirror with his fingers and imagined he was scraping ice from the window of a dug-up frozen submarine. A World War II sub discovered near the North Pole years after it was lost at sea. He pictured seeing the solid face of some old naval officer, frost in his moustache, eyes wide, staring out, frozen in the panic of realising he was about to be stuck forever.

He lowered his hand and saw only his own face, thirteen years old, flushed from the heat of the bath, his thick dark hair slicked back from getting out of the water.

Whenever Ryan looked into the mirror he felt an urge to slap himself in the face. Not because he was angry with himself and thought he deserved it, more because he'd seen it in a film once. The private investigator character staring at himself in the mirror after a crazy night of action and danger and slapping himself to make sure he was focused for a new day on the job.

Ryan lifted his hand level with the side of his face. He tensed the muscles in his arm, pulling his hand back ready to strike. His eyes narrowed as he prepared for the slap. Then he froze, staring at himself.

— Come on, you chicken, do it. Do it!

He let out a sigh, puffing out his cheeks as his arm moved back down to his side, and thought about how much space there was inside his mouth. How you could probably fit half a good-sized orange in each side between the teeth and your cheek.

— Yo!

The voice from outside the door came with a bang that shook the hinges and popped the air out of Ryan's face.

— I said yo! You better hurry up, weed, or I'll fold you in half.

Ryan stared at himself as the banging carried on.

He pictured Nathan's face on the other side of the door, getting more and more angry, twisting into shapes like some kind of mutant monster stepbrother. He reached for another towel and threw it over his head and shoulders like a boxer, getting himself ready for the title fight.

*

It was just over six months since Dad sat him down and told him that Sophia would be moving in and bringing Nathan too. Dad had asked him what he thought and he'd said it was a good idea because he'd seen the hope in Dad's eyes. They moved in the next week, which made Ryan realise it really didn't matter what he thought.

At least he didn't have to share his room. Dad's gesture to turn his office into a bedroom for Nathan meant Ryan at least got to keep his own space, although Nathan didn't seem all that clued up about the rules of privacy. He never knocked. He just barged in like he owned the place.

He was four months younger and yet a couple of inches taller and, truth be told, a lot stronger, although Ryan put that down to the fact that he seemed to eat non-stop. He even slept with a sandwich next to his pillow.

A month later Dad and Sophia got married in a small grey room in the council building. Ryan wore the same suit he'd worn to his mum's funeral. Back then it had been baggy; this time it fitted like a glove.

The night of the wedding Sophia had cornered him in the

kitchen, when Ryan was trying to find more cherryade, and told him that she wasn't trying to replace his mum. That she loved his dad very much and wanted this to be a new start for everyone. Ryan had seen the look on her round face as she stood there awkwardly in too much make-up, her dark hair tied up, wearing her peach dress with frilly edges. Ryan had smiled and said that's what he wanted as well and Sophia had hugged him slightly too tight and the pop bottle had fallen out of his hand.

When she went back to the living room, Ryan picked up the bottle and watched the bubbles inside fight to get to the top. Nathan came into the kitchen to get more food. He told Ryan his suit looked stupid. Ryan said nothing. Nathan saw the bottle of pop and snatched it. Ryan went to say something then stopped himself, stepped back and watched Nathan twist the bottle lid and soak himself in cherryade.

Ryan pulled on his Chicago Bears sleeping T-shirt and stared at his boom box. The shiny silver panels caught the light. The clean black buttons underneath the little windows that let you see the tape inside. The super bass circular speakers. Perfect. It had been his gift the Christmas before Mum died. He remembered tearing open the paper and seeing the corner of the box, spending the rest of the day in his pyjamas tuning the radio dial to all the different stations he could find.

Ryan pulled open the narrow drawer of his bedside table and took out a cassette box. Its white sleeve was empty of any writing. He ran his thumb along the edge of the box, feeling the plastic edge, then eased the box open and took out the tape.

He looked at the thin white label as he slotted the tape into cassette deck two. In block capital dark blue felt tip, the word MUM.

Ryan pressed rewind and wiped the little window with his fingertip as the tape motor hummed, spooling the tape back to the beginning.

The rewind button clicked up. Ryan moved the boom box to the edge of his bedside table so he could speak into it while lying in bed and, with two fingers, pressed the play and record buttons at the same time. The little red indicator light blinked on as the tape spooled round showing it was recording. Ryan cleared his throat.

Ameliah stares at what's left of her cornflakes. Her spoon makes waves in her bowl as her slender fingers turn it and she imagines each soggy flake is a tiny wooden raft floating in a milky white sea.

She moves her spoon in between them and watches as some sink, while others fight to stay afloat. Morning light cuts across the kitchen floor through the big window.

— Penny for 'em, Nan says from across the small square table through a mouthful of crumpet.

Ameliah knows what that means, she's heard it plenty of times before (mostly from Nan), but only this time does it occur to her that one penny for what someone is thinking seems like a really cheap deal.

— I've never been in a boat.

Nan stops chewing for a second to listen then carries on. Ameliah looks at her.

— I mean in proper water, like the sea.

Nan starts to spread butter on to another crumpet from the pile on the plate between them.

— You're still young, love. There's plenty of time.

She smiles as she pushes the new crumpet into her mouth.

— How old were you? asks Ameliah. When you went on your first boat?

— Me? Oh, now you're asking. It was probably with your granddad, long before you were born. Before I had your mum.

Ameliah looks down. A strand of dark curls falls across her face. She sweeps it back behind her ear with her fingertips.

— Are you sure you don't want a crumpet, love, strength for your last day?

Ameliah shakes her head.

— No thanks, Nan.

Nan takes another crumpet from the pile.

— She wasn't a breakfast person either.

Ameliah looks at Nan and tries to imagine her younger, sitting across a table from Mum, a pile of crumpets between them, Mum daydreaming about school.

— I guess it's genes, continues Nan, although she

certainly didn't get it from me.

Ameliah shrugs. Nan leans forward.

— Are you keeping up with your journal, like the lady said?

Ameliah pictures the empty journal pushed under her bed, the light brown recycled cover, the pages clean and new. She looks into her bowl. All but one of the tiny rafts have sunk. She stares at it, clinging on to the surface.

— Kind of. It feels weird.

— It will do, love, for a while, but trust me, it's—

— Important to get stuff out.

Nan smiles and lets out an old-lady laugh through a mouthful of crumpet.

— That's my girl.

Ameliah stares at the last flake clinging on to the surface of her milk as it bobs alone, refusing to sink.

Ryan stared out of the classroom window across the school

playing fields. The grey sky heavy with rain ready to fall. He saw a group of girls jogging in a loose pack, doing laps of the pitch, too far away to see faces. He focused on one girl, near the back, her dark hair bouncing against her shoulders as she moved.

— Ryan!

Miss Zaidel was standing in front of his desk. Everyone else in the class was watching.

— Do you have any thoughts?

Her voice was angry. Ryan looked across the room and saw Nathan smiling his smug smile.

— Sorry, Miss, I was—

— You were miles away, Ryan. Again. That's what.

— Yes, Miss.

— It's been like this all term, Ryan.

— Yes, Miss. Sorry, Miss.

Nathan pulled a face from across the room. Ryan scowled back at him.

— Right, well, if you've finished watching the girls outside, would you mind coming back and joining us for our last lesson together?

People giggled. Nathan's smug stepbrother smile widened.

Ryan felt his cheeks getting hot.

— Yes, Miss.

Miss Zaidel returned to the front of the class.

— Right, so can anyone else answer my question? How long has John Major been Prime Minister?

Nathan's hand shot up into the air.

— I can, Miss. Three years, Miss.

Miss Zaidel nodded.

— Thank you, Nathan, and somebody else? Who did he take over from?

Nathan smiled straight at Ryan as the rest of the class stuck up their hands. Ryan ground his teeth as the sky rolled thunder outside and it started to rain.

Ameliah scans the lunchtime selection in front of her. The dinner lady stares at her. Ameliah doesn't recognise the lady, but she knows that stare. She's felt it enough times. It's the stare people give when they know about her parents and feel they should say something, but don't really have a clue what words to use.

She grabs a ham roll and a carton of juice and moves away before the dinner lady can speak. As she queues up to pay, she thinks about how six months have flown by. She thinks about Dad, how he changed in the months after Mum. How the illness made him shrink.

— Is that everything, sweetheart?

Ameliah snaps out of her daydream. Corine on the cafeteria till smiles her Cheshire cat smile like always. The gap between her top front teeth big enough to fit a five-pence piece.

— No crisps today?

Ameliah smiles back.

— Not today thanks, Corine.

Across the room she spots Heather, sitting with some of the others, flapping her arms like a bird, calling her over. Ameliah sighs.

— Chin up, love.

Corine's face is round and warm like the grandmas in fairy tales and, as she makes her way through the busy lunch hall towards the table of girls, Ameliah decides that Corine would get on really well with Nan.

In the noisy lunch hall Ryan sat staring into space with a mouthful of ham roll. The seat opposite him was empty. He shook his head as he thought about being embarrassed in class earlier.

Liam sat down like a horse crashing into a fence.

— Summertime!

Ryan jumped.

— Got you! Big L strikes again.

— I told you not to do that!

Liam smiled and dropped his Tupperware lunch box on to the table.

— I know, but it's too easy, man.

He rubs his shovel hands together.

— Half a day left, Ryan, then six sweet weeks of freedom.

— Sit down, will ya? People are staring.

— What you got?

— I dunno.

— You're eating it.

— Oh, ham.

— You got crisps?

— Monster Munch.

— What flavour?

— Beef.

— Beef? Forget it. I was gonna swap you, but not for cow.

Liam started to eat, his square face chewing his sandwich like a camel that was in a rush. Ryan smiled. Liam had been his best friend since the infants and he couldn't think of a single day since they'd known each other that Liam hadn't made him laugh at least twice.

— I heard you got caught watching the girls do PE.

As Liam spoke, little bits of sandwich flew out of his mouth on to the table.

— I wasn't watching the girls. Jeez, Liam, can you keep the food in your mouth?

Liam shrugged his thick shoulders.

— That's not what I heard. Tracey said Miss Zaidel properly got you and you went bright red and everything.

— Yeah, well, Tracey's full of it.

Liam peeled a banana and took half of it with one bite.

— You should just pick one.

— What?

— Pick one. Any girl – there's loads of them. Look, there's some.

Liam stuck out his big arm. Ryan slapped it down.

— What are you doing?

Liam pushed the last bit of banana into his mouth.

— I would just walk up to one of them and lay it down.

— Lay it down? What does that even mean? Just eat your food, man.

— I'm just saying I'd do that.

Ryan took another bite of his roll.

— You don't get it.

— What don't I get, Ryan? You choose one and then you lay it down.

— Stop saying that. And you don't just choose one, do you? It's not an auction.

Liam looked confused. Ryan finished the last of his roll.

— And you wouldn't lay it down anyway.

— Yeah I would. I'd lay it down hard.

— Oh really? Big Liam? Mr Smooth, yeah? And what would you say?

— Call me Big L.

— You're an idiot.

Liam slapped the banana skin on to the table and puffed up his chest.

— I'd walk straight up to her and be like, look, baby, it's me and you, yeah? You can be the I S P to this Big L. What you sayin'?

Ryan shook his head and smiled. Liam looked offended.

— What? That's good. Big L. I S P, lips, like kiss.

— That spells lisp, you idiot.

— What?

Ryan watched Liam's face as his brain worked out the spelling.

— Oh yeah. Yeah, well, you know what I mean.

— Yeah. Big L can't spell.

Liam smiled.

— Big L can't spell, but you smell, like beef, you've got cow crisps in your teeth.

His big fists started to knock a beat on the lunch table. Ryan smiled and tried to think of a comeback rhyme.

Ameliah watches the girls around the table talking about things everybody expects girls to talk about. Their fast lips motoring through sentences.

Heather gives her a look that says 'Stop being so quiet' and Ameliah tries to say with her eyes that she's only quiet when she's around people talking about things she doesn't care about, that she's not interested in the fact that Simone has taken some of her older sister's foundation and eyeliner and is going to do makeovers for people after school on the field. Mom always said that foundation was what you build houses on and, if your face needs to be built on, then make-up isn't really going to make a difference, is it?

But Heather already knows.

Ameliah looks at her. Pretty without trying. The freckles scattered across her nose and cheeks making her seem that little bit more special. Thank God for Heather. The bridge between her and the others. Heather knows how to let Ameliah be in the group without having to do or say too much. She's always done it, since the infants.

— You OK, Am? Half a day left then freedom.

Heather smiles. Ameliah smiles back. She thinks about the two of them sitting inside Dad's tent in her room by torchlight, Heather hiding her face in the neck of her jumper as Ameliah tells her Dad's ghost stories, Heather screaming as she gets to the end and the big shock about the old man with no head.

— You wanna try it?

Heather holds out the little eyeliner pencil and smiles. Ameliah smiles back and Heather lowers her hand.

— I'm coming back to yours after school, right?

— Yeah?

— Yeah. We're gonna make a start on those boxes.

Ameliah looks around at the other girls, all engrossed in talk of makeovers and brush technique.

— We don't need to.

Heather reaches out for Ameliah's hand.

— Yes, we do. New summer chapter, Am. It's time to make it your room.